THE FLICKERING BRIDGE

TIME ALLEYS

BOOK TWO

J.A. ENFIELD

WAYZGOOSE PRESS

Edited by Dorothy Zemach

Cover art by Morgen Witt

ISBN 978-1-961953-24-6

Printed in the United States of America

Contents

For Magda, who worried about these kids.

Chapter 1

The Calm

Sweaty and sleepy in the early evening swelter, Mick lay limply on loose-packed wool fleece in a dim, quiet corner of the warehouse, savoring the sounds of others working when his labors were done for the day. Through the open doors came the bickering of canal boaters and the nickering of their horses, none of it needing his attention.

Mick had been at Demeter Farm and Demeter Academy a month and had fallen into its rhythms. He rose nearly as early as the real farmhands and did something useful with chickens or crops until attacking breakfast in the Academy's little dining hall. Then, like his classmates, he sponge-bathed and slipped on his scholar's cottons before marching through the Academy's oddly mixed curriculum of agriculture, history, geography, and temporal mysteries. After class or tutorial, he usually spent another hour or two in scratchy clothes doing arm-sapping work in the barns, the fields, or the warehouse nestled among a stand of tall trees across Hill Street on the pointed slice of land called "the Scythe." Altogether, it was exhausting but calming. This was the best he'd felt since involuntarily becoming a time-traveling "alley rat" by dropping almost two centuries backward in time to 1853 London.

It helped that he hadn't gone patrolling for time alleys since coming to Demeter. Being the best alley spotter at the Forsyth Institute sounded cool. Sometimes it even was cool. Mick had spent most of his eleven years being good or good enough at what he had to do, but until arriving at the Institute, he'd never been exceptional at anything. But being a gifted alley spotter carried a price. In bad times, it meant stress, sleeplessness, and sorrow. For a while there, he'd started to flinch at even a hint of a time alley. Blessedly, at Demeter, there were no kids falling dead from waylaid alleys. No villains lurking with hate in their guts and murder in their hearts. Nobody bursting into literal flames as they crossed forbidden thresholds enforced by the cruel and incomprehensible laws of time travel.

Sure, he was still stuck in 1853 London. Or 1853 Peckham, anyway—he still hadn't figured out when a place on the outskirts of London was a separate village of its own and when it was just London with sheep. Either way, he was stranded in a foreign past and sometimes woke in the middle of the night, missing his real life—Chicago with cars, electricity, streaming video, GPS. And his family, of course. His baby sister Emilia, Tía Verónica, Tía Julieta, dopey Uncle Dan, his dad hiding behind an ocean, and the rest. He especially missed Emilia. He wished he could see her hugging and gumming Swaggy Bear, the barf-orange, squinty, lopsided teddy bear their crunchy Tía Julieta had made, even stitching her first initial into one ear and Emilia's into the other. But he couldn't. Chicago, his family, it was all gone. So gone it hadn't even happened yet. Everybody told him there was absolutely, one hundred percent no way for him to go back home, and he worried that he was starting to believe them.

And sure, sometimes in the stifling, dark nights when flickering candle scraps were his only protection against a planet with its face turned away from the sun, he would jolt awake, remembering the grim warning from Miss Emmet, who seemed suspiciously aware of powerful people's secrets for a simple librarian. Before Mick had left for Demeter, Miss Emmet had gone out of her way to let him know that there were dangerous power struggles happening around him as shadowy figures fought to take control of the "Project," a secretive organization run by alley rats, supposedly to help alley rats.

So, no, Demeter wasn't perfect. But compared to the mess and stress of his first frantic months in 1853, it was pretty darn good. Most days, he was even able to struggle into his ludicrously complicated old-fashioned underwear in under five minutes.

Still, Mick missed the Squad, his friends Alison, Dolly, and Leech from the Institute. Several days earlier, a lot of students at Demeter had started getting on Tilling omnibuses back to the Institute, and Alison, Dolly, and Leech had been among them. He wasn't sure why he was still at the farm and his friends weren't, and he was starting to feel a bit uncomfortable without them. It was the first time since he'd dropped into 1853 that they hadn't been around to help him navigate the past and to just be his friends.

But at least he wasn't totally alone. Some of the Demeter full-timers were okay, and there were still about ten other Institute students, including his frenemy Stephen Burton, or, as Mick still thought of him sometimes, Stephen the Snob. As the summer had worn on, Stephen had moved further from "enemy" and closer to "friend." It helped that Stephen had stopped sulking as if being at Demeter was cruel and unusual punishment. To be fair, Demeter did have a reputation as the place where the Institute sent its problem pupils to grind some dirt into their fingernails and some humility into their souls. But it didn't feel like punishment to Mick. He liked getting his hands dirty, at least with real dirt rather than the sooty grime that millions of Londoners had been wiping off of their hands, one after another, since Julius Caesar came conquering. Plus, Mick really liked a lot of the oddball things they were learning —the history of barley one day, the history of insurgent warfare the next, all mixed up with the theory and practice of not destroying the future.

In terms of not destroying the future, there was a lot of emphasis on anachronisms at Demeter, just like at the Institute and, apparently, everywhere else controlled by the Project. Nobody knew if alley rats could change the future, but a lot of smart people thought there was a real risk. So they were supposed to work hard to avoid "conspicuous anachronisms," "connans" for short, because doing or saying something that conspicuously didn't belong in the past might suggest that the alley rat didn't belong there either, which might reveal that time travel was real and thereby change the future. And alley rats were *really* supposed to avoid "mortal anachronisms," actions or choices that might cause large-scale changes—and suffering.

Avoiding anachronisms could be surprisingly hard. Sure, some of it was easy. Mick was pretty confident he could avoid, say, building an aircraft carrier in St. Katharine's Dock, partly because he didn't know how and partly because big iron-hulled ships weren't allowed that far into London anyway. But it might be possible to cause a mortal anachronism by accident, maybe without ever knowing. Mick occasionally felt a wave of panic about that. For example, he might accidentally wipe himself out of existence by irritating the wrong bee, sending it buzzing angrily across the park to sting his multiple-greats-grandpa in the face right before his first date with Mick's multiple-greats-grandma, and she'd decide she didn't want to date some guy with a swollen face. Or maybe his multiple-greats-grandma had fallen in love with his multiple-greats-grandpa *because* the swelling from the bee sting made her giggle, but Mick might brush a flower and make the bee's life easier, and the bee would just go home to the hive and chill with its friends instead of stinging anybody. Either way, Mick would erase half his family from history, including himself.

People usually said changing the future couldn't be that easy or it would happen more often. Mick really hoped so. There were a lot of bees in 1853.

Whether it was possible or impossible, hard or easy, to change the future, the Institute believed it was better to err on the side of caution. All the Institute's students were alley rats who had dropped from distant futures into the past as babies or as terrified, confused children. And the Institute taught them that Rule Number 1 was to avoid doing anything that seemed likely to change the future. Mick had recently seen firsthand the death and horror that could result from breaking Rule Number 1. So he was glad to have it and the nice bright line it drew.

But brightness caused shadows, gray areas. Mick had only the dimmest understanding of the gray areas and the people who lived in them, mostly tidbits he'd learned from Miss

Emmet. But he did understand that even when people agreed that nobody should make improper use of knowledge about the future, they didn't always agree what counted as improper. The more he saw of Demeter—and the more he thought more about the Institute—the more he realized that wherever you found alley rats, you were going to find *inconspicuous* anachronisms, sneaky scraps of the future happening a little too early, tucked away where they wouldn't be noticed, at least not by "arrows," people who only traveled in time in the usual direction and at the usual speed.

For example, Mick suspected that if he could get somebody to unlock one of the heavy doors to the workshops run by the secretive, tight-knit group of "mechanicals," he would find at least a few hidden anachronisms. Most of Demeter was shielded from the outside, and that was especially true of the mechanicals' workshops, which, like the warehouse, were nestled on the Scythe. The warehouse loading dock had to be visible to the outside world because it faced the southern branch of the Grand Surrey Canal, but the workshops were all cloaked by fences, ivy, trees, and hedges. Only small patches and quick flashes of the workshops were ever visible to the waggoners clucking their horses along the bumpy road, the boaters drifting along the canal, or the Peckham farmers, villagers, and travelers who gathered to drink beer just south of the workshops at the Globe Tavern.

Even most people at Demeter never got into the workshops. Mick had definitely never been allowed inside. But he had caught a couple glimpses through open doors when tagging along with his friend Chris Biggs on one errand or another, including once at night when Mick had spotted an unnatural yellowish light, which at first had looked like what Alison's old books called the "eldritch glow" of a time alley. But Mick saw alleys better than anybody he knew, their shimmers and swirls, their colorful moods. He could even hear their silent songs in his bones, hymns that called to him like the sweet, deadly summons of the sirens. Whatever he'd seen in that workshop hadn't been a time alley, but he was pretty sure it hadn't belonged in 1853.

He wondered yet again what they were building in there. Time machines? Nuclear bombs to seize control of the British Empire? Steampunk microwaves to heat up the disgusting meat slop pies that 1853 Londoners actually ate on purpose?

But that afternoon, he was fine not knowing what the mechanicals were up to. He was drifting into sleep like a narrowboat on a lazy current. Soon, there would be chicken and buttered brown bread for dinner, maybe followed by a good game of tag with the students and the farm kids as the day's last light slid slowly from the fields. It felt good to have a break from the craziness.

He should have known it was too good to last.

CHAPTER 2

THE STORM

Mick woke up from his wooly doze to urgent shouting from outside the warehouse. It got louder as a canal horse's hoofbeats grew nearer. The shouting had started from a boat and was getting echoed and expanded by the warehouse laborers on the loading dock. The words were indistinct, but the urgency was clear.

He scrambled to his feet and ran out the nearest door to the loading dock. The warehousemen, Silas, Henry, George, and Miles, were all clustered at the north end of the dock, looking up the canal branch. Mick's friend Chris Biggs had been standing with them but was now sprinting up the tow path toward the canal bridge. Mick squeezed in among warehousemen to get a better view and found himself standing shoulder to shoulder with Ward Carlton, a boy about his age who did every errand Demeter threw at him.

Following everyone's gaze a couple hundred feet north, Mick

scanned along the sun-shimmered canal waters and spotted the familiar sight of the roan mare Jeanne pulling the canal boat *Baret*. Jeanne usually moved at a calm walk, but now her dark forelock was dancing to and fro as she trotted down the towpath. The forelock's movements revealed and concealed the white starfish marking on her forehead, and her hooves punched up small puffs of dust with each step. Before the horse, reins in hand, jogged Rosie Maxwell, a girl about Mick's age who looked younger because she was so small, even for somebody in 1853.

Then the shouting turned from sounds to words, and Mick understood that someone aboard the *Baret* was hurt. It probably wasn't Rosie's father, who was standing at the bow of the boat, waving and yelling. Mrs. Maxwell was kneeling a few paces behind her husband, but it wasn't her name they were calling out. It was Elmer's. Rosie's older brother.

Hardly slowing her pace, Chris leapt nimbly onto the *Baret* and knelt beside Mrs. Maxwell.

The boat drew closer with agonizing slowness. Eventually, Rosie led Jeanne to the main hitching posts, and Silas helped her tie off the towline while the other warehousemen grappled with the mooring lines to tug the narrowboat out of the main body of the canal and into the farm's protected dock.

Even before they had finished tying off the narrowboat, Chris hopped onto the dock's heavy boards. She looked at Mick and Ward. "Find Nurse Peck and tell her to meet us at the Maxwells' cottage."

Ward nodded. "I'll check the infirmary," he told Mick and took off running.

Mick was distracted by the sight of Mrs. Maxwell using the hem of her calico dress to wipe blood from her son's face. By the look of the dress, it wasn't the first time she'd done it. "Is he —" Mick started to ask.

"That's a question for Nurse Peck, Mr. Gunn," Chris said sharply.

Chris usually didn't use Mick's (fake) last name. For future-protection reasons, all the Institute kids had official fake names, and they weren't supposed to tell anybody their real ones. Mick's Institute name was Mitchell Edwin Gunn—"Gunner" to a lot of the kids and "Mr. Gunn" to everybody else. Chris usually called him Gunner, even though she wasn't a kid. Or a professor. She wasn't even one of the dons, the nerd ninjas who guarded against disturbances in the alleys. Dons needed good alley sight, and Chris was nearly alley-blind. She freely admitted it, and Mick would have guessed anyway. He could almost always spot alley rats by looking at their eyes. Even though he seemed to be the only person who could see it, rats' eyes had a subtle glow to them. Some were a lot brighter than others, and Mick was starting to feel pretty sure that the brighter the glow, the better the alley sight.

But Chris didn't need good alley sight. Chris was just ... Chris. One of a kind. Smart, funny, always at ease, usually half-smiling, occasionally half-frowning. She usually wore slightly disreputable men's clothes and a shapeless soft cap perched atop her mannishly short hair. She went, and was welcome, almost everywhere. The teachers let her inside Demeter Academy, even though it was off-limits to everyone who wasn't a student or professor. The Squad said the Institute's wardens let her come and go at the Institute also, although it was also off-limits to outsiders. The mechanicals let her into the workshops, and they didn't do that for anybody. Even the Maxwells let her ride on the *Baret* all the time, and they probably would have told Queen Victoria herself that they didn't want strangers on their boat.

But there was no half-smile on Chris' face now. "Mr. Gunn! Go find Nurse Peck!"

Mick started running. He cut back through the warehouse, along the gravel drive, weaving his way out of the Scythe, across Hill Street, and onto the main part of the farm. He struggled to pull his thoughts together as he ran.

Focus, he told himself. He was supposed to be a hotshot spotter, and being a good spotter wasn't just about seeing time alleys. It was also about thinking quickly and clearly. He or Ward needed to find Nurse Peck ASAP. Ward had said he was going ... where? The infirmary, right, which was on the ground floor of the schoolhouse. So were Nurse Peck's quarters. If she was in the schoolhouse, Ward would find her.

So Mick ran past the schoolhouse and along the gravel drive leading to the Manor, where Lady Penbrook lived. He was soon at the front door of the large, elegant building that he knew to describe as "Georgian"—and that he even knew was named for one of the King Georges, not the American state. Just like 1853 London was "Victorian" because Queen Victoria ruled it. And not just London—she ruled all of England and a lot of the world beyond.

Mick tugged energetically at the bell pull, and Mr. Anderson, the butler, soon opened the door. Like the Manor he ran, Mr. Anderson was large and elegant, nearly filling the front doorway as he looked down at Mick. His white shirt, dark suit, and gray hair were all crisp and controlled. He had mastered the fine butlering art of looking at you with an expression that should have been politely respectful but somehow said that he would rather be contemplating a chamber pot. His voice worked the same way. "Yes, young man?"

"Elmer Maxwell got hurt. Badly. Chris Biggs told me to fetch Nurse Peck immediately."

"Ah," Mr. Anderson said, dialing his disapproval back a couple notches. "As it happens, Nurse Peck is in attendance upon Lady Penbrook." Without turning his head, he called sharply, "Beryl!"

A teenage maidservant scurried into view behind the butler. "Yes, Mr. Anderson?"

"Pray inform Nurse Peck that her ministrations are urgently required."

"Yes, Mr. Anderson," the girl said, scurrying out of view.

"Was there anything else?" Mr. Anderson asked Mick.

Mick shook his head.

"Very well." Mr. Anderson nodded firmly and stepped aside enough to shut the door in Mick's face.

That kind of rank-pulling was one of the baffling and hilarious things about London for Mick. It was full of people who lived in cramped servants' quarters along the back hallways of their bosses' big houses but went around halfway convinced the houses were theirs.

Not that it mattered, Mick reminded himself as Nurse Peck bustled out the front door, still tying the drawstrings on her simple bonnet. He was there about Elmer.

"There's been an accident?" she asked. "Someone is injured?"

Mick told her what little he knew as they walked briskly toward the Maxwells' cottage. Partway up the manor drive, they met Ward. Nurse Peck sent him running off to tell Chris and the Maxwells that she was on her way.

Mick was feeling calmer now that he'd found Nurse Peck.

Mick's Tía Verónica was an RN back in his real life. She and Nurse Peck gave off the same no-nonsense vibe of calm competence. Tía Verónica sometimes talked about how terrible old-timey doctors were, and, basically, Victorian doctors proved her right. But those were only the regular doctors whose confidence seemed to be based on the fact that they had big hats and bigger sideburns. The nurses and doctors at Demeter and the Institute were much better at their jobs. Mick figured that one way you could tell whether doctors knew anything was by seeing if at least some of their patients actually got better. Sure, Nurse Peck often pretended to be a regular Victorian nurse, a friendly, motherly sort of woman who didn't do much besides sit in a chair next to sick people, drinking gin from a flask. But when she gave you pills, you probably started to feel better. And when she put a cast on your broken leg, you probably would be able to walk again. And her bandages and her hands were very clean, which was rare in 1853.

Nurse Peck looked around the tiny parlor, where Elmer was lying on the sofa. "If everyone would please leave the room. Except Chris. Mrs. Maxwell, I shall need you to boil some water, if you please. Clean well water, nothing from the canal."

Mrs. Maxwell stared blankly for a moment and then quietly nudged her way through the others into a separate room.

Most of the others filed out. The cottage door was still open when Rosie Maxwell asked Nurse Peck, "Mightn't I stay and help?"

"No, dearie," Nurse Peck told Rosie, pressing a stethoscope to Elmer's chest. "Your brother needs freely flowing, healthful air, so we must clear the room."

Victorian Londoners seemed to think you could cure anything—bronchitis, cancer, asteroid impacts—with enough fresh air coming through the window. Which sort of made sense when you thought about how rare fresh air was in London. Still, Mick suspected that Nurse Peck just wanted to work in peace.

Plus, he assumed she had some inconspicuous anachronisms in her battered leather satchel that she wanted to use undetected. At least he hoped she did. Before Chris closed the front door on everyone, Mick caught another glimpse of Elmer, and he didn't look good at all.

Most canal boaters lived on their narrowboats to save on rent and keep an eye on their cargos, and the Maxwells sometimes did sleep aboard the *Baret*. Mick didn't understand how four people could fit in the boat's tiny cabin, not even the short, small-boned Maxwells. Luckily for them, Lady Penbrook let them live in a small cottage near the warehouse, and the Maxwells spent most nights there. Elmer and Rosie even went to the farmhands' school several days a week, which was more schooling than most boat kids got.

Rosie and her dad were standing at the cottage's front door, Rosie snuggled under her dad's arm. Mick wanted to say something to them, but they looked so worried and withdrawn that he would have felt weird intruding. Turning away from the cottage, he spotted Ward leaning against the warehouse near the wagon entrance at the rear. Mick crunched across the gravel lane to join Ward.

"Poor Rosie," Ward said.

Mick was pretty sure that Ward had a crush on Rosie. "What happened?"

"The Maxwells was set upon just past the Greenwich bridge.

Headed for the docks, they was," Ward answered in a thick south London accent that Mick was finally starting to understand.

"Who did it?" Mick asked.

Ward shrugged. "Don't think nobody knows. A rough business, it was."

If Ward thought business was rough, it was. Ward had told Mick enough of his life story that Mick knew Ward had endured a lot of rough business. He wasn't a big, strong kid. In fact, Mick was a lot bigger, which was one of the weird things about being a time-traveler—Mick had gone from being smaller than average to being bigger than average, at least among arrow Victorians. Dr. Quinn said that most arrow Victorians were small because they didn't get enough healthy food. Ward got enough to eat now because everybody at Demeter did, but he hadn't always. Ward was an orphan and had spent half his life at the nearby St. Mary le Strand Workhouse, where they'd starved and beaten him. Ward's first name was Edward, but the adults at the workhouse had shortened it "Ward" to mock him for being a ward of the parish.

In a way, Ward also owed his last name to the workhouse. The workhouse hadn't granted him a last name of his own, not even a mocking one. But one winter day they'd beaten him once too often and, while he was on an errand, he'd just kept walking. He'd once told Mick that he'd decided to give himself his own last name based on whatever street he came to next, which had turned out to be Carlton Street. Eventually, cold and hungry, he'd stumbled into the Demeter warehouse, and they'd taken him in for a while. They'd tried sending him to the School for Orphans of the Empire, where the Project sometimes sent rats who went alley-blind. But Ward didn't like the crowds and craziness of central London, so a couple years ago, he'd returned to Demeter, where he fetched and carried for anyone and everyone, though he was hoping to get apprenticed to one of the mechanicals. Mick wasn't sure that would work out for Ward—if the mechanicals really were building time machines in there, they weren't going to let some kid apprentice see it all, especially not an arrow kid.

"But Rosie and her dad, they're— all right?" Mick's lip twitched with annoyance at himself. He'd almost said "okay." Miss Emmet said that some Americans were already saying "okay" but that English people had no idea what it meant yet. So they'd think it was weird, and, along with the American accent he was struggling to lose, it would be another reason to remember him. And he wasn't supposed to be memorable. Institute kids were supposed to fade into the background so they could patrol for time alleys unnoticed and not get the arrows wondering what exactly was going on over there at the Forsyth Institute. Or at Demeter Farm. It was harder at Demeter than the Institute. At the Institute, outsiders almost never entered the building, not past the kitchens anyway. All the students were alley rats, and so were the professors. At Demeter, though, it was more mixed up. Lady Penbrook was an alley rat, and so were Nurse Peck, the professors, and the mechanicals. And Chris. But past that Mick wasn't sure. He didn't think the warehousemen were alley rats. Or the farmhands, not all of them anyway. Ward wasn't.

Ward was too busy staring at Rosie to answer Mick's question. He uncrossed his arms, flapping his hands away from his chest in frustration. "'Twouldn't be so bad if a cove could have some smoke, would it?"

Mick still couldn't wrap his head around the fact that in

1853 London, kids could smoke, and it wasn't considered a terrible thing. It wasn't considered a good thing, exactly, but at least some kids his age did it in public and nobody came to yell at them or arrest their parents. Maybe they didn't have parents. Maybe it was because the whole city seemed like one big chimney—people smoking, fireplaces smoking, factories smoking. People from the countryside sometimes called London "the Smoke." But Lady Penbrook didn't allow children at Demeter to smoke, and she didn't allow anyone to smoke in the Manor or the schoolhouse. Mick was grateful for that. London was starting to feel real to him, and he was even starting to like parts of it. But not all the smoke.

Ward flapped his hands a couple more times, obviously worried about Rosie but unable to help. Mick was trying to think of something to say when Chris opened the cottage door and stepped outside. She said something to Rosie and her dad, who quickly went inside.

Chris beckoned to Ward and Mick, who hustled across the lane to stand on the small patch of stones in front of the cottage. "Is Elmer badly?" Ward asked.

"He's hurt and no mistake," Chris said. "But Nurse Peck says he should be recovered from the worst in a few days, leastway if he hasn't any broken ribs, which she thinks he hasn't."

Ward grinned broadly. "I'm glad of it. Elmer's a good cove."

"But he'll be abed this afternoon," Chris said, "so we shall have to unload the *Baret* for the Maxwells." She flicked her hands at them, shooing them toward the loading dock.

Ward nodded eagerly. Mick sighed and thought sadly about the soft bed of wool at the back of the warehouse. His mistake, he realized, was that when people started shouting about danger, he ran *toward* them, like an idiot.

CHAPTER 3

THE REFUGE

Usually, the *Baret* carried far more away from the Demeter warehouse than to it. Fruits, vegetables, grains, pigs, chickens, sheep, all weighed down the *Baret* as it departed the farm for anywhere the canal could take it, including the many docks near the River Thames. Sometimes the mechanicals weighed down the *Baret* or some other narrow boat with locked trunks or thoroughly nailed-up crates. Mick had heard that those usually went to the Outer Dock. From there, who knew. The other side of the Thames? The other side of the world?

But the *Baret* usually rode higher in the water on her way back to Demeter, and luckily for Mick that evening was no different. There weren't even any exotic delicacies for the Manor. Just a few light bags and boxes that Ward and Mick carried into the warehouse.

After that, it was time for dinner. Mick and Ward walked together for a few minutes until the main drive began to curve north, at which point Ward turned left for the farmhands' quarters and Mick turned right for the schoolhouse because they didn't sleep in the same building.

That was how things were in Victorian London. There was a pecking order for everything, and every place in the pecking order had a physical place. You could see it at the Institute if you paid attention, and you could see it at Demeter even if you didn't. At the Manor, the servants slept downstairs in the servants' quarters at the back, while Lady Penbrook slept in nice rooms upstairs. The farmhands and other laborers slept in the farmhands' building or one of the small laborers' cottages near the warehouse. The pupils and professors slept in the schoolhouse. The mechanicals were more complicated. They got greasy like ordinary laborers, but a lot of them had university engineering degrees and were thus respectable professionals. Still, they had their own places to sleep—either their workshops or in the small cottages nearby.

Everybody had their own places to eat. Some servants might wait at their masters' dining tables, pouring wine and hefting serving platters, but they would never dare to eat at those tables. The farmhands' kids even went to school in a different building than Mick and the other Institute students. And Heaven and all the saints forgive you if you messed up and called the wrong person by their first name. And almost everybody was the wrong person—for a people who spent so much time congratulating themselves on being thoroughly Christian, Victorians sure had something against Christian names.

The pecking order gave Mick the creeps. Still, the fact that the alley rat students and professors were the only ones allowed in their dining room did allow them to discuss time travel. And sometimes the students had to talk about time travel to make sense of their lessons. Or to make sense of their lives—sometimes, it helped to just talk to somebody else about falling backward in time a few generations. To protect the future, they weren't allowed to talk about it in detail, not even what year they had come from. But just knowing that you weren't imagining time travel was a huge relief. If you didn't talk about it, you'd go crazy. And if you talked to the wrong person, they'd think you were crazy and you might get locked up in a madhouse. 1853 London had a lot of horrible places, and madhouses were near the top of the list.

If Mick wanted to discuss time travel, or anything else, with a student, he'd have to do it with Stephen the Snob, who was the only student still at either of the cozy dining hall's two long tables. Chris was sitting at Stephen's left elbow because Chris was everywhere, like oxygen with a quizzical expression.

Mick hesitated at the door, wondering whether he had the strength to be polite to Stephen. On the other hand, Mick had been delayed beyond the regular dinner hour, so the plate of food at Chris' elbow that she kept pointing to was his only chance at dinner. Maybe that's why Chris was welcome everywhere, Mick realized—because she was always doing nice little things like that.

"Hello, Stephen," Mick said as he slid into the chair across from Chris and next to Stephen. "Thanks, Chris. Is Elmer all right?"

"I've not heard any news since I last saw you," Chris said. "But if he'd taken poorly, people would have raised the alarm."

"Elmer's a good chap," Stephen said with an intensity that surprised Mick. Stephen usually hoarded kind words like dragons hoarded gold.

Mick caught himself wondering if there were dragons. That

happened to him sometimes now. He knew dragons were made-up. Impossible. Goofy, even.

Just like time travel.

It was annoying, Mick thought. You grew up. You realized Santa wasn't real. You realized the Tooth Fairy didn't make sense. That Smaug would weigh too much to ever get off the ground. You felt a little dumb for ever believing any of it. You felt a little sad you couldn't believe it anymore. But that was how it was.

And then there you were, in a world full of time alleys that plucked you from your real life and dropped you in the past. There were books about alleys to study. There were classes. There were alley patrol routes that street teams like the Squad had to follow so that greet teams like the Snobs would know where to be when some scared kid dropped half-naked and half-dead from the future. And there was an Institute that ran all of that, and a Project that ran the Institute, and a bunch of alley rats trying to run the Project or just run cons on it.

And, once you had time alleys, anything was possible, including and especially the impossible. Maybe there *were* dragons. Maybe Smaug slept on a big pile of gold under the Antarctic ice. Maybe Santa Claus was real, after all. Maybe the reindeer pulled his sleigh through time alleys, and that's how he could deliver toys to billions of people on the same night. Maybe Christmas Eve lasted fifty weeks for Santa, and he spent the other two weeks on vacation with Mrs. Claus. On the moon. In 10,000 B.C. With Smaug.

Mick remembered the Alice books, which his mom had read to him before bed a bunch when he was in the first grade. He'd always liked when the Red Queen explained that she believed six impossible things before breakfast. Now, sometimes at breakfast, he looked up from his porridge and sliced black pudding and wondered if he still had any idea what was impossible.

One thing he did know, though, was that he couldn't trust people when they claimed to know for certain what was impossible, at least when it came to time travel. When he first got the Institute, everybody—including the professors—had said that it was impossible to turn drop alleys, which brought people from the future, into lift alleys, which took people to the past. But it was possible, at least if you were willing to hurt a lot of innocent people doing it. People had said it was impossible for adults to use time alleys. But it wasn't.

And they all said that it was basically impossible to use a time alley to travel to the future. And they all said, even more forcefully, that it was totally impossible to use a time to travel to one's *own* future because all alley rats who lived long enough to reach the day of their birth died at the very instant of their birth, devoured by birth flame. But Mick had to believe that was wrong too. Otherwise, he'd never get back home, and he didn't accept that. The other kids all seemed like they accepted being stuck in the past. He'd read a bunch of alley rat journals from the even more distant past. Kids who'd dropped into 1720 or whatever had started off saying how they just wanted to go home, but then two years later they were saying they wanted to go to the horse fair, or the theater, or to take the sea air. You could read those journals and watch kids just … forget their futures. It was depressing.

He realized Stephen and Chris were staring at him. He must have zoned out. His plate was empty, so he must have scarfed his dinner without tasting it. Too bad. He really liked chicken and brown bread. "Sorry," he said. "I was thinking about something."

Chris' half-smile twitched up to three-quarters of a smile for a second. "Evidently."

"What did I miss?" Mick asked.

"Naught of import," she said. "Save that the two of you are to go to the warehouse for morning labors."

"No sheep?" Mick asked. The farmhands were shearing the sheep to keep them from getting sick or just stuck on their backs, unable to stand up because the wool was so heavy, and he'd been told to go to the pasture in the morning to help.

"No sheep," Chris said.

That was okay by Mick. He didn't like shearing sheep. He knew it needed to be done to keep them healthy—and to get their wool, of course—but it somehow seemed cruel. There you were, a sheep, just chewing some grass or sprinting with all the other sheep from one end of the meadow to the other for some obscure sheepy reason. Then *wham*, a couple humans were grabbing you and cutting off all your wool, including flipping you on your back and holding your hooves. And then the humans would let you go, and you'd have no wool and no idea what had just happened. It was a lot like being an alley rat, really. Except that the sheep got to go back to their family and friends.

Mick tried to cheer up. He didn't usually spend so much time feeling sorry for himself, but the attack on the *Baret* and Elmer's injuries had stirred up memories of how battered and scared he'd been when he'd dropped into 1853. It was another reminder that you could be drifting smoothly along on a sunny day, and life would sneak up and smack you around with a heavy club.

After dinner, Chris headed back to the Scythe. Standing in the liquid sunny air of an evening just starting to go orange at the edges of the sky, Mick could hear but not see the cheerful calls and taunts of kids playing tag or some other game, probably on the Manor lawn. He thought about joining them, but the day had worn him out. Stephen, who at thirteen was too old and dignified to play with other children, said he was going upstairs to revise for his courses. Mick told himself he was going to do the same and even pulled out his notes to read. But he made the mistake of trying to read in his cot. The thin, lumpy mattress had never felt so soft, and the next thing he knew it was morning.

It turned out that Stephen and Mick—along with Ward and a couple of the older Institute students—were needed at the warehouse because Silas and Henry from the warehouse were replacing Mrs. Maxwell and Rosie on the *Baret* while Mrs. Maxwell and Rosie stayed home to look after Elmer. Having Silas and Henry aboard would help scare off any crooks who were thinking about taking another shot at the narrowboat. They were tall, broad-shouldered men with heavy, callused hands, and they definitely would have made Mick think twice about trying anything.

Mick and the other kids tried their best, but there were a lot of heavy boxes, bales, and oddments that they couldn't begin to budge. So they moved the lighter items until there weren't any left. The two remaining warehousemen, George and Miles, looked at one another and shrugged before Miles shooed the kids away. The sound of faraway church bells said it was nine o'clock, which meant that there was breakfast in the dining hall. Mick's rumbling stomach said it couldn't be soon enough.

Instead of listening to his stomach, Mick joined Stephen and Ward in stopping off at the Maxwells' cottage. It was a warm, sunny day, with a gentle breeze, and the Maxwells had taken Nurse Peck's comments about healthy air to heart—the door and the front window shutters were wide open.

Mick, Stephen, and Ward stopped when they got where they could see through the doorway and realized it wasn't just Mrs. Maxwell, Elmer, and Rosie in the tiny parlor. There, in Mr. Maxwell's chair, was Lady Penbrook herself. That was highly unusual. Mick couldn't remember ever seeing Lady Penbrook on the Scythe, much less in the Maxwells' cottage. She mostly stayed in the Manor, though occasionally she stepped into the schoolhouse to observe a lesson or strode forth to inspect Demeter's fields and paddocks.

Hovering just outside the door, Stephen, Ward, and Mick looked at one another uncertainly. Lady Penbrook solved their uncertainty by turning her eyes to them. "Ah, boys, your timing is most opportune."

Ward gulped and tried to straighten his back while tilting his gaze downward as if something really fascinating were happening on his bootlaces. Fancy people made Ward nervous. "Nobs and nabobs give a chap a shiver," he'd told Mick more than once. Stephen also looked down, but that was just to show respect. Stephen loved being near nobs and nabobs.

Mick stood up straight but kept his eyes on Lady Penbrook's face. Mick got the sense that some people thought looking straight at fancy people was "impertinent." 1853 English people loved calling other people impertinent for not sucking up enough. But until Lady Penbrook actually told him to stare at his toes, he wasn't going to do it. He learned a lot more with his eyes up.

"Ward, do fetch a bucket of water for poor Mrs. Maxwell," Lady Penbrook said.

"Yes, Lady Penbrook," Ward said, turning around and scurrying out, his feet crunching on the gravel as he headed for the well.

"Mr. Burton," Lady Penbrook told Stephen, "please inform Nurse Peck that she is to attend to Elmer before luncheon."

"At once, Lady Penbrook," Stephen said, bowing. Though he left more calmly than Ward, he was still speeding up when he turned out of sight.

Lady Penbrook tilted her head at Mick, her eyes alight with a bright alley rat glow and, he thought, with curiosity. Her lips might have twitched with a wry grin before her face settled into its usual neutral expression.

Mick didn't blame Ward for finding Lady Penbrook intimidating. She reminded Mick of Miss North, a professor at the Institute whom he admired and feared. They both had the same no-nonsense tone of voice, the same sharp eyes, and the same air of command. But while, as a professor and as Headmistress of the Institute's mostly fictional Girls' School, Miss North got obedience from students and some professors, Lady Penbrook got it from everybody. Even Chris did a little bow whenever she talked to Lady Penbrook.

Mick was still trying to make sense of the pecking order in Victorian England, but he did know that Lady Penbrook was a big deal. She was a Viscountess who had somehow inherited, or half-inherited, the title from her late husband even though titles usually went to male relatives. That made her a "peer of the realm," which was very fancy indeed. There were some notches above viscountesses, including the royal family, but there were a lot more notches below, including barons, baronets, and knights. And, of course, everybody else.

Pretty much everybody in England was everybody else. "Commoners," they were called. Even half the English version of Congress—the Parliament—was the House of Commons, and it wasn't as important as the House of Lords, which was for people like Lady Penbrook. Well, for male people like Lady Penbrook. The House of Commons was for fancy ordinary people. Actual ordinary people didn't seem to matter much, not even pasty white ordinary people. Less white ordinary people like Mick or Stephen or Miss Emmet, well, that could get awkward. Not inside the Institute or at Demeter, mostly. Because he wasn't too obviously off-white, it was usually okay for Mick even outside the Institute, especially when he was wearing the respectable suit the Institute made him wear whenever he went out. But Miss Emmet didn't like to go outside if she could avoid it. And Stephen, well, maybe that was why he acted like such a jerk sometimes. From the start, because Stephen and his greet team members had picked on him, Mick had thought of them as "the Snobs," but he'd recently learned that in 1853, "snob" didn't mean "somebody who thought they were better than everybody else." It meant "somebody who wasn't better than everybody else but wanted people to think they were." Maybe that definition was better—maybe Stephen figured it was safer to come across as an uptight rich kid than a humble and vulnerable commoner.

Lady Penbrook was still looking at Mick. He felt tempted to

ask if he could do something for her, but he'd learned that Victorian adults mostly wanted kids to keep their mouths shut.

The pause dragged out until Lady Penbrook said, "Mr. Gunn, pray accompany me back to the farm."

Mick hadn't expected that. "Yes, Lady Penbrook."

Lady Penbrook took her leave of the Maxwells and gracefully eased her wide, sea-green gown through the narrow front doorway, like canal water flowing through a lock.

Mick fell in step as she walked briskly back toward the main farm. It occurred to him that a surprising benefit of the long, poofy gowns Lady Penbrook wore was that you couldn't see her legs and feet. She could move quite fast without anybody being able to see whether she was working hard to make it happen. Her calm face and almost motionless arms almost made it seem as if she were standing still.

Other than noting that the weather was "most fine," Lady Penbrook hardly spoke a word. After a long silence, they entered the south end of the main drive, and Mick started to wonder whether he was in trouble.

But he didn't think he'd done anything wrong. At the Institute, he'd gotten busted for a few different kinds of sneaking around, but at Demeter, he'd been a good boy. He'd only been sneaking around at the Institute because there had been bad things going on and he'd thought sneaking around would help stop them. Besides, there wasn't anywhere good to sneak to at Demeter. The Institute had creepy cellars, hidden vaults, and secret passages, and it was in a part of London full of people and excitement. The only cellars at Demeter were pantries, and the farm was in the middle of Dullsville. No, worse, it was in the middle of Boring Little Village, a suburb of Dullsville. Mick would have had to take two trains to get to Dullsville. Some of the farmhands liked to go to The Globe, the pub next door to the Scythe, to drink beer and play skittles (the bowling game, not the candy). But Mick didn't like beer or ye olde bowling. So unless he wanted to get stuck in a haystack or fall into the canal, there was no reason to go sneaking.

Still, even though Mick hadn't done anything wrong, Lady Penbrook had the knack of making him feel like he might be in big trouble. That feeling intensified after she led him past the farmhands' quarters and the schoolhouse but didn't turn onto manor drive as Mick had expected.

They had walked halfway around the main drive, just past the stand of trees separating the hayfields from the crops, when Mick got confused enough to risk speaking first. "Ma— Your Ladyship, aren't we going to the Manor?"

"Not at present, Mr. Gunn." Although pleasant, Lady Penbrook's tone discouraged further questions.

Still not speaking, they walked almost all the way around the main drive until it intersected with the paddock path. Turning onto the path, they passed chickens, pigs, sheep, cows, and horses. The farm hands were still shearing sheep, and the further Lady Penbrook took him, the more Mick felt like a sheep being led to the shearing.

After the horse barn, the paddock path turned into a narrow strip of dirt cutting across the pasture, and Lady Penbrook continued onward. The path was too narrow for Mick to walk beside her, so he dropped a couple paces behind. He kept a nervous eye out to avoid stepping on the hem of her dress, which skimmed the grass to either side of the path but mostly avoided dragging along the damp earth of the path itself.

Belatedly, Mick realized they had to be heading for the Refuge, the ancient stone building hidden behind the bushes and thick trunks of birch and London planes at the northeast edge of the property. The trees were tall, maybe eighty or a hundred feet, and their branches and leaves mostly didn't start until the roof of the two-story Refuge. Mick liked the trees, especially the London planes, which were common in the Institute's neighborhood. Alison said they helped pull pollution out of the air, which made them heroes in Mick's book.

Stepping through an old wrought-iron gate cloaked with ivy, they entered a courtyard Mick had never seen. The ground was covered by heavy, dark gray stones, fuzzed over in many places by moss that grew thickest in the cracks between stones. Pushed up by massive roots, the stones nearest the trees swelled and dipped like waves on an uneasy ocean, some of them nearly turned on their sides by a few especially thick and gnarled roots. Even on a hot summer morning, the dense canopy of trees left the air cool and the light dim. Mick half-expected the Refuge to be a ghost town shell, but there was only a light coating of dust on its windows, and, when Lady Penbrook unlocked it, its door swung open on silent, shiny brass hinges.

Mick found himself standing on the rough floorboards of a large, squarish room with a low ceiling. At its center, dominating the room, was a circular table with a lot of chairs. None of the oil lamps hanging from the exposed ceiling beams were lit, so the room was illuminated only by the soft light sneaking through the high windows. On the white plaster walls, Mick could see a few paintings hung from wires, but the only ones in good enough light to be seen clearly were two portraits of the same Black woman, her round face peeking out from fancy clothes and showy jewels, her sharp eyes scrutinizing him from across the room. At the Institute, all the portraits were of pale people, almost all men, and it was startling to see a sort of face that was familiar to him from his real life.

"Has Mr. Webster steeped you in the history of Demeter Farm?" Lady Penbrook asked Mick.

Mr. Webster was the professor who did most of the teaching at Demeter, at least for the Institute kids. "Yes, ma— Yes, your Ladyship."

"When conversing, the proper form of address is 'my lady,'" she said. "Or 'Lady Penbrook,' when first you address me."

"I'm sorry, your— my lady," Mick said.

"Oh, it's of no matter to me, personally. If people do as I tell them, I don't concern myself with what they call me." She smiled slightly. "So long as no coarse oaths are involved. Still, a boy born in this time and place would be expected to know the proper form of address, at least a boy whose life occasionally brings him into the presence of peers."

"Yes, my lady," Mick said.

"Good, good," she said. "Now, do tell me what you know of the farm's history."

Mick briefly wondered what was going on. Lady Penbrook sometimes summoned students to her to discuss what they had learned during their time at Demeter. But those were usually groups of a half-dozen or so students, including the one that Alison, Dolly, and Leech had been part of a couple days before they left. And those discussions happened in one of the Manor's parlors, not the Refuge. Mick started to worry that he'd done something wrong.

But he couldn't worry about it too long with Lady Penbrook looking at him expectantly. He launched into the version of the farm's history that Mr. Webster had drilled into his head over the summer. Demeter Farm was on some of the land that had belonged to the Institute when it was founded back in 1592. Although, back then, it had been called the Refuge School. In 1658, a bigger, fancier school called Young Scholars had been founded in London, and the Institute had eventually replaced it. The London schools had become the main schools, and the Refuge had become a farm first and a school second, a sort of retirement home for professors who hadn't saved their salaries and a dirty detention hall for problem students. By 1688, the school had been pretty pitiful, and the farm hadn't been all that much better, and that was the year the Nye twins had dropped from the future.

Mick looked at the portraits. Right—those weren't two portraits of the same woman. They were portraits of twins, Gemma and Athena Nye. He remembered Alison having said something about Lady Penbrook discussing the Nye twins during their talk.

He tried to remember what Mr. Webster had taught them about the Nye twins. The best evidence indicated that their late point—the date in the future when they stepped into a time alley and were pulled into the past—was pretty close to 1800 and that they had been about ten years old when they dropped in 1688. They had probably been enslaved in their original lives, but nobody really knew much about who they had been before they went into their time alley because, like most rats in those days, they hadn't left future journals. And it wasn't as if the Nye twins would have needed help remembering the future, or anything else. All the stories said they had almost supernaturally good memories. Around 1711, they had managed to buy all the Refuge's land and everything on it, one of the many properties they apparently bought before they both died at ripe old ages. Of course, people always said they probably hadn't officially owned the properties, or at least not all of them, because back then the laws had made it even harder for women to own property, especially women of color.

Stumbling a little over dates, Mick recited that history to Lady Penbrook, who had turned a chair away from the table and sat in it so that she could watch Mick as he spoke. She hadn't invited him to sit, so he was standing a few feet away from her, looking over her shoulder at the Nye twins to avoid her unnerving scrutiny.

"Well done, Mr. Gunn," she said when he finished.

"Thank you, my lady."

"Yet, one wonders whether children here and now can fully appreciate how remarkable the Nye twins were. All alley rats fall penniless and friendless from the future. Profoundly vulnerable, as you well know."

Mick nodded, remembering how terrified and confused he'd been.

"Imagine, then, being the Nye twins."

Mick could imagine some of it. As hard as it had been for him to end up in Victorian London, it could have been so much worse. Something had gone wrong with his friend Alison's alley, separating her from her twin brother and stranding her in a distant city with no Institute. She'd been maybe five or six then. She'd made her way to London, alone, searching for her brother and living for years on the street with other street kids, kids she was close friends with even now that she was at the Institute, and she'd made sure her friends had been taken in at Orphans. Whether in the proud houses on fancy streets or in the filthy alleyways inhabited by those too poor to rent a piece of dirty floor in even the meanest slum dwelling, Victorian London was dangerous for girls, even lily-white girls like

Alison. London almost two hundred years earlier had been far worse, especially for girls of color. The fact that the Nye twins had survived at all was amazing. The fact that they managed to become so rich they could buy a big chunk of Peckham... Well.

Staring at the Nye twins' identical faces and nearly identical expressions, Mick thought it was lucky the twins had been together. He thought of his sister Emilia and felt a pang of sadness. He missed her a lot. He wondered if she missed him. Did babies miss their brothers?

He liked to think that he could return to exactly the moment he left the future so that nobody would miss him because they'd never know that he'd left. But the longer he was in the past, the more he doubted that would work. He was already a few months older. According to Miss Weathers' measurements right before he'd come to Demeter, he was almost an inch taller, which might be tricky to explain if he returned to the future at the exact same moment he had disappeared. On the other hand, Uncle Dan wasn't too sharp about stuff like that. He might not notice even if Mick popped back into the future a foot taller and speaking in a London accent. And even if Uncle Dan did notice, he'd never guess—or believe—what had actually happened. Nobody would. So the main thing was to get back to his real life and sort out the rest when he got there. He just wanted to see Emilia giggling and gumming Swaggy Bear's paws.

Thinking of Swaggy Bear made Mick think of Tía Julieta. In addition to making ugly teddy bears out of all-natural materials, Tía Julieta was into horoscopes. She was always talking about how she loved to talk loudly and laugh louder because she was a Gemini. "Kiddo, when you're born under the twin sign like me, you gotta have enough personality for two people."

Mick's attention snapped back to the world around him. He was still staring at the Nye twins' portraits. The twin sign. He laughed.

"Something amusing, Mr. Gunn?" Lady Penbrook asked.

"Gemma Nye. Gemini. The horoscope sign for twins. It was a little joke, wasn't it? Like the Forsyth Institute?" It had taken Mick a while to realize that "Forsyth Institute" was a play on words for "Foresight Institute."

Lady Penbrook grinned. "Astute of you to notice, Mr. Gunn. Do sit," she said, turning her chair partway back to the table and patting the chair beside it.

With a bit of grunting, Mick turned the chair to face Lady Penbrook and clambered into it, his feet dangling above the floor.

"Were you in fact imagining being the Nye twins just now, when your attention wandered far from this room?" Lady Penbrook asked.

"Sort of, yes, my lady. They must have been really sma—intelligent. And brave."

"Both of those things, very much so," Lady Penbrook said. "And their phenomenal powers of memory were doubtless useful for people trying to blend into a new place and time."

"I bet it also helped to be able to remember the future really well," Mick said. These days, alley rats weren't supposed to take advantage of knowing the future because doing so might change the future. But back in the day, especially as far back in the Nye twins, it had been different. Alley rats hadn't worried about breaking the future and had done a bunch of crazy stuff. So either they hadn't broken the future because the future couldn't be broken, or they had broken it, and now everybody lived in a broken future but didn't know it.

Lady Penbrook tilted her head at him slightly. "Indeed," she said. "Though sometimes it hurts very much to remember a future beyond one's reach. Does it pain you still?"

Mick suddenly felt moisture in his eyes but managed to hold back the tears. "Sometimes."

"And if you could return to that future, you would?"

He nodded. "But..."

"But of course you cannot, or so all the wise professors solemnly say. Then again, the wise professors once solemnly and incorrectly said that dust can give birth to actual rats and that we dusty humans are the center of all the heavenly spheres. So we alley rats may yet surprise the professors and even the heavens themselves."

Mick nodded. He didn't know what she meant, but she'd used the I Am Speaking Wisdom voice, and when grown-ups did that, it was usually best just to nod. Besides, he was willing to listen to any adult who didn't say that returning to the future was flat-out impossible.

Lady Penbrook tilted her head again, just a little. Mick got the sense she knew why he was nodding. "Moreover, regardless of whether we are indeed doomed to plod forward through time in the ordinary way, our painful memories can be blessings. I am of the mind that our pain can spur us to build something better." After a long pause, she added, "You have rather cheated me of a chance to deliver one of my favorite sermons."

"I'm sorry," Mick said.

"Oh, you needn't apologize. In truth, I have delivered that sermon more than once of late. I risk numbing myself to it with repetition."

"What's it about?" Mick asked. "Your sermon?"

"The Nye twins. Their perseverance in defiance of adversity

and injustice, their cultivation of the inner dignity that allows one to suffer outward indignity. But you appear already to understand the Nye twins as well as can be expected. So let us press forward. Do you know the story of Demeter herself?"

He tried to remember what Mr. Webster had told them on the first day of class. "She was a farm goddess or something."

"Indeed. She was a Titan, a sister to Zeus and Hades. Their father ate the three of them when they were infants, along with their other brothers and sisters. Titans were forever eating babies, usually because there was a prophecy that the babies would grow up to be more powerful than their parents. They were a ravenous passel of gods. And shockingly poor parents, in the main. After Demeter escaped her father's stomach, she grew to adulthood and had a daughter by Zeus named Persephone. One day Persephone was out picking flowers, and Hades, who had become king of the underworld, dragged Persephone down to the underworld to be his bride."

Mick did the math. Persephone's father was also her uncle. And her husband was a different uncle. Yuck.

"Indeed," Lady Penbrook said, seeing the expression on Mick's face. "Demeter grew so despondent—that means sad—at losing her daughter to the underworld, she abandoned her duties as goddess of the harvest. The crops failed and mortals everywhere began starving to death. So Zeus, who was by then the king of the gods—"

"He's the one that throws lightning?" Mick asked. All the professors talked about the Greek and Roman gods like they were cousins everybody knew from the barbecue, but Mick had trouble keeping them all straight.

"Quite," Lady Penbrook said. "Zeus told Hades to let Persephone return to the world above, our world. However, because

Persephone had eaten food in the underworld, she couldn't remain in our world year-round. She had to go back to the underworld for part of the year, as she still must, even today. Each time she goes back, Demeter refuses to let the crops grow. That's why crops only grow part of the year."

Mick knew this was all just mythology, but he was having the dragon problem. If time travel was real, maybe the Greek gods were too.

"The Nye twins," Lady Penbrook continued, "gave Demeter Farm its name, you know. I usually weave that into the sermon I've just spared you. It's important to know what the Nye twins knew: that triumph can grow even out of the soil of violence and loss. Consider also, Mr. Gunn, that Athena Nye named herself for Athena, goddess of both wisdom and warfare. Some say Athena was born from Zeus' forehead after Zeus ate her mother while her mother was pregnant with Athena. I rather suspect Athena Nye chose the name because she knew that wisdom and victory can spring forth from violence and loss."

There was the Speaking Wisdom voice again. Mick nodded dutifully.

"Being an alley rat means suffering violence and loss, Mr. Gunn, some more than others. That is partly why I give the sermon, to remind children of what I remind you now: you can take that loss and pain and transform it into life, into purpose."

For a moment, Lady Penbrook's gaze held his unblinkingly, her face intense. She clearly was telling him something important, though Mick couldn't tell what. Then her neutral expression slid back into place, and she stood up, patting him lightly on the shoulder before leading him out of the Refuge and toward the Manor.

Mick got back too late for breakfast, so a few hours later, he really dug into lunch. As he took his nearly full belly and very empty plate to the courtyard, he thought about Persephone getting stuck in the underworld because she had eaten there. Had he doomed himself to being stuck in the past by eating too many meals there? He told himself it was just stories.

He even believed himself, mostly.

CHAPTER 4

INHALING THE SMOKE

Chris and Ward were waiting for Mick at the schoolhouse door when he left tutorial that afternoon. As usual, Ward looked nervous to be near the schoolhouse, and Chris looked amused by the world and its contents.

"Nurse Peck said it were all right to visit Elmer," Ward said. "We reckoned you might want to go too."

Mick checked his pocket watch to see if he had time before he had to be in the fields.

"Don't fret, Gunner," Chris said. "You're at liberty the rest of the afternoon."

"I am?" Mick asked, grateful but confused.

"You return to the nobs tomorrow morning," Chris said. "We leave after breakfast." She gestured toward the footpath, and the three of them all started walking toward the Maxwells' cottage.

Mick was surprised to be leaving Demeter. He'd known he would be going back to the Institute soon enough. But when

Leech, Alison, and Dolly had gone back, they'd gotten a few days' notice.

"I didn't mess u— I didn't mess it, did I?" Mick asked as they turned onto the drive. "Being at Demeter, I mean?"

"If they didn't tell you that you did something wrong, you likely didn't," Chris replied.

"Adults like to tell a chap he's done something wrong," Ward added. "Even when he never done nothing. Though those around here aren't so bad as— other places."

In the Maxwells' tiny parlor, Elmer had recovered enough to be sitting up in the armchair, though the bruises on his face were vividly purple and the dark hair on the side of his head had been shaved to reveal an angry red gash. It was hard to tell in the dim light, but Mick thought he might have seen stitches in the gash.

Elmer grinned broadly at Chris and Ward, including Mick in the smile. Then he winced, probably because smiling hurt.

"Nurse Peck managed to stuff your brains back in your skull, did she?" Chris asked.

"She said it was all straw and sawdust to start with," Elmer said.

"Nurse didn't say nothing like that," said Rosie, who was hovering at her brother's side.

Mick couldn't tell if Rosie had stood up from the couch to make room for Chris, Ward, and him, or if she'd been hovering there for hours. In any case, nobody sat down, so everybody just stood around awkwardly until Chris said, "Oh, for heaven's sake, Rosie, do sit. You're in your own parlor."

Rosie sat grudgingly, as if putting her full weight on the sofa might reopen her brother's wound.

"Greetings, Rosie," Ward said, his voice a little strangled and his face tomato-red with blushing.

"Ward," Rosie said, smiling shyly.

"There's tea for them as wants it," called Mrs. Maxwell's voice from the kitchen.

"We shouldn't wish to be a bother, Missus M," Chris called back.

Mrs. Maxwell poked her white bonnet into the room. "If my tea is good enough for Lady Penbrook herself, I'll thank you not to turn up your nose, Chris Biggs."

"I suppose we can't possibly refuse," Chris said, winking at Ward and Mick.

"Too right you can't," Mrs. Maxwell said, disappearing back into the kitchen.

Moments later, Mrs. Maxwell brought tea for everyone. Elmer and Chris got the good porcelain teacups and the nearly matching saucers, and everyone else got wooden cups.

Mrs. Maxwell couldn't bring herself to sit down. She fussed and hovered over her son. That was enough to make Rosie pop back to her feet. Mother and daughter stood there stiffly, hands and arms twitching, as if they kept trying to do something but didn't know what.

Mick sipped his tea, glad to have a wooden cup. He didn't mind drinking from the Vicar's wafer-thin teacups because the Institute could afford to replace a cup if he ever dropped one, although he never had. But in 1853 London, most working people didn't have fancy cups, except maybe family heirlooms or wedding gifts.

In a vivid flash of memory, Mick was six years old, holding his mom's hand in a gift shop at O'Hare Airport before flying to Los

Angeles to visit his dad's family for Christmas. He remembered being eye level with dozens and dozens of cheap Chicago souvenir mugs emblazoned with the Cubs logo or photos of the Willis Tower. Never mind everything else at the airport—the airplanes and the electric lights and the moving sidewalks—even the coffee mugs would have blown Victorians' minds. Color photographs? Unheard of. Color photographs on mugs? Probably witchcraft.

That moment in the fluorescent lights of the O'Hare gift shop, the warmth of his mother's hand, the sounds of the loudspeakers, even the hum of the refrigerators packed with diet sodas and overpriced egg salad sandwiches, it all rushed over him, for a moment overwhelming 1853 and erasing the Maxwells' parlor.

As if he'd jinxed himself by thinking about dropping it, Mick nearly let the wooden cup slip from his hands. But he recovered just in time, splashing a few hot drops of tea on the back of his hand.

Once again, he realized that even if he could manage to do what everybody said he couldn't do, if he could somehow get back to his life in the future, his mom would still be dead. Unless he could do the doubly impossible and go back *before* she died and somehow save her even though the doctors couldn't, but that felt wrong, even as a fantasy. It was one thing to wander around in a past that felt like an alien world, a museum world full of weird accents and weirder worldviews. It was another, scarier thing to imagine changing events that he had lived through. Even events he hated. Because if he could undo them, he could undo himself. And he was already struggling to hold on to himself.

"Gunner?" Chris asked.

"Sorry— what?" Mick asked, letting the future fade back into memory.

"Never mind," she said, with a small grin. She turned back to Elmer. "You're quite sure you're not planning to die? Only, I've my eye upon your churchgoing hat, if you are."

Elmer laughed and then flinched, putting a hand to his ribs. "I'll be keeping my hat, Chris Biggs, so I shall."

"Ah, how selfish some are, how selfish," Chris said. "Gunner, Ward, if you've quite finished drinking Mrs. Maxwell's very fine tea, we ought to tend to our own business."

Mick and Ward gulped down the rest of their tea, and the three of them took their leave, each shaking Elmer's hand. Ward mumbled something friendly to Rosie that might have included actual words.

Then they were back in the warm sunshine. Ward said something about cows and took off toward the farm at a trot.

"That boy will have lungs like a horse, running about as he does," Chris said fondly. "I don't know if his ribcage will be big enough for them, especially with his heart already swollen for Rosie."

She turned her gaze to Mick. "As you are a gentleman of leisure this afternoon, follow me to the Crow's Nest, if you will."

The Crow's Nest was a little tower atop the warehouse that you got to by climbing the ladder to the loft and then another ladder through the roof. The warehousemen and the mechanicals sometimes used it to keep an eye on the farm and the canal. Students weren't usually allowed up there, but being with Chris was like having a letter from the Queen saying that the rules didn't apply to you.

After they clambered up the ladders and into the Crow's Nest, Chris lowered the trap door back into place.

The Crow's Nest had a fantastic view in all directions, including of the sprawling, smoggy mass of London to the north. It felt a lot like a screened porch, and that feeling intensified when Chris slid a large window to one side, allowing her to swivel a hefty brass telescope outward.

Chris fiddled with the telescope's focus for a while, swiveled the telescope a bit, and fiddled with the focus some more. "Ah, there she is."

"Who?" Mick asked.

"The *Baret*," Chris said. "See for yourself."

Following the direction of Chris' waving hand, Mick spotted a box hanging below the windowsill. It held two pairs of old-timey binoculars. He slipped the strap of one pair over his neck and turned his gaze in the same direction the telescope was pointing, a spot on the main canal not far beyond the trees surrounding the Refuge. Mick turned the focus knob until a dark blur on the canal resolved itself into the *Baret*, with Jeanne plodding ahead. They were drifting slowly and unhurriedly toward the turn to the south branch that flowed past the Scythe. Mick couldn't see anybody's faces, but he could see two people aboard, presumably Mr. Maxwell and one of the warehousemen. He thought he might have recognized Silas' thick ginger hair and beard.

"No sign of pirates, I should say," Chris remarked. "Am I missing a Jolly Roger?"

"I don't think so," Mick said, scanning both directions along the main branch and then along the south branch for good measure. He knew Chris was mostly kidding about pirates, but Elmer's beatdown had been pretty brutal, and it didn't hurt to keep an eye out. When he'd finished scanning for ambushers, he looked north to see if he could spot the Institute. But the air was dull with distant rain, and the smog had swallowed the Thames and the buildings, like the Institute, that lay beyond of it.

Lowering his binoculars, Mick found Chris staring appraisingly at him. "If I'm not mistaken," she said, "Lady Penbrook took you to the Refuge for the sermon this morning?"

Chris always knew things and always managed to not explain how she knew them. "Sort of, yeah," Mick said. "There was a lot about Demeter. Not the farm. The goddess and her whole inbred family."

"Am I right to suppose that the theme was that violence and loss can be the rich soil of justice? With some discussion of Athena, goddess of war and wisdom?"

"Basically."

Chris raised her eyebrows. "Well, your education in the classics is proceeding apace. I shall be most interested to follow what you learn."

Mick didn't know what that was supposed to mean. "Why did she tell me all of that? Am I in trouble? Is there something wrong with the alleys again?"

Chris raised an eyebrow. "Lady Penbrook's thoughts run deep as the oceans and subtle as a Sphinx's riddle, so I can only speculate. But I doubt you are in trouble. Quite the opposite, in fact. I suspect she sees promise in you. And she may also foresee... Well, let me not cast my wee boat into deep seas." She smiled. "No need to wallow in worry on such a beautiful day."

Chris' cheerfully bland expression conveyed that she had said all she intended to say. After holding her gaze for a moment, Mick shrugged and looked away. The farm's green and golden fields were thick with life, and he felt a little pang of sadness to realize that he would be leaving them soon, them and the people he'd gotten to know and like. Maybe leaving them forever. Institute kids usually did only one summer at Demeter. Looking beyond the farm to the brooding blur of the great city, he realized that if he figured out how to get back home, he'd be leaving behind London and all the people there he knew. It was a gloomy thought, that whether he went forward or backward in life, he would keep leaving people and places behind.

He shook his head. He wasn't just leaving things behind. He was also going toward things. Returning to his people and his place. After his mom died, people had kept telling him that he couldn't live in the past. And that was true, even when he was literally living in the past. The future might look blurry and smoggy now, but he needed to head in its direction and hope the skies cleared up by the time he got there.

At breakfast the next morning, Mick had bread and butter. He had a lot of gripes about Victorian England, but the butter was *way* better, especially at the farm. Packing went quickly. He was already wearing the respectable suit the Institute made him wear in public. His required ready money of one florin, one shilling, and threepence was in a small leather purse tucked in his jacket pocket. Other than that, he only had his half-empty leather satchel from the Institute, which, as required, contained three calling cards for the Institute, a small notebook, two pencils, and a penknife. It also contained an optional copy of *Wilson's London Guide*. It felt like he should be taking more with him, but he didn't know what. Maybe a tablet and charger.

Maybe a Demeter Farms souvenir mug decorated with a cheesy picture taken from the Crow's Nest.

Downstairs, he found Chris waiting in the courtyard. "Ready to inhale the Smoke?" she asked, standing up from a shady stone bench.

Mick nodded. He was looking forward to seeing his friends again.

"Good, good. I am informed that, although the esteemed faculty of the Institute treasure you beyond all measure and are counting the seconds until you return"—she grinned a little at him and he couldn't help but grin back—"they are nonetheless willing to let you take the slow way with me. I've quite a few errands, and I thought you might want to see some parts of London that don't show up on the rashers and the greet sheets."

For a minute, Mick was surprised to hear Institute patrol slang from Chris. He kept forgetting that she'd also gone there. As they started strolling toward the Scythe, Mick wondered yet again what Chris' late point was. She seemed so comfortable in Victorian England that he was tempted to think she couldn't have come from too far in the future, maybe from 1953 in some backward village that had been a hundred years behind the times. On the other hand, she seemed perfectly comfortable wandering around in men's clothes with a man's haircut, even though Victorian ladies got judged and mocked if they didn't have ridiculously long hair and wear girly-girl dresses. Letting strangers' confused stares and side-eye slide off you, that seemed like the sort of thing you'd expect from Tía Verónica's edgy friends with pink and green hair and three layers of tattoos.

The skies were sunny and clear, and the air was gently warm as they reached the warehouse dock, where the *Baret* sat low in the water, already heavy with the goods still being loaded onto her. Near a hitching post, Jeanne was nuzzling bits of apple out of Rosie's hand, meaning that Elmer must have been well enough for Rosie to get back to work. There was no sign of Mrs. Maxwell, though, so she was probably still looking after Elmer.

Near the edge of the dock, sitting awkwardly on a smallish crate, was Mr. Yardley, a mechanical who looked like a college student but was apparently a full member of the King's College Engineering Society. He was a tall, skinny guy, made mostly of knees, elbows, and neck, a fact driven home as he unfurled himself from the crate when he spotted Chris. He doffed and waved his shapeless gray cap in greeting before jamming it back over his thick sandy curls and bending down to pick up the crate. He handed it to Chris, who accepted it with a little grunt suggesting it was heavy.

"Thankee, Oliver," Chris told Mr. Yardley, stepping carefully onto the canal boat and wedging the crate into a convenient spot. "We're off to the palace."

"Returning when?" Mr. Yardley asked Chris in a voice so deep that it startled Mick, as it did every time. A voice like that had no business coming out of somebody who looked like a pencil wearing a waistcoat.

"Perhaps tomorrow or the next day."

Mr. Yardley nodded and turned and walked back toward the workshops with a wave over his shoulder.

By the time Mick had stepped carefully onto the *Baret*, Rosie was untying Jeanne's reins from the hitching post, and just like that, the narrowboat was underway, pulled along by the big roan's calmly flexing muscles. Mr. Maxwell was up front, holding a pole in case he needed to push against the edge of the canal, and Miles was farther back, holding a cudgel, in case he needed to bash in a pirate's head.

Mick and Chris sat fifteen or so yards behind Mr. Maxwell, close to the rear of the narrowboat. Chris chatted cheerfully, but she stayed standing and was scanning in all directions. They'd only been floating a few minutes when Rosie unhitched Jeanne from the tow rope and led her over the Hill Street bridge. With Rosie and the horse now on the other side of the canal, the tow rope was reattached, and they continued on their way, only now set up to carefully take the tight left turn onto the main branch of the Grand Surrey Canal. Mr. Maxwell waved at the toll collector on the far bank, but they didn't stop at the tollhouse. Lady Penbrook had some arrangement with the toll collector that Chris had once tried to explain to Mick.

Something had been bothering Mick. "You're not actually taking me to the Palace, are you?"

Chris smiled. Speaking softly so that her voice wouldn't carry forward to Miles and Mr. Maxwell, she said, "Not the Queen's Palace, if that's what you mean. 'The Palace' is what we simple folk call any of the rarefied buildings associated with the Project, including the Institute."

Mick nodded. That was a relief.

After drifting quietly for about a quarter hour, they stepped off the boat at a lane leading away from the canal. A teenage boy, maybe sixteen or seventeen, with broad shoulders and a dirty face, was waiting for them, leaning against an oversized wheelbarrow. Mr. Maxwell called hello and tossed one mooring line to the teenager, then the other.

Chris hefted the crate out of the *Baret* and into the wheelbarrow, working it carefully into the straw. Mr. Maxwell handed her a couple sacks of vegetables of some kind, which she draped over the crate. She raised her eyebrows at the teenager. "If you will, Mr. Davies."

Mr. Davies raised his eyebrows back. "But of course, Miss Biggs." He flashed a set of teeth so white that Mick double-checked to make sure that his eyes didn't have an alley rat glow.

With that, they began a long, pleasant walk that was probably less pleasant for Mr. Davies, who was pushing the wheelbarrow along the uneven and occasionally rutted roads. Mick wanted to offer to help, but he was wearing his fancy suit, and kids in fancy suits didn't push wheelbarrows. He started to feel guilty about acting like a spoiled brat, even though that was sort of his job.

After a bit, Mick realized that they were at the southern outskirts of Zoo Cluster. It was one of the least active time alley clusters in London, but it was still a cluster, which meant that he might spot a time alley, or at least sense a stirring of some kind. But he didn't see anything, and he couldn't hear even the faintest note of alley song. That wasn't surprising. When streets and greets went on patrol, they went to the places most likely to have a time alley that day, and still, mostly, nothing happened. And even if something did happen, probably nothing *really* happened—maybe you'd get a stirring or two that never turned into an alley. Or you might get a fawkes, an alley that opened but didn't have an alley rat in it. Real alleys and real alley rats were rare, when you got down to it.

After about a quarter hour, they stopped at a dusty intersection. Mick closed his eyes to call up the map of London that long hours of study had tattooed onto his brain. By now, he had a pretty decent sense of where London's important roads and notable neighborhoods were. Somehow, being at Demeter, in an area of London without a cluster, he'd felt like he was a million miles from the Institute. But now that he was in an area near the dark purple triangle marking the Zoo Cluster, he was suddenly reconnected with all of it.

When he reopened his eyes, he realized that a wagon had pulled up just in front of them and that Chris was loading the heavy crate and the sacks of produce into the back, among some other crates and sacks. Chris clambered into the bed of the wagon, sitting atop her crate. She gestured for Mick to join her, so he climbed up the short ladder attached to the side of the wagon and found a crate to sit on.

"Mr. Davies, if you please," Chris said. At first, Mick thought she was talking to the teenager, but the teenager was doffing his cap to say goodbye.

"Yes, Miss Biggs," the waggoner in the front seat said, flicking the reins at the pair of swaybacked horses, who grudgingly began to walk forward. Mick assumed the waggoner and the teenager were related, maybe father and son. The waggoner's eyes also showed no hint of an alley rat glow.

Moving slowly and joltingly, the wagon eventually made its way past the bright green expanse of Kennington Common. After closing his eyes to conjure up the Plan, the Institute's map of London and its time alley clusters, Mick accurately predicted they would be crossing the Thames at the Vauxhall Bridge. The river sparkled with sunlight and teemed with boats and ships of all shapes and sizes except the tall-masted ships and enormous iron-hulled steamships coming from or going to the farthest reaches of the globe, which didn't come so far west.

After clattering down the bridge, they turned to roll beside the river. A couple kids not much older than Mick waved at Chris from the Millbank stairs, and she waved cheerfully back. The wagon bumped along between the river and the high walls and deceptively cheery spires of Millbank Prison. They were probably in the Scholars Play Ground cluster, although it was hard to be sure. Scholars Play Ground was the only London cluster that "twived," meaning that it wandered around a bit from day to day. Mick wondered if unlucky alley rats ever dropped into the prison. He'd never heard of that happening, but you never knew, especially since the prison's layout supposedly was so weird even the guards got lost.

After a while, they turned away from the river, stopping while Mr. Davies pushed some of the crates around in the back and Chris chatted with a grimy urchin who apparently spent all day watching the horse ferry. The urchin somehow talked Chris out of a penny in exchange for telling her about all the boring stuff that had gone across the river on the ferry that day. It went on long enough that Mick dozed off and woke up only when the wagon started rolling again.

Not too much later, Mick realized that they were near the Seat. "Seat" stood for the Society for the Enlightened Advancement of Trade, which was secretly the headquarters of the Project. Mick hadn't been inside, but a couple months earlier, he had spent a memorable night following somebody up to no good through the streets of London, sometimes at a flat-out sprint, and the chase had ended at the Seat. His heart sped up a little remembering it.

After fighting congestion and nearly fighting a couple surly coachmen and waggoners over who had the right of way, Mr. Davies turned the wagon onto a narrow drive leading to the courtyard at the rear of the Seat. The courtyard was a calm oasis, where elegant stone walls and soaring London planes muffled the grumbling city. Spending so long in Demeter's sleepy pastures had made Mick forget how noisy and bustling

London could be. In the courtyard, once Mr. Davies' mares came to a rest and their hoofbeats stopped echoing off the Seat's walls, the only clear sound was the quiet nickering from the mares and from the sleek, broad chestnut horses hitched to the enamel black carriage waiting at the bottom of the short stairway thirty or forty feet distant. Mick could just make out a large brass "H" on the side of one of the carriage's four doors.

"One of Lord Harrowgrave's carriages, I think, Mr. Davies?" Chris said conversationally.

"I believe you have the right of it, miss."

Mick sat in the back of the wagon, leaning his head against a large crate and staring up at the half-dozen stories of tall windows and the crisp blue skies above, savoring the gentle warmth of a friendly summer morning. He had just started to doze off again when the wagon bed shook as Chris stood up and waved lazily.

Mick followed her gaze to see a square-jawed, square-shouldered Captain America-looking guy in an expensive suit jogging down the short flight of stairs near the fancy carriage. Well, it wouldn't be Captain *America*. Captain England? Captain Empire?

"Mr. Blake," Chris said with a smile as the man came to a stop at the side of the wagon.

"Chris," the man said, raising his hat a few inches above his thick blond hair. His eyes twinkled with mischief and with a fairly bright alley rat glow. "My heart flutters like a butterfly freshly freed from its cocoon." He held his hands to his chest and made exaggerated flapping motions.

Mick tried to remember Uncle Dan's comic book digital subscription. He was pretty sure there'd been a Captain Britain.

Chris stuck out her tongue at Captain Britain's corny flattery and squatted to grasp the small crate she'd taken from Mr. Yardley at the Demeter loading dock. She hefted it up and balanced it on the wagon's box board. The man lifted it down easily, still grinning.

"His lordship will be waiting for that, I'd wager," Chris said, tilting her head toward the elegantly dressed man with a dark beard stepping down the small stairway toward the fancy carriage.

Over the top of the coach, the coachman's hat jogged forward a couple paces as the bearded man approached the carriage. Mick heard the carriage doors open, and the carriage shimmied a bit. One of the curtains on the near side opened partway, and Mick caught a glimpse of a young woman in an expensive, cream-colored hat and matching high-necked dress.

For a moment, Mike thought he recognized her, like maybe he'd seen her at Kosciuszko Park when his family was taking their old dog Scootie for a walk. That was a weird thing about going somewhere new—part of his brain would try to make everything familiar, and he'd keep thinking he recognized people even though he couldn't possibly. Brains were strange.

"A pleasure as always, Miss Biggs," Mr. Blake said, turning and carrying the crate toward the carriage.

The glossy black carriage shimmied as Mr. Blake hoisted first the box and then himself inside and again when the coachman closed the doors and clambered into the driver's seat. The carriage started rolling and soon disappeared from sight.

Mick wanted to ask Chris what had been in the crate. But since the crate came from Mr. Yardley, it had almost surely come from the mechanicals, meaning it was probably something Chris couldn't talk about, especially not where Mr.

Davies could hear. So Mick just asked her how often she went to the Seat, and she replied, "More than enough."

Mr. Davies was already removing the chocks from the wagon wheels, and soon the mares were tugging the wagon back into London's stink and clamor. It wasn't even noon yet, and they were only a couple miles from the Institute. Mick figured that even with sluggish horses plodding along crowded streets, it shouldn't be long until they got there.

Mick hadn't counted on all the stops. Meandering along a mazy route that more than once doubled back on itself, they wound their way through some of the fanciest parts of London. Mick got more and more impatient every time a turn took them away from the Institute. And it didn't help that they stopped frequently to pick up and drop off boxes, parcels, sacks, and stacks of who knew what. Annoyingly, sometimes they simply stopped to chat.

Mick tried to soothe his impatience by guessing what Chris and Mr. Davies were up to. A lot of the pick-ups and deliveries and much of the chatting happened at places that belonged to the Project—the Seat, the Ladies Society for Moral Advancement, the Learned Society of the Great Globe, and Lady Grenville's Academy. Those were all places where well-dressed people with fancy accents smiled tightly at one another with what Victorians considered good teeth. But they weren't stopping at just the fancy places. They often pulled over in unremarkable places for unclear reasons. Each time that happened, Mr. Davies swung down from the driver's seat and fussed with items in the bed of the wagon. Mick eventually realized that was just for show. And he was starting to suspect that the ragged street urchins who always managed to beg a coin from Chris in exchange for their street news weren't actually street urchins, at least not all of them. A lot of them had what Victorians considered to be good teeth, and, if you looked past the generous layer of grime, they didn't look unhealthy enough to be poor people in a place where even rich people's medication often made them sicker.

Mostly, the Institute's streets and greets wore their Little Ladies' and Little Gentlemen's clothes when they patrolled, but sometimes they went out in disguises, including going disguised as street urchins. The more Mick got used to Victorian England, the better he was getting at spotting the subtle flaws in those disguises. Of course, with streets and greets, it was easy for him to know when to take a close look. Streets and greets had glowing alley rat eyes, which they couldn't cover up with dirt and tattered clothes from the Old Clothes Exchange. But the kids and teens coming up to Chris didn't have alley rat eyes. Still, they did have a similar way of looking around. Most street kids in London were always looking around carefully, just like the kids coming up to Chris. But real street kids also had a wariness caused by worrying about someone getting the drop on them. The kids who kept coming up to Chris were a little calmer, somehow. Mick didn't know what to make of it. Several times, he almost asked Chris who the kids were and why she was dragging him on such a long tour of London, but it might not be safe to ask where Mr. Davies could hear him, not if whatever Chris was up to involved time alleys. Although Mr. Davies obviously was involved in whatever game Chris was playing, there was no way she had told him anything about time travel.

At Lady Grenville's, Chris took a long break to stroll along Hyde Park with Lady Somebody, the Academy's headmistress, and a grim-looking young woman who seemed to be Lady

Somebody's assistant. Chris told Mick to follow them, keeping an eye out for pickpockets. He doubted Chris needed any help with that, but he did as instructed. From fifteen yards back, it looked like a casual, friendly conversation, though Chris was doing the hat tugs and head bows that Victorian London expected from a working-class person attending on a nob. Specifically, she was doing a pretty good impression of being a young tradesman of some sort. Chris didn't go around telling people with words that she was a man, but she was pretty good at saying it without speaking.

Eventually, they returned to Lady Grenville's. After Lady Fancyface went back inside, Mick followed Chris around the corner, where they settled back into Mr. Davies' wagon.

"Do you know," Chris said to Mick as the wagon rattled away from Lady Grenville's, "I rather miss the old gal."

"The headmistress?" Mick asked.

"Lady Eunice?" Chris asked, laughing. "Dear me, she would utterly detest being called 'gal,' much less 'old gal.' And I don't much miss her, to be frank. I meant Lady Grenville's. I rather enjoyed my time there, much to everyone's shock, including my own."

Mick was surprised that Chris had gone to Lady Grenville's. Kids from the Institute always described Lady Grenville's as a place where female alley rats learned to wear silk gowns and to pretend that dull men were witty. Alison and Dolly used its name to scare each other straight when they didn't want to study.

His surprise must have shown on his face. Chris chuckled.

After a few minutes, they were heading east on Oxford Street along a stretch of road that, before going to Demeter, Mick had walked nearly every day going to and from the Institute. Even with the pavements crowded with handcarts and pedestrians, he could have walked it in twenty minutes. So it would probably somehow be hours before they got there. His stomach muttered at him, reminding him he'd already missed lunch.

Chris said, "Your tragic expression suggests that you are unenthused about the prospect of further errands."

Mick blushed but didn't deny it.

"Well, you're a patient young chap, but I suppose it's right enough for you to wish to see your friends again." Shouting to be heard over the London din, Chris said, "Cavendish Square, Mr. Davies."

Soon enough, Mr. Davies had brought the wagon to a halt in front of the Royal Polytechnic, where Chris hopped over the side of the wagon and Mick followed suit. "You can finish the deliveries, Mr. Davies, I should think," she said. "I shall attend to my business and spend the night at the palace, if they'll have me." She pointed to the plump, elderly horses. "Try not to let our fierce fillies trample too many pedestrians."

Mr. Davies raised his eyebrows at her. "I'm but one man, miss." He flicked the reins at the horses, raising his cap in farewell. Chris raised hers back.

Mick did the same, not sure if that was right. He was never sure what to do with his cap. In public, Victorian men basically lived in their hats, but there was a whole semaphore around when, how, and how much to take them off and put them back on. Luckily, boys Mick's age got a little bit more flexibility, or at least forgiveness. Which was good because Mick disliked wearing hats. Hats were just one more thing to make you sweaty when you were trying to run to a time alley before it opened, and one more thing to lose to the wind when you were trying to buy a baked potato from a street vendor. Thinking of street vendors made Mick miss his real life again. Elote. He missed elote. And granizados on hot summer days, like this one. Baked potatoes were okay, but they weren't elote. They weren't even fries. He looked around the park at the center of Cavendish Square, hoping that somehow it would turn out to be a real park—something with jungle gyms and kids yelling twenty-first-century words that he could yell back without destroying the space-time continuum.

Nope. Still a bunch of pasty English people, each one wearing enough clothing to make a four-person tent. Wherever Chris was taking him, it was still in 1853.

CHAPTER 5

SPIES AND SNEAKS

Chris led Mick to a stone bench beneath tall trees. She gestured that he should sit, even though she remained standing, apparently casual but quietly alert.

Mick sat. He couldn't sense or see any time alleys, and he didn't know what Chris was looking for, so gradually he let himself relax, staring blankly at the statue of Lord Bentinck. It was a pretty good statute. Lord Bentinck looked like a person, mostly, which was a nice change of pace. Most of the sculptures in Victorian London looked like what you'd get if influencers could turn selfies into marble and metal—stiff expressions, weird body language, and a general "look at me, look at me" vibe that always made him want to stick googly eyes on them.

"Have you any reflections on the day's errands, Mr. Gunn?" Chris asked in an exaggerated schoolmarm voice.

"Yes." He stopped there, pretty sure his answer would make her roll her eyes.

It did, but she grinned so that he'd know she understood his game. "Such as?"

"Well, I have questions. The big one is, what was in the crate? The one Mr. Yardley gave you. But also, who were those kids who kept coming up to you? I have other questions too."

"Why didn't you ask me at the time, Mr. Gunn?" she asked, still in the schoolmarm tone.

"I didn't know if it was all right to talk about in public, especially with Mr. Davies there, and all."

"I trust you won't be too shaken to learn that I'm not going to tell you what was in the crate or even whether I myself know."

Mick was a hundred percent sure she knew.

"What else? Ah, yes, the kids. And why, pray tell, do you ask about those endearing scamps?"

Mick explained how a lot of them seemed too healthy to be real street urchins.

She smiled at him and dropped the schoolmarm voice when answering. "Just so, Gunner. But they're quite good at playacting, though of course playacting is often unnecessary because most people have trained themselves never to look at the poor. Or at least to look only enough to make sure that nearby poor people don't appear dangerous. That's often the key to being dangerous, by the by. Don't look dangerous." She gestured at her humble, worn clothing and grinned.

Mick raised his eyebrows at her to show he was still waiting for an answer about who the kids actually were.

"Spies and sneaks," she said.

"Spies?"

"Observers. There are people throughout London, including real and counterfeit urchins whom we call 'Eyes' because they keep their eyes on important people and places. There are a great many 'lookouts,' points that Eyes watch over because something important or interesting might happen there. Important buildings. Busy roads, especially the ones entering and leaving the city. Railroads. Canals. Thames bridges. The docks."

Mick thought about their route that day. It checked out. They had made a lot of stops at Project buildings, including the Seat. "It's for the Project, right?"

"Well done, Gunner."

"But not time travel." Their eyes had shown they weren't alley rats, so they couldn't have been looking for time alleys.

"Well done, indeed." She kept her usual joking tone, but Mick was pretty sure she meant it. It felt good to impress Chris. "Clearly you spotted at least some of the Eyes and the lookouts. Where would you say you saw them?"

Mick closed his eyes and tried to retrace their route. He hadn't really noticed anything until they got north of the Thames. "Other than the kids who came up to the wagon?" he asked.

"You may pass over those."

They had taken so many detours that Mick couldn't entirely remember the order in which he had seen the potential Eyes, but he was pretty sure he remembered the places. He closed his eyes so that he could run a mental finger over the Plan. "The Millbank stairs," he said. "The horse ferry. The Old Palace Yard. Off Parliament Street before we passed the Board of Control. The Treasury. Where St. James's meets Pall Mall. And maybe the Stationery Office. Did I already say Trafalgar Square? Oh, and I think maybe Green Park, right by Hyde Park."

"Anywhere else?" Chris asked.

Mick thought for a minute before opening his eyes. "I can't remember any." He looked across Cavendish Square. "There are a couple of fake urchins over there right now, but I'm pretty sure they're a greet team. Maybe from Tory Four, at least the tall girl." He squinted. "Yeah, she's a Four."

"I'm told you have very good alley sight," Chris said. "But your street sight is quite good as well. Most rats with good alley sight forget to use their ordinary eyes."

"Alison tries to teach us," Mick said. "She's really good. She always remembers where things were, including people. So she always sort of knows who's moving, and where."

"Miss March? The young headmistress?" Chris said with surprise.

Mick liked "the young headmistress" as a nickname for Alison. But as book-smart and prim and proper as Alison was, there was more to her. "She lived on the streets before the Institute found her. For a really long time," he said. "She sees the streets better than any kid at the Institute, probably."

Chris cocked her head and stared into space for a while before tapping a fingertip to her temple. "Foolish of me to miss that."

Mick waited for Chris to explain, but she went back to the earlier thread of the conversation. "Still, even with help from Miss March, you must be a quick study. That's good. Alley sight is a prized gift at the Institute. But a cultivated street sight is also a worthy ability, even if no professor ever pats your head for it."

Mick nodded, keeping an eye on the Tory Four fake urchins. As if responding to his gaze, they ambled away, crossing the street and disappearing from sight.

"A trifle obvious," Chris said, watching them go. "We teach the Eyes better."

Mick wondered if Chris was supposed to be telling him about the Eyes. At the Institute, or Demeter, or anywhere in 1853 London, adults usually didn't tell kids anything. The most he got was an occasional hint from Miss Emmet.

As if reading his mind, Chris grinned and said, "Not to worry, young sir. I'm not speaking out of turn. I've charge of a great many of the Eyes, in my own way, and it's my right to discuss them as I see fit."

She raised her eyebrows at Mick, asking him to agree with something, though he wasn't sure what. He nodded.

"Now, the young headmistress, I'm sure she's pointed out that the London streets are filled with people signaling one another. Beggars, thieves, street sweeps, even the peelers, all of them whistling, hooting, waving arms, and the like."

Mick nodded again. Alison hadn't needed to point it out. *Hyde's Practical* had several pages on it, and it was pretty obvious once you got used to the London streets. But Alison had helped him get better at spotting the less obvious watchers and giving him some handle on who all the watchers were and what they were doing. It had been an adjustment. In twenty-first-century Chicago, technology was almost always watching you—security cameras, cookies, GPS—but probably actual people weren't, at least not with their own eyes. You were lucky if people looked up from their phones long enough to avoid plowing into you on the sidewalk. In Victorian London, on the other hand, the tech couldn't watch you, but everybody was looking around with actual human eyeballs, and the odds were pretty good that some of those eyeballs were tracking you. The watchers probably didn't care about you personally or plan to do anything about you, or to you, but they were watching.

Chris continued, "And there are more Eyes in London than any other single group of watchers, more than even the peelers, I should say. All ages, many sorts of livelihood. But the difference isn't just the number of Eyes. The difference is the Mind."

Mick could hear the capital letter. He could tell Chris wanted him to ask what the Mind was. So he didn't.

She stared at him for a bit before realizing he was messing with her. She chuckled. "'The Mind,' you ask, 'pray tell, Chris, what is this Mind?' Well, I'm glad you ask, young sir, I'm glad you ask. The Mind is the people who try to understand what the Eyes see. Men and women from the Project. Dons, if there's alley business afoot, others if not. They try to puzzle it out. To see sequences, connections, oddities, and so on. There are a few levels of the Mind, from the street right up to the Seat."

Mick nodded. Like tall ships to the Channel, information always flowed to the Seat eventually. "And it's not just about alleys?"

"Indeed not. Of course, in the murky world of the Project, things that seem not to be about alleys sometimes are." She shrugged. "And things that seem to be about alleys sometimes are not."

"So you're part of the Mind?" Mick asked.

"I suppose I am," Chris said. "I like to think of myself as Good Sense. The Mind tries to make pictures from what the eyes see. But sometimes it tries too hard and makes pictures of something that isn't there. Or misses something that is. Here is a tidbit of erudition I acquired at Lady Grenville's: the *punctum caecum*. That's the spot at the back of your eye where the optic nerve attaches to the eyeball. The optic nerve is how information gets from your eye to your mind. The tricky thing is, the optic nerve actually creates a dead spot where it touches the eyeball. So when the light coming into your eyeball hits that spot, your eye doesn't notice it and can't tell the brain about it. The very thing that carries the information destroys some information. It's a literal blind spot."

Poonk-toom see-coom. Mick repeated it in his head a couple times. It seemed like the sort of thing he could drop into conversation to make Alison wonder if he was smarter than he looked.

"But if the human mind does its job," she continued, "it fills in the missing information and you're never aware you have a blind spot. And if it does its job properly, what it fills in is actually there. That is what the Mind is supposed to do for the Project."

Mick started looking for the blind spot, closing one eye, then the other. He stopped when he saw Chris smirking at him.

"So, some blind spots you can live with. Maybe you even need some of them. But sometimes the Eyes miss something. Maybe by accident, maybe because somebody's deceiving them. Maybe the Eyes are deceiving the Mind. And sometimes important information falls into a blind spot that the Mind doesn't know about, and that information goes unseen. And sometimes the Eyes are simply looking the wrong way altogether, and the information marches by while their backs are turned. I try to prevent that from happening. I look for the blind Eyes, the lazy Eyes, the lying Eyes, the misdirected Eyes, and the Eyes in need of spectacles."

"Isn't that the Mind's job?" Mick asked.

"Yes and no. The Mind likes words, especially written words. I'd swear some of them think the words have magical powers, like sorcerers' spells. But words aren't deeds, and a great deal may be missed between the word and the deed. Some truths can only be learned out in the world."

He'd known that Chris often disappeared from Demeter for days at a time. Now he knew why.

Chris frowned thoughtfully for a moment. "When one spends so much time fearing that something important is escaping one's notice, one can easily begin turning harmless shadows into lurking monsters."

Mick could hear the "but" very clearly, so he waited for it.

"Nonetheless," Chris said. "I believe the Eyes may be seeing signs of something important. Vexatiously confused and confusing signs, but signs even so. I have conveyed something of my suspicions to Lady Penbrook, which may have contributed to her decision to speak with you when she did."

"What's going on?" Mick asked.

"Vexatiously confused and confusing," Chris repeated. "I cannot say whether something of import is happening, much less what it might be. But I do suspect something is indeed afoot. And I fear it may prove ... unwelcome."

"Is what happened to Elmer part of it?" Mick asked.

Chris shook her head in frustration. "I often ask myself the same question."

Before Mick could think of his next question, Chris said, "I cannot safely or wisely say more, except that you have proven to be an observant child, and not without some glimmers of wisdom. Do continue to be as observant and as wise as you can in the coming days."

"What should I be—"

Chris cut him off with a smile. "You must be looking forward to seeing your friends again."

Mick knew she was telling him that she had said all that she planned to say. But that was okay. He did want to see his friends.

Letting the city's din fill the friendly silence between them, they walked the few short blocks to the Institute. As they went, the self-serious young men who attended the Royal Polytechnic thinned out, largely replaced by a more varied crowd of well-to-do Londoners. As they reached Mortimer Square, there were a few groups of kids, mostly within a few years of Mick's age. He recognized most of them, and the rest fit the model of Institute students. These were streets and greets, going to or returning from patrol. Like him, they were dressed like children of moderately prosperous doctors and lawyers—fancy enough to get respect from cops but not fancy enough to be gossiped about by status-obsessed Londoners.

And, of course, their discussion about the Eyes had him looking around carefully while pretending he wasn't. He knew Eyes sometimes looked like urchins, but Chris had basically said they could also look like rich kids. Or rich adults. Or not even be visible. Pretending to brush dirt off his suit, Mick spun slowly around, trying to figure out where he would put people to watch the Institute, especially if he didn't want them to be seen. Well, you could set up easily enough across Little Castle to watch the Girls' School entrance, but if you wanted to watch the more frequently used Boys' School entrance you'd need one of the homes facing Mortimer Square. This time of year, the tall trees rising high above the fence around the square would interfere with your view, but maybe one of the top floors would work. But those were expensive houses. It would be way cheaper, and maybe more useful, to watch the professors' and dons' doors on Berners Street. You could just set up a baked potato cart or a coffee stall next to the County Court. If it was decent coffee, you'd actually turn a profit. Leech said the man with the only coffee stall on Berners made pretty good money even though what he sold was more chicory than coffee.

He caught Chris staring at him with an amused expression.

"In theory, only a very few people from the Project are authorized to keep watch on the Institute, and only then to make sure that nobody else is spying on it." She paused. "Then again, some people never will believe the rules apply to them."

That afternoon, Mick weirdly enjoyed going through the rigamarole of getting into the Institute. Ringing to announce himself, opening the heavy Boys' School door if Mr. James didn't open it for him, walking down the dark, low-ceilinged corridor to check in with the warden, and, finally, emerging into the soaring white marble surprise of the Great Hall. That morning, the Great Hall was sparkling in the late August sunshine pouring through the enormous skylight a half dozen stories above the lobby.

He looked around, half-hoping to see the Squad waiting for him. They weren't, of course. They probably didn't even know he was coming. And they might be out on patrol. Mick was a little distressed to realize he didn't know their current patrol schedule.

Chris led him to the dons' wing, climbing some stairs and unlocking a couple sturdy doors along the way. Eventually, she opened another heavy door, which opened into a pleasant, airy hall not nearly so imposing as the Great Hall but larger and more elegantly appointed than the common room in Tory Six.

"The dons' lounge," Chris said.

Mick looked at the dozen or so dons scattered throughout the room. He was pretty sure that he and Leech had hidden from one or two of them while sneaking around the Institute after curfew trying to catch the Mysterious Interloper. And there was Miss Mitchell, the head don, at a table in a patch of sunlight at the far side of the lounge. Gail Atkinson, the thane of Mick's greet team, was sitting with Miss Mitchell, even though Gail wasn't a don. Gail waved cheerfully.

As they started in that direction, Mick asked Chris, "Were you a don?"

"You know I wasn't," she said. "Poor alley sight. Lady Grenville's."

Right, right. "So why do you have keys?"

"A pure heart and a kind soul unlock every door," she said with a lopsided grin.

Mick couldn't quite manage to get annoyed. He tried to think of a better way to ask the question, but then they were in arm's reach of Gail and Miss Mitchell. Both of them used it as an opportunity to give Chris a hug. Chris' short hair nearly disappeared as Miss Mitchell's frizzy dark hair covered it from one side and Gail's straight, dark hair fell over it from the other.

Mick grinned at how stiff Chris got. She definitely wasn't a hugger.

He escaped with just pats on the shoulder and had mixed feelings about that. It was like family picnics. He always steeled himself to get hugged by a bunch of aunts, "aunts," and miscellaneous other family members, and if all he got were waves and fist bumps, he was relieved and disappointed at the same time. He didn't want to be hugged, exactly, but he did want people to want to hug him, especially cool people like Miss Mitchell and Gail. Miss Mitchell wasn't just the head don. She was also the one who had taught Mick how to do the required "condy" (constitutional development) exercises that improved his concentration and agility. And he'd stolen part of his fake name from her. And Gail was, well, Gail. She was the day prefect, which made her sort of the highest-ranking student at the Institute. She was the best spotter, best thane, and baddest all-around boss on the streets. Also, he might—might—just have had a little crush on her, even though she was several years older and several times smarter.

Chris took a seat without waiting to be asked. Mick threw caution to the wind and did the same. Miss Mitchell and Gail sat back down.

"And thus," Chris said in a deep, theatrical voice, "I return unto ye a son of the palace, pardoned at last from his sentence of exile."

Mick rolled his eyes.

Gail grinned at his reaction. "Welcome back, Gunner."

"Yes, welcome back, Mr. Gunn," Miss Mitchell said. There was a little question mark at the end of it, and she raised her eyebrows at Chris. Mick guessed that Miss Mitchell was asking why he was in the don's lounge.

"Lady Penbrook gave him the goddess Athena speech," Chris said. "And I've just given him a primer on the Eyes."

That didn't seem like an answer to Mick, but Miss Mitchell and Gail nodded as if it were.

"He spotted most of the lookouts on the way here, by the by," Chris told them. "He credited Miss March's instruction."

Gail nodded. "Miss March is admirably alert."

"In any case," Chris said, "you needn't hide the Eyes from Gunner here as you continue to guide him on patrol." She told

Mick, "Dons and sometimes greets receive information from the Eyes."

"Some of it even proves useful," Gail said dryly. "On rare occasions."

"Omniscience is bad for the soul," Chris said. "Consider it part of your spiritual development."

"I'm halfway to sainthood, I should think," Miss Mitchell said with a grin.

"Well, Gunner," Chris said, "I believe we ought to show ourselves out." She stood, and Mick did the same. "Though, ladies, after I finish my rounds, I may have a tale or two to tell you. Scandal at society balls and the like, don't you know."

With that she turned and swept toward the exit. Mick shrugged and followed her, stopping partway to turn and wave awkwardly at Gail and Miss Mitchell. Gail waved back, but he was pretty sure it was a pity wave, so he felt like a doofus and turned away fast. Before Chris swung open the door, Mick noticed that carved into a single line running near the top of the door was the phrase "Count Every Second. Consider Every Instant."

Once they were back in the hallway, Chris led him to the familiar parts of the Institute, where she shook her arms to free her sleeves and stuck out a hand to shake his. "And with that, Mr. Gunn, I leave you to your palace and return to the perils and the pleasures of the streets."

She walked briskly down the corridor and disappeared from sight by turning onto a side corridor that Mick would have sworn led only to a broom closet. Mick stared for a minute, his head tilted to one side, and then trotted after her, turning into the same side corridor and opening the only door, which indeed was for a broom closet. Mick was about to decide that

Chris was actually an elf or a fairy when he noticed a small door at the back of the closet low enough that he had to duck to step through it. He found himself in a side corridor that led quickly to the Great Hall. Chris was nowhere in sight. Mick thought must be nice to have all the cheat codes to life.

Mick started looking for the Squad in the Tory Six common room but didn't find them. He shrugged and decided to drop off his satchel before figuring out whether to mount a search or take a nap.

Leech wasn't in their room, but his laughter was. It threw Mick off for a second until he noticed that the rope ladder to the roof was fastened in place. He followed Leech's voice up the ladder and slid out the window that opened onto the roof. His friends were seated nearby, in the shade cast by a tall copper cistern. Alison spotted him first, of course, and smiled broadly. Leech and Dolly followed her gaze and then her example. "Gunner!" Leech exclaimed.

There they were. Tall Alison with a narrow face and sleek, dark hair. Dolly, who was about Mick's height, with a roundish face framed by frizzy brown hair with an occasional strand popping up like an exclamation mark. Leech, taller than Dolly and Mick but shorter than Alison, pushing his wavy hair out of his eyes and back from his square forehead. They were all still desperately pale, though a little tanner after the summer.

Mick grinned. It had only been a few days, but he really had missed them. They'd been the first people he'd seen when he'd dropped into the past. If it had been anybody else, he might have gotten killed or gone crazy. Assuming he *hadn't* gone crazy, of course.

Mick rolled off the window ledge and stood upright just in time to get his hugs from Dolly and Alison. When they were done, Leech shook Mick's right hand and grabbed his left elbow like an MMA grapple. Leech was stronger than he looked.

When Leech eventually let go, he asked Mick whether Elmer Maxwell really had been attacked. Apparently students returning from Demeter had brought the news back with them. Mick told them what little he knew. They all looked as worried and baffled as he felt. When their speculation about the attack wound down, Mick asked, "What did I miss here?"

"Well," Leech said, interrupting both Dolly and Alison. "Something very peculiar has been happening with the alleys."

Mick tensed up, picturing the dead kids who had fallen from the waylaid alleys. Picturing the raging and disappointed Cassandra Halliwell, who had almost cut him apart with a knife before his friend Ellen Weathers had bashed her over the head. "What?"

Leech took a deep breath and said, "They're behaving properly."

Leech grinned. Alison punched him in the shoulder.

Mick let himself unclench. "Jerk."

Leech rubbed his shoulder and cast Alison a reproachful look. She sniffed disdainfully.

"Sorry, Gunner," Leech said. "But you must admit that it's actually quite peculiar for the alleys to behave themselves, of late."

"It has been pleasant to consult *Broome's* and have it be useful once again," Alison said.

"Sure, and if the books are useful again..." Leech said.

"Shall I punch him this time, Alison?" Dolly asked with a tiny smile that, for her, was the same as roaring laughter.

"But, really," Mick asked, "the alleys are all right?"

"To our knowledge, yes," Alison said, knocking for luck on one of the wooden legs supporting the cistern.

"And Miss North isn't angry with us?"

"To our knowledge, no," Alison said. This time, Dolly and Leech joined her in knocking on the cistern support. No kid at the Institute liked having Miss North mad at them.

"Mr. Victor is still terrifying?" Mick asked. "Mr. Phillips still wants everyone to sing? Miss Emmet still talks to her books? Mrs. Robbin still can't tell students apart?"

"Yes to all," Leech said. "Miss North did say that you were to see her if you arrived by four o'clock, but it's gone quarter past already, so it will have to be tomorrow."

"Did she say why?"

Leech shook his head. "But she didn't seem angry."

They sat on the roof for a while, chatting about everything from the castle-shaped cloud in the blue sky to the thick raven curls on the new boy who had dropped a few days earlier near the Fever Hospital. At some point, Mick must have found everything so soothing that he dozed off. He woke up with the others already standing, their dark instisuits surrounding him. He flashed back to dropping into 1853 five months earlier and waking up surrounded by his friends' legs before he'd known they would become his friends. Back then he'd been battered and baffled. Now he was drowsy with sunshine and sleepy with safety. It was a nice feeling, he thought as he pulled himself to his feet.

CHAPTER 6

THE LIGHTNING CENTURY

A few days later, Mick reminded himself not to lean too heavily on any feeling, good or bad. Feelings shifted like cloud castles in the winds. This time, the few clouds at the edges of the sky didn't look like anything in particular, except possibly rain toward the west. And the sky above was clear, so the ground-level lighting that he was watching from the stand of Lord's New Cricket Ground was probably related to time alleys. He and the Squad had spotted the stirrings the day before, and Gail had led him and the Snobs there that day. Stephen was with them, having gotten back from Demeter the day before.

They'd had to cross the canal to get to the cricket ground, which had reminded Mick of Elmer Maxwell, who had mostly recovered, according to Stephen. Mick had been hoping that Miss North might have some information about who had attacked Elmer, but she'd had to postpone their meeting. Then it had been postponed again when Mick, Gail, and the Snobs had been called out to the cricket grounds to look at the lightning.

Mick felt a little guilty that he was starting to get bored. He was worried, of course, because the lightning might be connected to an alley, and any time an alley acted weird, there was a chance that the alley rat inside it would be hurt or killed. If there was an alley rat inside it, of course. There often wasn't. And weird activity was extra ominous given Chris' vague warning to be on the alert. Still, the lightning hadn't changed since they'd gotten there, except for occasionally getting a little brighter or duller. And, of course, cricket itself was impossibly boring, unless you'd been infected with Englishness at birth, in which case you might be one of the Londoners in the packed stands buzzing with excitement because "Wilkinson was on a century." Even the Snobs were hyped.

Mick didn't understand cricket, but he assumed a "century" was a description of how long each inning of a cricket match lasted. It definitely felt like a couple centuries had passed since they'd gotten there. After the novelty of the scoreboard's being operated by telegraph wore off, the only thing keeping him awake was that, on the way to the ground, he could have sworn that he'd passed a group of fake street vendors selling roasted chestnuts and coffee on the St. John's Wood Road. He was hoping to catch a glimpse of what they were up to, but they were too far away for him to see much.

Mick wondered what would happen if an alley rat dropped onto the cricket pitch right in the middle of the lightning storm. Alley rats usually dropped with their clothes in tatters or with no clothes at all. He was trying to picture how a bunch of Englishmen in peaked caps and shin guards would react to that.

During an especially bright flare of lightning, Gail said,

"Odd." Mick followed her gaze across the cricket field to a cluster of spectators a couple hundred feet away. He had to squint through the lightning to see anything, so at first he wasn't sure what Gail meant. Then he realized that a couple of the people, a fashionably dressed man and woman, were shielding their eyes.

"You see?" she whispered out of the side of her mouth.

Mick nodded. "Alley rats."

"Indeed," she whispered.

They were too far away and too blurred by time lightning for Mick to see their faces, but they were adults, not students. Professors, maybe? Or dons? But if there had been professors or dons on Institute business in the area, the warden would have made a big fuss about it to Gail. Besides, their clothes were too showy.

"I wish I had field glasses," Gail said. "Ah, well, Nothing for it." She stood and started to walk behind the stands. Mick followed. Belatedly realizing something was afoot, the Snobs started to stand up. Gail subtly waved them off. "Hands in pockets," she told them.

The Snobs sat back down. "Hands in pockets" was Institute slang that meant to "stand by and keep watch."

Mick followed Gail around the stands, which were tall enough to block their view of the unknown alley rats, which was probably why Gail had told the Snobs to stay where they could see the unknown rats. Moving at a trot, Gail and Mick soon reached a break in the stands that let them cut back toward the unknown rats, but there was no sign of them.

Mick wondered whether to do a lap around the cricket ground to search for the vanished alley rats. But he stopped wondering when the time lightning changed color. It became a shimmering mix of pinks and purples and then sort of sucked back into a ball in the middle, like a tape measure pulling back into itself with a hiss and a click. The ball started shimmering and appeared to rotate slowly. In seconds, it was an ordinary glow-orb, probably an aperture Eight. About a yard away, the batter and the umpire stood oblivious to the whole thing.

Mick belatedly plucked out his pocket watch and started the stopwatch. One minute and eighteen seconds later, the glow orb framed up. Two minutes and fourteen seconds after that, it stopped rotating. Then came the flash of the aperture opening followed by a bright but unsurprising coronal flare, and a few seconds after that, the glow orb blinked out of existence. There was no sign that an alley rat had dropped from the alley, which was just as well because the batter on the century had gotten another hit and was sprinting pell mell where a dropper would have appeared.

Walking back to the Institute, the Snobs confirmed Gail's and Mick's observations of the alley. They also reported that the two unknown alley rats had left their seats right when Gail and Mick had started toward them. The Snobs hadn't seen their faces, either. When the woman had stood up, she'd opened a large parasol that had covered both unknown rats' faces until they'd turned away. Stephen reported that they had left by a side gate leading toward the Asylum for Orphan Children of the Clergy.

"Amazing stuff, what, Gunner?" Stephen asked him as they turned toward York Terrace.

"Definitely unusual," Mick responded, making sure his tone was friendly. This was the first time he'd patrolled with Stephen since they'd gone to Demeter for the summer. Before, when they'd been on patrol, Stephen had usually been trying to undermine him, and Mick realized that he was still tensing up every time Stephen spoke. But so far, Stephen was being more like his Demeter self—polite, even friendly. So Mick was trying to do the same.

"A hundred forty-one runs in a single innings," Stephen said, shaking his head. "He's a marvel, Wilkinson. They say he can see stitches on a shirt at fifty yards."

Mick forced himself not to smile. "Lucky for him he can't see time lightning, though. That would have ruined his batting."

Stephen grinned and slapped him on the back. "That it would, that it would."

Gail caught Mick's eye and grinned, and he smiled back. Soon, they were at York Terrace, and Gail let him take a detour to Mayor Cakes' bright red cart to buy spice cakes. The only reliable way to get a big smile from Dolly was to hand her a spice cake from Mayor Cakes, an old man with a face as red as his cart and teeth as brown as his frayed wool jacket. Mick checked the change in his pocket. He had enough to get a cake for Alison, Leech, and himself, but then he wouldn't be able to buy any snacks for himself the next day. Maybe just a cake for Dolly. Mick liked the spice cakes okay, but he'd never enjoy eating one as much as he enjoyed watching Dolly eat one.

After that, he tried to catch up with Gail and the others. He assumed they'd go back along Portland Place because it had more interesting shops and people-watching, so he trotted that direction and soon spotted them. He was about to pick up his pace to join them when he noticed that he wasn't the only one following them. On the far side of the street, a few dozen paces ahead of him, a pair of ragged kids, maybe in their early teens, were keeping pace with Gail and the others, slowing when they slowed, stopping when they stopped.

Remembering his lessons from Alison, he moved to the inner edge of the pavement, so that his shoulder nearly rubbed the buildings as he walked, and scanned the street for signs that the ragged kids were working with other people. Nobody caught his eye, though Mick knew he probably wouldn't spot anybody if they were good at it. He decided to think of the ragged teens as Blue and Green, based on the colors of their jackets. Blue was short and stocky. Green was short and skinny, with a slight hitch in his step.

Mick considered catching up with Gail and the others to warn them. But, betting that Gail had already spotted Blue and Green anyway, he decided to hang back to try to get some clues about them. Before Chris had told him about the Eyes, Mick would have assumed that Blue and Green were up to something shady, maybe part of a pickpocketing gang. But now that he knew about the Eyes, he saw fake urchins everywhere, even when they turned out to be real urchins. He wasn't sure about Blue and Green yet.

The furtive parade continued for another couple blocks. Gail and the Snobs strolled along Portland Place, first on the west side, then crossing to the east side when there was a break in the traffic. Instants after Gail and the Snobs crossed the street, Blue and Green crossed in the other direction, bringing them close enough to Mick that he felt pretty sure that they were actual ragged kids. They looked genuinely ragged, for one thing. And at one point they stopped suddenly, and Mick ended up near enough to hear them speaking in the kinda-Cockney accents you heard north of the river near Limehouse. A little later, when Gail and the others split into pairs at the circled columns of All Souls Church, Mick got a good sample of how Blue and Green talked when they started loudly cursing each other, the Lord God, and the Lord Mayor. After a brief argument, Blue and Green also split up.

After checking to see if anybody was tailing him, Mick followed Green because Green was following Daniel and Flora, who were more likely to need help than Gail and Stephen. Or at least Gail.

Mick half-expected Daniel and Flora to start running as soon as they turned the corner, but they sauntered along, turning away from the Institute at Union Street. Looking care-free, they chatted nonstop and stopped frequently, inspecting every statue and tree they ambled past. Green stayed about thirty yards behind them the whole time, and Mick stayed the same distance behind Green.

Eventually, Daniel and Flora entered the British Museum. Green lurked at a corner of the building while Mick watched him from across Great Russell Street.

Mick wasn't close enough to see Green's face, but Green's body language showed that he didn't know what to do. He kept taking a half-step toward the museum entrance and then taking a half-step back. Probably he wanted to go into the museum but realized it wouldn't work. Like much of London, the museum had an unwritten but strict dress code. Flora and Daniel would be fine, but the porters would take one look at Green's dirty face and cheap clothes and chuck him right out.

Mick wandered across the street toward the opposite end of the museum, cooling himself in the shade of a tree about a hundred yards from Green. Watching Green from the corner of his eye, he pulled out his copy of *Wilson's London Guide*. Mostly, the book was just a prop, but it also let him confirm that the museum was open until seven. So Flora and Daniel could be in there for hours. Or they could sneak out any of the back and side doors, if they hadn't already.

Down the block, Green continued pacing indecisively for a few more minutes until, as if a faulty gear had finally engaged, he turned and disappeared around the corner.

Mick returned *Wilson's* to his satchel and hustled after him. In case Green was watching, as Mick rounded the corner, he slowed down and pretended to consult his pocket watch.

There was no sign of Green. The only thing Mick could do was return to the Institute the long way, trying to make sure he wasn't followed.

CHAPTER 7

POPPY'S PALS

When Mick got back to the Institute, the warden handed him a note from Miss Emmet instructing him to meet her in her office.

In Miss Emmet's office, which as always was overflowing with books of all description, Miss Emmet was engaged in an animated discussion with Gail and Miss North. It was interesting how similar and how different Miss North and Miss Emmet were. Miss Emmet was short, and Miss North was tall-ish. Miss Emmet was a roundish woman with chestnut skin whose face came to rest in a faint smile. Miss North looked like she only went outdoors at night, and her sharp-featured face came to rest in a faintly skeptical frown. But when they talked about something of interest, they suddenly looked very alike—focused and intense. And, of course, like Gail, they both had the unnaturally bright eyes that marked them as alley rats with good alley sight.

Miss North looked up at him, and Mick straightened his tie nervously.

"Welcome back, Mr. Gunn. Do sit," Miss Emmet said, gesturing at the empty chair next to Gail.

Mick squeezed into the chair.

"We do send Mr. Gunn to the excitement only *after* it happens, yes?" Miss Emmet asked Miss North. "And it therefore would be unjust to accuse him of *causing* it?"

"One does occasionally wonder," Miss North said.

Miss Emmet looked at Gail and then at Mick. "Miss Atkinson was providing us with an account of today's events. Miss Atkinson, if you wouldn't mind repeating yourself, perhaps Mr. Gunn will have additional insights."

Gail walked them through the time lightning on the cricket pitch, the unknown alley rats, and being followed by Blue and Green. It was impressive how clearly she was able to describe everything, including things Mick had done when he could have sworn she wasn't watching him. He was briefly distracted by the unsettling realization that, since she noticed everything, she almost surely had noticed he had a bit of a crush on her. On the other hand, she hadn't made fun of him for it, so he was probably okay. Except for being painfully embarrassed.

He managed to return his focus to Gail's story. She and Stephen had led Blue west as far as St. Clare's, the little Catholic church where Leech went sometimes for Mass. They'd waited inside for a half hour before ducking out different side doors and making their way back to the Institute separately and, as far as they could tell, without being followed. Daniel and Flora had snuck out of a side door at the Museum and gotten back to the Institute even earlier.

Mick was able to add a few details about the alley

phenomena that Gail hadn't seen and a few points about Green that Flora and Daniel hadn't noticed. Then he remembered the fake urchins he'd spotted, or thought he'd spotted, when entering the cricket ground. Miss Emmet and Miss North asked him a few questions, mostly to confirm that the fake urchins were not the same people as Blue and Green.

"Grove End and St. John's Wood," Gail said, raising her eyebrows.

"Ah," Miss North said. "Quite."

Mick took a guess. "Eyes?"

Miss North looked at him sharply.

"Chris Biggs," Miss Emmet explained. "She told Mr. Gunn about the Eyes when she escorted him back to the Institute."

"I see," Miss North said.

It was almost impossible to know how Miss North felt about anything unless she wanted you to know. Her expression almost always made her look quietly exasperated. Mick was pretty sure she'd look that way if she won the lottery and cured cancer while eating her favorite dessert.

"Yes," Gail told Mick, "those were Eyes."

"But Blue and Green weren't, right?" Mick asked.

"I very much doubt it," Miss North said. "Sadly, however, doubt is the best one can do when one gets dragged into cloak and dagger foolishness."

"The Headmistress," Miss Emmet said, grinning at Miss North, "has no problem with the dagger. She simply disapproves of cloaking it."

That actually got a tiny smile from Miss North. "Well, I must inform the Vicar of the day's events. Miss Atkinson, please join me. Mr. Gunn, our discussion has been much postponed, but Miss Emmet knows its purpose, so perhaps I might impose on her?"

Miss Emmet nodded, and Gail followed Miss North from the door, patting Mick on the shoulder as she squeezed past his chair.

When the door clicked shut behind Gail and Miss North, Miss Emmet raised her eyebrows at Mick. "It was so peaceful when you were at the farm. Perhaps I might prevail upon them to take you back. Though I suppose they cannot afford to have any more canal boaters attacked by time pirates."

"Is Elmer all right?" Mick asked.

"At last report, young Mr. Maxwell was regaining his vigor most admirably."

Relieved, Mick thought back to the rest of Miss Emmet's remarks. "Time pirates?"

"More romantic than 'canal ruffians,' wouldn't you say?"

Mick grinned. "The time lightning wasn't me. Really."

Miss Emmet grinned back. "I wasn't truly accusing you. Indeed, I have just learned that the time lightning didn't begin today. There was an episode two days ago near Foundling's Cluster, only the warden of the day misfiled the report under 'Routine' rather than 'Urgent,' and we've only just discovered it. The poor thing was taken rather poorly that afternoon with a case of the grippe. Given the state she was in, we're fortunate she didn't file her report in the fireplace."

Miss Emmet pursed her lips and drummed her fingers on the desk. "And it's possible it wasn't just those two instances."

"But you're not sure?" he asked. He wondered whether Chris had somehow known about the other time lightning. Had that been one of the signs she'd been trying to make sense of? Was it somehow related to Blue and Green or the unknown alley rats at the cricket match?

"Many, perhaps most of the people in London with useful alley sight live within these walls," Miss Emmet said. "We cover a mere two and a half alley clusters. Admittedly, those are the busiest clusters by far, accounting for perhaps ninety percent of activity in London. But if we need to know about the other ten percent, including whether that ten percent is becoming fifty percent, well, we must rely on a handful of dons and other rats with alley sight. Or hope that the Eyes will recognize the secondary signs of alley activity without being able to see the actual alleys—and without being told that there are such things as time alleys, which is rather awkward. I rather wonder whether many of the Eyes simply conclude that their mysterious superiors are lunatics with an unhealthy fixation on peculiar winds and overexcited dogs."

Mick nodded. "So, there might be a bunch of time lightning going on, and we don't know about it because it doesn't happen on our patrol sequences?"

"Just so," Miss Emmet said.

Mick sighed.

"Why the ponderous sigh?"

Mick thought about mentioning Chris' warning to be alert, but he wasn't sure if he was supposed to repeat that to others. "I was just getting used to not worrying all the time, I guess."

"Worrying?" Miss Emmet asked.

"Like it was before. Going out in carriages at three in morning to look for echo phantasms. Worrying about alley rats getting hurt or..." Mick remembered how exhausted he'd been by the time the craziness had come to an end. He remembered not being sure if he had another week, another day, left in him.

"I see," Miss Emmet said, looking concerned. "Well, I'm afraid a little worry probably is in order. But I shouldn't wish you to be too extravagant in your dread. Thus far, there have been none of the troubling signs we saw during the recent dark times. There has been no increase in the proportion of fawkes alleys. No unusual deviations from the predicted timing and magnitude of the apertures. Indeed, the time lightning that was misfiled accompanied a whirlpool Nine that dropped a perfectly healthy alley rat precisely where and when the signs indicated. So, whatever this is, it doesn't seem to be the sort of nightmarish, deadly selfishness perpetrated by Cassandra Halliwell."

"Really?" Mick asked.

"Truly," Miss Emmet said.

Mick's shoulders unclenched. He hadn't realized how tense they'd become. "That's good. That's great."

Miss Emmet nodded. "Indeed. Still, we ought to investigate. It does seem to be *something*. And that, by the by, is what Miss North wishes me to discuss with you."

Mick felt his shoulders starting to tighten again. Miss Emmet spotted it and smiled reassuringly. "Take heart. You might even consider this good news. We shall be asking you to spend considerable time outside the walls. If indeed this time lightning—or whatever it may be—is scattered more broadly throughout London than time alleys usually are, we must also have people with good alley sight scattered more broadly throughout London than usual."

"Is this one of those things where I have to do a bunch of extra work outside the walls but I also have to do all my regular tutorials and chores and everything else?" Mick asked skeptically.

Miss Emmet grinned. "Fortunately for you, we're in Lammas term now, meaning you needn't be in tutorial at all unless the Vicar or Miss North so decrees. And they're agreed upon this plan. You'll be on patrol a good deal more than many students, but I'd encourage you to think of it as a guided tour of London. People like to be out and about in the allegedly sunny months."

Mick raised his eyebrows at her. Miss Emmet had admitted that she hesitated to leave the Institute because being a woman of color in Victorian London was often uncomfortable and sometimes dangerous.

Miss Emmet blushed. "Yes, well, little boys in fancy suits who look merely bronzed from the sunny months often like to be out and about. And, in truth, I've realized that for my profession, and my pride, I need to be outside the walls more than previously, and I've been doing just that. Though I do take rather a lot of carriages. Still, inside a carriage is outside the walls."

Mick smiled at her and thought of the Nye sisters, of how certain activities could be whims for some people but had to be carefully planned acts of courage for others. Although he couldn't wrap his head around it, the Civil War hadn't happened yet in the U.S., and it was still totally legal to enslave people in a lot of states. Mick still wasn't totally clear on how much slavery there had been in England itself, but it had definitely been legal in the British Empire for a long time before finally being abolished about twenty years earlier. And wasn't like abolition had magically fixed everything, in England or in its colonies.

"So you will be spared lessons," Miss Emmet said, "at least those requiring books. Indeed, you'll be spending some time in

Chris Biggs' company, and I believe she regards most books as snares for the unwary."

Chris again, Mick thought. *Interesting.*

They chatted for a little bit more before Miss Emmet shooed him out. He went back to the Squad, got a rewarding smile from Dolly for her spice cake, and filled them in on the day's events, which everyone thought were interesting but confusing. Mick decided that was okay. He'd started to think that if he was confused, he knew what was going on, and when he wasn't confused, he was clueless.

For another week or so while the professors put together their plans, Mick patrolled both with the Squad and with Gail and the Snobs, sometimes on the same day. Since both teams were lucky enough to have Sundays off, Mick and Leech got up early enough on Sunday to play soccer or, as Mick was trying to train himself to call it, "footie."

After freezing roof-water showers from the locker room's complex system of copper pipes and janky nozzles, Leech and Mick met Alison and Dolly for breakfast at the Sixers' table. Alison and Dolly had saved them some food with the help of their fellow Sixer Owl, a pleasant enough kid. He was a year or two older than Mick, making him about Alison's age, and was one of the few students immune to Leech's charm. Mick admired that.

As she often did on Sundays, Alison would be visiting her former street kid friends at the School for Orphans of the Empire, a Project school for arrows and alley-blind alley rats.

Mick had always watched Alison head off to Orphans without thinking too much about it. Sure, he admired her for surviving as long as she had on the streets of London after being yanked out of the future and having her brother torn away from her partway through their time alley. Mick was glad she had friends who'd helped her survive and helped her look for her brother, even though finding him again had meant finding him dead. But ever since dropping in 1853, Mick had been so focused on alley emergencies or getting back to his real life that he hadn't really thought about Alison's friends. Or the rest of his friends' lives, really. But listening to Ward describe what it was like to grow up in a workhouse and seeing Elmer beaten nearly to death had driven home that people in 1853 were, well, *alive*. Even if Mick didn't want to stay in the past, the people around him were real people with real lives, and he was ashamed that he'd been too up his own butt to notice.

Alison had just finished sneaking food into her satchel for her friends and was gathering her skirt to leave when Mick asked if he could go with her.

Alison tilted her head. "Pardon?"

"I wanted to see the city when we're not on patrol and maybe meet your friends. Make their acquaintance. If that's acceptable, of course."

Alison's head was still tilted. "They're— they aren't in danger, are they?"

"No. Why?"

"Oh," Alison said. "Good. You were talking with Miss North and Miss Emmet yesterday evening. I thought perhaps..."

"I would've told you," Mick said. "You know I would've."

Alison's face and shoulders relaxed. "Yes, you would have done, wouldn't you? I do apologize, Gunner."

Mick shrugged. "You're worried about your friends."

Alison nodded absently as she stared into space. She squared her shoulders and said, "Today is… It was seven years ago today that I dropped in Manchester. This day always makes me think about my friends, who looked after me once I made my way here. And, naturally, about J— my brother."

"I'm sorry if it isn't my place to say this," Owl said to Alison, "but it was awful about your brother. I thought you were very brave."

Alison's brother had been a passenger in her alley and had died when something had gone wrong with the alley. Mick and the rest of the Squad never brought it up because Alison never brought it up.

"How did—" Alison began. "You knew about my brother?"

"I was prenticing on the street team that found him—and you," Owl said.

"Prenticing" meant "being an apprentice." Sometimes, Institute kids went out with street teams as apprentices even if they were too young to do much for the team. That usually only happened when the apprentices had been at the Institute long enough to get a good handle on the basics, which usually meant the prentices had dropped from the future as really little kids. Mick wondered how old Owl had been.

"I am sorry if I oughtn't have mentioned it," Owl said.

"I don't remember seeing you that day," Alison said.

"I doubt you did," Owl said. "I gave you my coat, but I don't think you ever turned around."

"Was that really you who put the coat over my shoulders?" Alison asked wonderingly. "The cobblestones were chilly on my knees—it was such a foggy day—and I remember being glad of the warmth but terrified I'd be put before the magistrate for stealing such a fine coat. In those days, any coat without mud in the lining and holes in the elbows was impossibly fine, and it was quite obvious that I wouldn't have had such a coat unless I'd stolen it."

"It was too small for you," Owl said. "I was not yet the strapping giant that I am today," he added with a small grin.

Although Owl wasn't tiny, he was a bit small for his age by Institute standards, except for the big eyes and big head that had given rise to his nickname.

Alison smiled faintly at him and patted Owl's hand. "Thank you for the very fine coat, Owl."

Owl blushed and mumbled that she was most welcome.

Alison stared into space again for a moment before turning to Mick. "If you wish to accompany me to Orphans, you would be most welcome. If any of you wish," she said to the rest of the group.

Owl said, "Including me? I have a friend there, Jeremiah. He went alley-blind when I was prenticing, and he had to go to Orphans. I don't see him nearly so often as I'd wish."

Alison smiled at Owl. "You're most welcome, Owl."

In the end, after everyone but Alison ran upstairs to put on outdoor clothes, they all joined Alison, and the don at the warden's desk didn't even make them beg much before allowing them to leave the Institute.

It was a mild, sunny day that made Mick glad he'd asked to come along. It was nice to get outside when he wasn't patrolling. He was getting more and more used to Victorian London—the sights, the sounds, the aggressive smells. He could walk through the neighborhoods near the Institute and know without paying attention whether it was a plain vanilla day, a festival day, a market day, or if something else unusual was afoot. He had a better idea who people were and how they fit into things. The man with the enormous gray sideburns and expensive clothes turning onto Grays Inn Lane was almost certainly a fancy lawyer enjoying his day off. The teenager skittering along Cheapside in a plain cotton dress and cheerful blue bonnet was probably a domestic servant just leaving an early church service. Mick was about seventy percent sure the middle-aged woman in the green dress that still looked expensive at a distance was working with the middle-aged man in a drab gray suit who was picking pockets along Bishopsgate Street.

Mick poked Leech and pointed out both the woman and her partner. The Squad all did that for Leech, who had eyes in the back of his head when playing soccer but might as well have had a sack over his head when it came to pickpockets.

It was still all surreal, when Mick stopped to think about it. A whole city without electricity or cars. The streets were snarled with horses and carriages, and words were snarled between surly drivers. The biggest thing that ever flew overhead was a hawk or a falcon because in 1853, planes were a kind of tree and drones were a kind of bee. Another surreal thing was that he and the Squad and Owl, none of them older than thirteen, were wandering by themselves through one of the biggest and most dangerous cities in the world. Heck, their education—their jobs, really—*required* them to wander that city for hours at a time on their own. And they definitely weren't the only ones, nor the youngest ones. There were six-year-olds running about on some kind of business, even if it was just sweeping the street in front of you as you crossed, hoping you'd toss them a farthing for their troubles. As Mick and the others drew near the stairs leading up to Orphans, he realized yet again that London was a tough town, including for a lot of kids.

Alison went up the stairs to ask the school's porter about her friends, while Mick and the others waited on the bottom steps ten or fifteen yards away from a dull black carriage that Mick was pretty sure belonged to the Institute. The carriage rolled away while Mick and the others discussed reports of another recent time lightning incident.

Alison skipped back down to report that her friends were still at church. "Mass should have been finished a half hour ago, but Margaret says the new priest at Christ Church Spitalfields is very high church and services take simply an age, particularly the homilies. Oh, and do remember that my friends are arrows who haven't the faintest inkling of time travel or what the Institute really is. So be sure not to mention time lightning or the like."

"You never told them?" Leech asked. "Not even before the professors taught you to fear eternal damnation for discussing time travel?"

"I mentioned time travel to the first few people I met after I dropped," Alison said. "Most called me mad. One old crone tried to brain me with an egg basket. I never spoke of it again until I arrived at the Institute. And after that, naturally, I knew better than to discuss such matters with arrows— Ah, there they are." She waved.

From a large group of kids of varying ages and heights, all in their Sunday finery, three kids broke off and stopped in front of Alison. The first thing that Mick noticed was that they were all older than Alison, probably by three or four years. The boy had the beginnings of a mustache and maybe even a beard. The girls were very definitely female, even more obviously than Gail Atkinson.

Each of them hugged Alison, who then dug into her satchel to press into their hands the food she'd filched from the dining hall.

"They do feed us, Poppy," the brunette girl said affectionately.

"Nevertheless," Alison said.

Alison introduced everyone. The brunette was Margaret Corcoran, the blonde was Anna Baker, and the boy was Charles Tanner. But when Alison spoke to them, she called them Tips, Hoot, and Gristle, and they called her Poppy. Mick could tell that Leech was dying to ask about the nicknames, but so could Dolly, who smacked Leech's arm.

Owl arranged to meet them back at the front stairs in an hour and then went inside to visit his friend.

The rest of them wandered along, chatting gaily, except for Mick, who didn't want to draw too much attention to his accent. Also, he was starting to get an uneasy sensation. He wondered if it was an early stirring, but he couldn't see anything that looked like a time alley and couldn't hear even the faintest alley song.

As soon as they neared Finsbury Circus, however, he realized his uneasy sensation had nothing to do with a new alley. He was being bothered by an old alley. Earlier that year, toward the end of figuring out why so many alleys had been misbehaving, Mick had been summoned to Finsbury Circus after Gail had spotted a stirring beside the same wrought fence in front of St. Mary Moorfields that Alison and her friends were now passing. A couple days later, the stirring had turned into a damaged alley, out of which a dead alley rat had dropped. Mick remembered how the dead dropper had slumped heavily to the ground, an ungainly corpse lit first by the fawkes' sickly flickering, then by the square's dim gaslight.

"Gunner?" Dolly's voice came from a distance, partly because Mick's attention was far away and partly because she and the others were already partway across the circus, nearly at the front entrance to the London Institution.

Mick waved to Dolly but didn't move. His legs were too shaky. He stood for a moment, regaining his balance.

Smiling, Leech glided down the church steps, stopping just in front of Mick. "I've just popped into the pro-cathedral. Nobody can say I didn't go to church this fine Sunday." Leech looked at him more carefully and his smile disappeared. "Gunner?"

"There was an echo phantasm here. An alley rat died."

Leech looked around. "That's right. I'd forgotten."

For a second, Mick wondered how Leech could possibly have forgotten seeing a dead kid. Then he remembered that Leech and the rest of the Squad hadn't been there that night.

Dolly was waving to encourage them to rejoin the group. After Leech raised his eyebrows and Mick nodded, they started toward the group.

As they walked, Leech said, "Perhaps it's a thing best forgotten today, with Alison's brother already in her thoughts."

Mick nodded. If he felt like this for a dead kid he'd never met, Alison must be struggling way worse because of her brother. No need to dump more on her.

Fortunately, Alison was tough and enjoyed being around her old friends. When Leech and Mick rejoined the group, she was chatting comfortably with Tips, Hoot, and Gristle. She kept doing so as they left Finsbury Circus and continued meandering through the small part of the city of London that, to Mick's occasional confusion, was called the City of London.

Alison and her friends were so caught up in their conversation that they mostly forgot the others were there. That was fine with Mick. He didn't really feel like talking, especially not if he had to fake a London accent. Although Dolly and Leech were obviously snooping on Alison and her friends, they mostly bantered with one another, Leech using one of the London accents he could do so effortlessly. Mick tuned them out, alternating between listening to London and to Alison and her friends.

Alison asked a lot of questions about how things were going at Orphans. Mick supposed it was easier to get her friends talking about their lives than to try to explain her life at the Institute without mentioning time travel.

Kids at the Institute always made Orphans sound like a pitiful dumping ground for alley-blind rats. But Alison's friends made clear that it was actually a good school, with Latin, Greek, and French, and algebra and science and all that. That's why, Dolly had once told Mick, as soon as Alison had gotten to the Institute, she'd bullied the Vicar for weeks until he pulled some strings to have her friends admitted to Orphans. Also, Orphans wasn't just for alley-blind rats. The school presented itself to outsiders as a school dedicated to educating orphans of British soldiers or kids whose fathers had died in a war and whose mothers couldn't support them. And it actually did educate quite a lot of kids like that. As Leech whispered at one point, the British had stolen a lot of land, which tended to kick off a lot of wars that orphaned a lot of kids.

From what Mick could gather, Alison's friends made it a point to try to welcome new kids to Orphans because they'd been snubbed for months when they'd gotten there. For a while, Tips talked about their efforts, especially a new girl who'd been refusing to talk to them, and everybody else, since she'd arrived at Orphans a couple months earlier.

After that, Alison and her friends got to talking about the bad old days, when they'd lived together on the street. It was funny to listen to their accents. Normally, Alison spoke with a very correct, upper-class accent that you might have expected from the daughter of a knight or a baronet. Her friends' accents weren't as fancy, but they were respectable. As they talked, however, all of them gradually fell into the accents they'd had on the streets seven years earlier. At least to Mick's ear, Alison's friends sounded a lot like Blue and Green. Tips' accent might even have been stronger, and he was pretty sure she was dropping in some Cockney rhyming slang. Alison's accent started to sound a lot like her friends' lower-class accents, but there was something else to it also. Maybe something from one of the northern cities. And then one of them would hear how lower-class they sounded and snap back to a fancy accent, and the others would do the same. They went through a few cycles of that before their meandering progress brought them back to Orphans' front door. Alison and her friends hugged goodbye, and Owl emerged from the school not long after Alison's friends had gone inside.

Owl and the others nodded at each other and started walking in the general direction of the Institute.

"How was your friend?" Alison asked Owl in her familiar accent. "Jeremy? No, that's not right," she said, sounding weirdly upset.

"Jeremiah," Owl said. "You very nearly had it. Jerry's well.

Receiving excellent marks, apparently, and will matriculate at St. George's for Trinity term, or possibly Epiphany."

"Well done, Jerry," Alison said with a slight smile.

Leech told Owl, "Do be sure to tell Jerry not to request elocution lessons from Monsieur Gristle and Mademoiselles Hoot and Tips. Or from Mademoiselle Poppy here. Several drunken sailors stopped us along the way to reproach them for the low, coarse nature of their speech."

"Sure, and it's a feckin' perfect model o' pure aristocratic elocution that you are, Leigh Charles," Alison snapped in a surprisingly good imitation of Leech's real accent.

Leech looked at Alison in surprise and burst out laughing. "Stop that, or I'll fall in love out of pure homesickness."

Alison looked startled for a moment and started laughing too. Owl, Mick, and Dolly looked at one another and shrugged. Laughter was like accents, Mick figured. Fun to listen to even if you couldn't understand it.

CHAPTER 8

THE FLICKERING BRIDGE

Chatting and laughing in the mild summer sun, Owl and the Squad strolled through the City of London, pausing at St. Paul's again to watch the fine people milling around the cathedral in order to be seen and, ideally, envied. The other kids commented on the ladies' gowns, the men's beards, and a few particularly fine carriages and the sleekly muscled horses pulling them. Mick didn't know enough about gowns and beards to say much. He hadn't cared about horsepower when it had meant cars, and he didn't care much more when it meant carriages.

After that, not far from St. Clement Danes, Alison stopped to buy a nosegay from a dirty-faced flower girl who didn't look older than eight.

"Thankee, miss," the girl said when Alison gave her an extra farthing.

Alison smiled at her and drifted away from the girl, finding a comparatively calm spot nearby.

"Everyone continue smiling and looking at me," Alison instructed them. "Do not look away from me. Understood?"

Everyone nodded.

"Has anyone else the sense that we're being spied upon?" Alison asked. "Look at me," she said sharply.

Mick blushed. Even though she'd warned him, his head had started swiveling as soon as she'd asked about being spied on.

They all said they hadn't noticed anything. "Have you actually seen anyone?" Dolly asked Alison.

Alison shook her head. "It's just a feeling I have. I might be mistaken. Possibly it's simply spending time with Tips and the others. They taught me how to keep alert, you understand." She raised the nosegay to her face, her eyes flickering subtly behind the poppies.

Mick wondered if Alison's old friends called her Poppy simply because she liked poppies.

"Leech, Gunner, if there is anyone, perhaps you could flush them out," Alison said slowly, thinking aloud.

Mick and Leech both shrugged.

"Yes, I do think," Alison said. "Take Wych to Drury Lane and wait for us a half mile hence, at Long Acre or Castle. Avoid Bow Street. Anyone following us might disappear if you approach the police station too closely. We shall come behind and see what may be seen," she told them. "And don't constantly look over your shoulders and the like."

Mick and Leech set off walking, trying hard to look casual. When you shouldn't look back all the time, it was amazingly hard not to look back all the time. They walked slowly, making themselves easy to follow. After a few blocks, Mick spotted a couple of flashy young men who might have been following them, but even Leech noticed them, so Alison couldn't have missed them. By then, he and Leech had reached Castle, so they turned left and walked a couple dozen yards until finding a little nook in the front of a building where they could stand with their backs protected.

The flashy young men paused down the road but without looking at them. Mick started to suspect they were pickpockets, cutpurses, or possibly just rakehells wandering Covent Garden in search of "immoral congress." The phrase "immoral congress" always made Mick laugh because it made him picture the U.S. Congress taking big cartoon bags of bribe money. But it actually meant "sex" or, usually, "sex work." The phrase showed up several times in *Wilson's London Guide*. Although *Wilson's* was secretly written to give alley rats a guide to London that they could safely carry outside the Institute, it was published by a real publisher and popular with tourists from Canada and the United States. More than once, that had made Mick's life simpler. An American was unusual in London, and unusual could be memorable. If he pulled *Wilson's* out of his satchel, pointed to the little black and white map of the West End and said he was trying to meet his parents at "Lye-kester Square," people thought he was a halfwit tourist and forgot about him five minutes later. Also, honestly, with a lot of Londoners, life was easier if he could get them to focus on his accent rather than his skin color.

Not too long after Mick and Leech had taken up position in their little nook, the flashy young men turned onto Castle, walking directly toward them. Mick and Leech tensed up. The young men were way bigger, so Mick and Leech would have to rely on shouting and sprinting away if things turned ugly. But the young men wandered past harmlessly, burbling at each other about the theater and somebody named Betsy.

"You watch them," Mick whispered to Leech. "I'll watch the rest." For a few minutes, he scanned the street for anybody who seemed connected to the flashy young men but didn't see anything.

"Our peacocks have turned the corner and flown away," Leech said.

Mick nodded. Alison and the others had just turned onto Castle and were walking toward them. In case Alison and the others wanted to pretend that they were strangers, Mick kept himself from waving. But Alison and the others walked straight for him and Leech.

"Anything?" Leech asked.

Alison shook her head. "Quite possibly I was mistaken."

"Or they're good enough to evade you," Leech said.

"Perhaps," Alison acknowledged with a nod. "I do fear that I have gone soft in recent years."

"Soft enough to forget your razor?" Leech asked.

Alison flicked her forearm, and a man's shaving razor, still folded shut, slid out of her lacy sleeve and into her hand before disappearing with another flick. "Never so soft as that, poppet," she said in her Poppy voice.

For the thousandth time, Mick reminded himself to stay on Alison's good side.

They turned onto Charles, paralleling the Thames, and walked for a bit before Mick stopped suddenly. The others stopped with him.

Mick turned to look down a side street that felt oddly familiar. Why did everything here seem so— Oh, of course.

"Your drop site," Dolly said. "'Tisn't it, Gunner?"

Mick nodded, following his feet down the side street and then into an alleyway. He'd tried to forget where it was. But he remembered every detail. He'd been collapsed on the cobble-stones, too sore and exhausted to stand. The cobbles had been cold and slick with rainwater. His clothes had been in tatters from his trips through an endless series of way-worlds that had kept trying to strand him or kill him. Everything had reeked like a landfill, though apparently he'd gotten used to London's odors because now the smell didn't seem too bad. He'd heard hoofbeats, same as he was hearing now, and he'd refused to look up from the cobblestones because looking up might have made things real.

"You dropped here?" Owl asked.

"They found me," Mick said, nodding at the Squad.

Compelled by memory, Mick walked deeper into the alley-way, squatting in a few spots, trying to match what he saw to the view he remembered from when he'd first looked up at 1853 London. He finally found what he thought was the exact spot.

"Yes," Alison said, reading his mind.

Mick felt his shoulders tensing, then shaking. He managed to hold back his tears, or at least most of them.

"Your first time back?" Owl asked.

Unable to speak, Mick nodded. Not only had he avoided returning to his drop spot, he'd avoided even thinking about it. Now he knew why. It was the same reason he'd avoided looking up from the alley cobblestones right after dropping. He hadn't wanted it to be real. He knew the alleyway, was real. But it was painfully empty. Not empty of physical objects—there were plenty of nightsoil buckets, scurrying rodents, and other things you didn't want to dwell on. But there wasn't even the faintest hint of the time alley that had brought him. Experience, tutori-als, the repetitive pages of *Broome's* and *Clayton's*, they all told him that even the showiest time alleys eventually went dark and disappeared. But he realized he'd been secretly hoping that his would be different. That he'd get to his drop spot and see some faint glimmer or hear the softest whisper of alley song. Anything that would give him hope that he could somehow reopen the alley and go home, despite what everybody said.

But there was nothing. It was just 1853 London. Dirty stones and dirty air. The endless sounds of solid objects and real people bumping into each other for miles and centuries in every direction. He could close his eyes, cover his ears, and stop his nose, and it would all still be there, exactly where and when it was: far from his home and his family.

Leech rested a friendly hand on his shoulder, and Owl offered him a hand. Mick stared at Owl's hand for a moment before clasping it, and Owl tugged him to his feet. "Thanks," Mick said.

Owl suggested taking a slight detour to Trafalgar Square to see how the bronze reliefs at the base of Nelson's Column were coming along, and the Squad approved. Mick smiled a little, impressed that Owl had found something that would both distract Mick from his sadness and troll Leech into complaining about the British military. Keeping watch for any signs of a tail, they wandered to the square, enjoying the gurgling fountains, the spectacle of Sunday promenaders, and some delicious soft-centered boiled sweets that Alison bought from a street vendor.

After that, Leech wanted to watch the Thames from the new Hungerford Market. Owl started to say he didn't want to go, probably just to troll Leech more, but he shut up when Alison said it sounded nice.

Leech treated them all to small shells of vanilla ice cream

from the stand owned by Mr. Cats (actually Signore Gatti). When Mick's tongue touched the ice cream, he found himself back in Chicago at the Renegade Craft Fair, with his mom and Tía Julieta, eating vanilla ice cream and trying to convince his mom to go back to the stall selling the steampunk lamp that lit up when he rubbed its base. He'd really wanted that lamp.

The moment passed as the ice cream melted, and he found himself still standing in the open square of the Hungerford Market, surrounded by its fancy buildings and it shabby benches and stalls, ensnared in the thickly woven smells of people, produce, and butchers' shops, plus the pushy waft of the Thames.

Owl looked at him, raising his eyebrows and smiling slightly. "Memories of the future?" he asked. "I always get them when I eat ice cream."

Mick nodded.

They climbed the steps to stand near the entrance to the Hungerford Bridge, staring across the big, busy river. The Thames could be beautiful, and it was at its best that day, its waters sparkling in the sunshine and dotted by countless rowboats, sailboats, and steamboats of various shapes and sizes.

Mick's mom had always liked looking at the Chicago River, especially from the State Street bridge or one of the restaurants on the riverwalk, and Mick had always thought of it as a big river. But the Thames was in a totally different category. In London, the Thames was maybe five times wider and busier than the Chicago River. And it was a thousand times more important to its city. A lot of London worked on the Thames, and depending how you looked at it, most of London lived off it. On the ceiling of the Institute's dining hall, there was a big map of the world, with England connected to other places by lines, and all the lines stopped and started in London. The lines represented ideas—trade, power, and weird mystical stuff that the students snickered about—but even on that map, the Thames was a very real line connecting London to other parts of England and the world beyond. If you kept going east from where Mick and the others were standing, the Thames went to the sea, and the sea went to the world, British ships coming and going, packed full of tea, spices, guns, cash, and schemes.

Some people, including Miss Emmet, suspected that so many time alleys started and ended in big, powerful cities like London, Peking, Rome, and Constantinople because alleys dropped kids in places that had shaped their ancestors' lives in some important way, and that big cities tended to have shaped almost everybody's lives somehow if you went back enough generations. If so, being stuck in Victorian London was probably his dad's fault, or at least his dad's family's fault. If it had been his mom's family, Mick probably would've dropped in Mexico City or Chicago.

But he didn't know how his dad's family was connected to London. He realized how little he knew about them. His mom's family was everywhere in his life. His mom had sometimes joked about needing to get a broom to sweep stray relatives out from under the sofa. But except for a couple trips to LA when he was a little kid, he never really saw anybody from his dad's family except Uncle Dan. Not even at his mom's funeral. And his dad and uncle almost never talked about them.

"All right, Gunner?" Leech asked.

Mick nodded, taking deep breaths and trying to focus on the shimmering water and even the faint shimmering of afternoon sunshine on the long cables of the Hungerford Bridge stretching to and from the two tall towers rising from the river.

Wait.

He stared along the footbridge a little longer. "Anybody, um, notice anything about the bridge?"

The others shrugged. "Such as?" Leech asked.

Mick stared for a minute, wondering if he might be imagi—nope. There it was, the faintest alley song and an unnatural shimmering that went beyond the crisp summer sun. "Time lightning," he said.

They all squinted, obviously not seeing anything yet. Out of the corner of his eye, Mick saw Alison and Owl remove their pocket watches and start timing. With Alison softly asking Mick questions and discreetly taking coded notes on his answers, the group spent several minutes pretending that they weren't staring hard at the footbridge as Mick watched the increasingly bright tentacles of yellow and white light wrap themselves around it. There were the same flashes of pink that he'd seen at the cricket ground, plus little flares of purple now and again.

Eventually, the purple flares turned into several roundish blobs big enough to cover the width of the bridge, and they started to pulse across the bridge from one side to the other like wax dripping down the side of a candle, moving about the same speed as the people walking across the bridge and passing through one another. That was when the others started to see the lightning. Alison took furious notes without looking at her notebook as each kid described what they were seeing, one after the other. After about fifteen minutes, the purple blobs were moving as fast as cantering horses when everything flashed brightly before disappearing.

Except it wasn't everything. The alley song from the time lighting was replaced by another song—a little louder, a little more familiar. There was a time alley getting ready to open somewhere nearby.

As always, Mick felt summoned by the alley song and had to wrap a hand around a wrought iron railing to remind himself not to run off in search of its source. He closed his eyes and swiveled his head slowly, checking whether the song seemed to be coming more from one direction than another. He was pretty sure that alley song wasn't actually a sound and that he didn't really hear it with his ears the way he heard a real sound. But his brain treated it like a regular sound, more or less, and listening to it like a regular sound seemed to work.

As best he could tell, the alley song was coming from the footbridge itself. He looked closely and saw what might have been the first flickers of an aperture. He stared until he was pretty sure it was real.

"Aperture," he said quietly.

"Where?" Alison asked.

"On the bridge, there." Mick pointed with his chin at a spot forty or fifty yards away.

"I don't see anything," Owl said.

"With Gunner, we never do," Leech said. "Until we do."

"Any notion when it might open?" Alison asked.

Mick shrugged. He was extremely good at seeing alleys. But knowing when an alley would open, how big it would be, what kind it would be, that took a lot of experience and math. He was starting to get experience, but the math was a struggle.

"Not even a guess?" Dolly asked.

"It doesn't look like right now," Mick said, staring at the still subtle alley shimmer. "But I bet it won't be more than a couple hours."

"I shouldn't think there will be a greet team," Dolly said. "We're beyond the main sequences."

"The dons?" Owl asked.

Alison shook her head. "Not unless they're present by chance," she said. "The nearest outpost is more than a mile away."

Mick pictured the Plan in his head. Alison and Dolly were right. They were in a dead zone for patrol sequences and nowhere near a dons' outpost. The Seat was the nearest Project building. He didn't know whether the Seat sent out patrol teams, but he doubted it.

They debated how to get word to the Institute. Mick knew he couldn't mention the Project's secret telegraph system or the Eyes, so he stayed out of it and tried to keep watch on the aperture as much as he could, occasionally sparing a glance around to see if they were being spied on. He hadn't forgotten Blue and Green or the flashily dressed grown-up alley rats at Lord's. But there was no sign of them, or anyone else.

In the end, Owl volunteered to run back to the Institute. With luck, he would be back with a greet team before the alley opened.

A quarter hour later, the aperture had started to grow bigger and brighter, though not so much that the others could see it. They stood there for a while, pretending to be casually enjoying the view. Dolly and Leech bickered with one another until Alison snapped at them to "stop behaving like children," which made Mick laugh.

Alison stared at him sternly.

The young headmistress indeed. "We *are* children," he reminded her.

"That's hardly an excuse," she said stiffly.

Dolly and Leech laughed. Alison frowned at them but eventually chuckled at herself. "As may be," she said. "Stop acting like irritating children. Any changes, Gunner?"

Mick filled her in and continued to do so until the aperture became bright enough for the others to see. They then followed the usual procedures, whispering to Alison what they saw so she could write it down in the coded shorthand required by the Institute. Over the next half hour, it took clearer form, turning slowly into a fairy path Seven. Then it gradually framed up and took a more solid form before the random flickering turned into a steady, rhythmic pulsing that signaled it would probably open in a quarter hour or so. Alison handed some coins to Leech and Dolly, sending them to get in line for the footbridge. Describing the alley to Alison, Mick watched Leech and Dolly pay the toll and step onto the bridge, halting ten yards or so from the farthest boundary of the alley, trying to keep out of the way of people crossing to the south side of the river.

Alison and Mick took turns looking around to see if they could spot anybody taking an interest in the alley—or in them. They saw nothing.

Eventually the alley opened, erupted with a blinding flash of purple light, and then disappeared, leaving a dropper in its place. The dropper looked like a small child.

Leech and Dolly walked casually but briskly toward the dropper. Leech put his jacket over the child's shoulders and lifted it easily to his chest.

Without waiting for someone to take an interest in the miraculous appearance of a child, Leech and Dolly started to weave their way back to the north bank to rejoin Alison and Mick.

"All's well," Leech called ahead,

Mick relaxed and saw Alison do the same. They'd been wound tight with worry, especially Alison, who took the child —a baby, really—from Leech. The baby appeared to be fast asleep, which was sort of amazing. Mick's baby sister Emilia would have been screaming her head off. But the baby seemed healthy enough, so Mick figured they should take the win.

"I often wonder why some droppers arrive with clothes intact like this little one," Alison said, "while some of us arrive half-naked."

Mick was about to say maybe it had to do with how many way-worlds a rat passed through between their late point and their drop point, but Dolly spoke first. "At the risk of a connan..." she began.

Mick and the others perked up. Dolly never risked a connan.

"There are, far enough into the future, I believe," Dolly said cautiously, "materials woven and stitched into clothing that are manufactured, rather than taken directly from crops and livestock. It seems to me that such materials do not survive passing through an alley."

Mick considered that, surprised. He tried to remember what he'd lost in his alley. The elastic from his socks, for sure. The smooth stuff on the t-shirt that made the logo. Zippers? He was pretty sure he'd lost zippers. Metal didn't come from crops or livestock. "You know," he said, "you never see kids at the Institute with braces." He cut Leech off. "Not suspenders for trousers. For teeth. Like metal and plastic."

"Orthodontia," Alison said. "One doesn't see that, does one?"

Leech and Dolly looked at one another like they'd never heard of such a thing.

All four of them resumed walking out of the Hungerford

Market. Leech focused on carrying the baby, and the others kept an eye out for help and for trouble.

Fortunately, help came before trouble could. Owl arrived with a greet team from the Institute led by Florence Dylan, the sober-faced, broad-shouldered girls' prefect for Tory Six. Florence and her team escorted them to the dull black Institute carriage waiting nearby. Leech handed the baby to Florence, who hopped with her team into the carriage, which lurched promptly into motion. For a second, Mick wished 1853 London had bumper stickers so that he could slap a "Baby on Board" sticker on the back of the Institute's carefully unmarked carriage.

Owl and the Squad kicked around some ideas about what to do next and decided in the end just to go back to the Institute. They were out of spending money, and the grown-ups would probably have questions for them about the time lightning. Soon after they started walking, another black carriage caught Mick's eye. This one was shiny, with a big brass "H" on the side. He dug through his memories until he found himself in the back of Mr. Davies' wagon in the courtyard behind the Seat. Right, the carriage with Captain Britain and the woman who had reminded Mick of somebody. And Lord Starts-With-An-H, of course. Mick tried to point the carriage out to the others, but it had disappeared into traffic.

CHAPTER 9

GUARDING THE SILENCE

W hen Mick and the others got back to the Institute, the adults did indeed have questions. As usual, the Vicar gathered them onto the solarium's comfy sofas and chairs and pushed hot tea and sweet biscuits into them while he and Miss North pulled information out of them. This time, Mr. Victor and Miss Emmet were there too. But Mr. Victor wasn't actively trying to terrify them, so it wasn't too bad. Other than saying hello in the hallway, it was the first time Mick had spoken to the Vicar since returning to the Institute, and it was reassuring to see his twinkling eyes and horsey teeth.

Afterward, Mick, Leech, and Owl played footie for a while. Stephen was there, and Mick felt very mature when he and Stephen were polite to one another once again, especially in contrast with Owl and Leech, who needed each other the whole game. Their sniping continued through showers and dinner until Mick caught Alison's eye and then told Leech and Owl,

"Do stop acting like children, if you please." Leech and Owl didn't laugh, but they did shut up when nearby kids laughed.

The next morning, still on the early rising schedule he'd gotten used to at Demeter, Mick woke up while Leech was snoring and realized he wouldn't be getting back to sleep. He went downstairs to the gym, where he found Miss Mitchell and a few of the other dons running course. That day's obstacle course was devious, especially because each don would occasionally move something around to try to trip up the others.

Miss Mitchell waved at Mick to give him permission to join them. She'd been letting him run course with the dons for months, at first because he'd been so awful at course that the Snobs had made fun of him and later because he just enjoyed doing it. As always, he made sure to stay out of the dons' way. He'd gotten way better, but the dons were all at least a half dozen years older than he was, and way stronger and faster. One of them in particular was absolutely flying through the course, moving like a blend of parkour expert and jungle cat. It wasn't until the don finished a lap and started jogging toward where Mick was waiting in line that he realized it wasn't a don. It was Chris, who waved at him cheerfully.

Mick made himself keep going even though he suddenly felt as slow and clumsy as when he'd first arrived at the Institute.

After a half hour of struggle, Mick stepped away from the course to sit with his back against the wall to catch his breath.

Chris flowed through the course like floodwaters for a few more laps, then jogged over to sit beside him. "Hail, fellow, well met," she said.

Mick nodded to say hi. "You're really good at that."

She waved a hand dismissively. "I went very nearly alley-blind when I was too old for Orphans and too uncouth for Lady

Grenville's. So I spent a great deal of time doing concentration and course while the faculty here civilized me for Lady Grenville's. I rather disliked being civilized, so I exerted myself all the more at concentration and course." She turned her head to look at him appraisingly. "Also, my mother was a very gifted hurdler. My fondest memories from the future include watching her run."

Mick nodded. That might have been the first time an adult had told him anything about her future. It wasn't forbidden, exactly, but alley rats had to be so careful not to give too much away. And, from what he could tell, his late point was way further in the future than almost anybody's, right around the time of the mysterious and potentially very important "Shroud" that seemed to be the latest possible late point for any alley rat. So he had to be extra careful about what he said. If he said something like, "That's cool about your mom. My Tía Verónica ran track at college for a while," he'd be announcing that there was a time in the future when at least some women went to college and did sports. They mostly didn't do either in 1853, at least not arrows. Even at the Institute, the pick-up footie game was usually at least eighty percent boys because a lot of the girls preferred to do calisthenics in the girls'-only room of the gym. Some of the girls who didn't play footie got judgy about the girls who did, and vice versa. Mick guessed that made sense. Although it was hard to be sure because everybody had to dance around exact dates, most alley rats got carried back in time just over a hundred years, meaning that most of the kids his age had probably come from somewhere around 1950 or 1960, and Mick was pretty sure the women's World Cup hadn't been as big a deal back then.

"Are you still present, Mr. Gunn?" Chris asked lightly.

Mick nodded.

"Good, good," Chris said. "I spoke with Clara North yesterday evening. I am to serve as your escort through London for the next few days. Miss March will be joining us as well."

"Just Alison?" Mick asked.

"This time," Chris said.

"Miss Emmet said that I wouldn't need a bunch of books while I'm out with you?" Mick asked hopefully.

Chris grinned. "Miss Emmet spoke aright."

"I'll warn Alison to leave the library here," Mick joked.

After showering, visiting the Scriptorium to write in his future journal, and eating breakfast, Mick returned to his room to put on his outdoor clothes and pick up his satchel. Alison was waiting for him in the Tory common room, so they started downstairs together to meet Chris at the garden gate.

"At breakfast," Alison said, answering his unspoken question about where Leech and Dolly were.

"Will they have to patrol alone?" Mick asked, a little worried. Street teams usually had three or four kids.

"Owl will be their thane, temporarily," Alison said. "He's to become a street thane when Michaelmas term begins, Miss North said."

Mick grinned, amused by the idea of Leech having to take orders from Owl.

"Let us hope Dolly can make them behave," Alison said.

At the gate to the Institute's garden, Chris was helping a couple new scullions unload produce from a wagon. The wagon and the gentle, elderly mares belonged to the elder Mr. Davies, but there was no sign of Mr. Davies himself. After a couple final trips, the unloading stopped and Chris hopped into the driver's seat. At a gesture from Chris, Alison climbed up to sit on the bench beside her, while Mick sat in the bed of the wagon, facing backward and resting his back against the wagon bed's lip. The mares walked gently out the gate, which one of the new scullions laboriously tugged shut so that Mrs. Robbin could chain and lock it behind them.

"Why don't the scullions ever stick around?" Mick asked, speaking up to be heard over the clatter of wheels and hooves. "Is Mrs. Robbin that bad to work for?"

"I'd imagine the girls would prefer to work for someone who remembers their name," Alison said.

"There's some truth to that," Chris said. "Still, it's typically a good sign when a scullion leaves the Institute. It signifies they are destined for some more desirable position."

"In service?" Alison asked.

"In the main," Chris said. "Are you an impatient person, Miss March?"

"I endeavor not to be," she said.

"Successfully?" Chris asked.

"Increasingly so," Alison said, sounding a little confused. Mick didn't blame her.

Chris chuckled. "I ask because today will be a very purposeful day, and yet it will appear aimless. Gunner and I spent a similar day not long ago, and he strained his eyes rolling them with impatience. I shouldn't wish you to damage your eyes."

Mick was facing backward and couldn't see either Chris or Alison, but he assumed Alison was smiling one of her quiet little smiles.

"If I may ask..." Alison said gently.

"You may," Chris said into the pause.

"What is our purpose today?" Alison asked.

"As is so often the case," Chris said in a comically philosophical tone, "one has many purposes, including those of which one is unaware."

She let that sit for a moment. Alison waited her out.

"Very good, Miss March, you do indeed endeavor not to be impatient. My purpose today is to collect certain words and objects and to deliver other words and objects. And, of course, to ferry you two about town so that you may keep watch for time lightning."

"I take it we are traveling beyond the main sequences?" Alison asked.

They had been moving in a generally northerly direction since leaving the Institute. They were still within the Institute's patrol area, but Mick could see why Alison asked. There would be no point using a wagon to patrol what the Institute teams would cover on foot anyway.

"Correct," Chris said.

After stopping at St. George's, the fancy Project school for older boys near Euston Square, to trade a small crate for a leather bag, they went west to St. James's Chapel near the Birmingham rail line, where Chris spoke with a couple fake urchin Eyes for ten minutes. Mick understood about five percent of it, so Alison translated after the wagon rolled away. Next, they zigzagged through Pancras and Camden Town as if testing the mares' willingness to turn corners. Mick kept alert for signs of time lightning or other alley phenomena. But there was nothing.

After that, they clattered east beside Regent's Canal for a

while. Chris exchanged shouted hellos with the crews of a couple of narrow boats, further proving she knew half the people in London.

"Do the Maxwells ever bring the *Baret* up here?" Mick asked.

"I am shaking my head to say 'no,'" Chris said. "Why not, Miss March? Or, Alison, if I may."

"You may," Alison said. "The *Baret* is horse-drawn, is it not?"

"Indeed," Chris said.

"Then I believe it would be unable to cross the Thames under its own power," Alison said.

"Correct again," Chris replied.

"Oh," Mick said, embarrassed he hadn't figured that out. "But Elmer is all right, isn't he?"

"Fully recovered," Chris said. "He's been out on the *Baret* for the better part of a week."

That was good to hear.

They came to a halt in front of a drab, lonely brick building that looked like an oversized brick garden shed and called itself "Claremont's Cartography." Chris told them to keep an eye on the wagon as she slid to the street and entered the store.

"Oddy's Outpost," Alison said. "It's in the cartographer's."

Mick's mental version of the Plan got blurry and unreliable this far north, but Alison was almost always right about that sort of thing.

Chris came out a quarter hour later, saying nothing. From there, they worked their way east, meandering through the neighborhoods south of the canal until Mick and Alison confirmed that they couldn't sense any alley activity. After that, they swung so far north that they occasionally went beyond the edge of the Plan.

That far out, there weren't any alley clusters or dons' outposts, but there were several lookouts where Eyes kept watch on people entering and exiting the city. At least that was what Mick assumed they were. He didn't think he could ask Chris with Alison right there, and Chris didn't volunteer any information.

They moved briskly along, stopping occasionally so that Chris could exchange cryptic conversation with various Eyes. Given the thick accents and the gibberish vocabulary, Mick hardly understood anything, though Alison promised they really were speaking English.

They covered a lot more ground than Mick had expected. Since there weren't any alley clusters that far from the city center, they didn't have to go slowly to look for alley phenomena. Also, although the roads were often rutted, uneven dirt, it hadn't rained recently, so they were hard enough for the wagon's wheels to turn smoothly. Even so, it was past noon when the mares came to a stop in front of a tallish, narrow building with "Fuller & Sons" painted on the front window. Mick assumed it had to be another lookout keeping watch on the comings and goings nearby.

Chris was inside for a while, leaving Mick and Alison to sit shoulder to shoulder in the wagon bed. Alison seemed to be staring blankly into the distance, but Mick knew that she was keeping a watch in all directions. Trying not to be too obvious about it, Mick watched the traffic and also watched the Eye across the road pretending not to watch the traffic. Aside from a single, stately stagecoach and a cabriolet that jittered by faster than seemed wise, the traffic was mostly the occasional wagon and a fair number of folks on foot. There were probably twice as many people headed south into the city as in the opposite direction.

"Do you suppose they're science or magic?" Alison asked out of nowhere.

"What?" Mick asked.

"The peculiar phenomena we observe."

As usual, Alison was trying to avoid talking openly about time travel in public. Mick respected that, even if it seemed like overkill given that there was nobody in earshot except the rabbit munching a shrub on the other side of the road.

"I don't know," he said. He thought about it sometimes but never got anywhere. He didn't like the idea of magic, somehow. But time alleys seemed more ... alive than he expected from technology. "My un— Somebody I knew always used to say that if the tech is advanced enough, you'll probably think it's magic. Like, I bet a cave person would know that a fancy sword is technology, even if cave people didn't have steel. Cave people didn't have steel, did they?"

"Assuredly not," Alison said with a tiny smile.

"Right, so, the cave person would know that people made the sword. But a steam engine? That would blow his mind, I bet." As soon as he said it, he realized that "blow his mind" was probably a connan. Oh well.

Alison nodded thoughtfully and they sat silently for a while.

"Wait," Mick said, "why?"

"Curiosity, in the main, I suppose," Alison said. "And then too Miss Mitchell was showing me some of the equations the dons are using to try to predict the phenomenon we observed at the footbridge. The new phenomenon."

Time lightning. Mick nodded to show he understood.

"I shouldn't think that magic could be predicted with integral calculus," she said.

"Can it be predicted?" Mick asked. "What we saw on the bridge?"

Alison shrugged. "The dons seem optimistic. Miss Mitchell said that some clever rats devised some equations before the Collapse that are giving the dons some insights."

Mick thought about that. Back before the 1767 Collapse, a few rats had been able to travel—on purpose—a few years into the past and then return to their starting point, which they had called "shuttling the alleys." But nobody had been able to do it since the Collapse. "Rats aren't shuttling the alleys again, are they?" he asked.

"Miss Mitchell and the other dons think not," Alison said. "But they do seem to think something is in motion. Chris does too, I believe. Today she seems … ill at ease. Watchful."

Now that Alison said it, Mick agreed that Chris seemed more alert than usual. Besides, after their first long trip through the city, Chris had basically told him that there might be something to watch out for.

"I wonder why we're here," Alison said. "In truth."

"You don't think it's like Chris said? She runs mysterious errands, and we keep an eye out for—for the new phenomenon?"

Alison frowned. "That's certainly part of it. But not, I think, all of it."

"What's the rest?" Mick asked.

Alison shrugged. "I wish I could say. It feels, somehow, like a test, though perhaps more for me than for you." She frowned in thought for a moment. "We shall see."

They chatted idly until Chris returned. After sliding up into the driver's seat as if gravity didn't entirely apply to her, she reached into her small leather shoulder bag and pulled out a small loaf of brown bread, which she tore in half, handing the pieces to Mick and Alison.

Thanking Chris, Alison clambered back into the passenger seat and asked Chris, "Should we give her some bread?"

Mick looked over his shoulder to see who Alison meant. She seemed to be looking at the Eye he'd been watching earlier. Huh, he probably would have guessed the Eye was a boy.

Chris had been about to flick the reins at the horses, but she returned her hands to her lap and looked appraisingly at Alison. Mick turned around to face them in case it got interesting.

"And why, other than our bottomless reserves of Christian charity, would we do that?" Chris asked Alison in a pleasantly curious tone of voice.

"She works for the Project, does she not?" Alison asked.

"And what leads you to that conclusion?" Chris asked in the same tone.

"She was watching when you spoke to those drovers near Forest Row," Alison said. "You signaled to her then, and she left a quarter-hour before we did."

Chris looked at Mick and raised her eyebrows questioningly. "You haven't been discussing topics of a delicate nature with Miss March, have you Gunner?" Chris asked.

Assuming she meant the Eyes, Mick shook his head. Chris nodded impassively and turned back to Alison. "He truly hasn't?"

Alison shook her head. "Gunner has been watching the girl, but he tried to conceal it. And he didn't speak of her. And I don't think he saw the young man above Fuller and Sons watching Well Street and the canal through a spyglass."

Mick shot a quick glance up at the row of windows just below the roof. Yes, there was indeed a guy with a telescope. Mick had to assume that Alison was right that the guy could see the canal from there. Alison remembered where objects were almost perfectly and seemed to know what everything would look like from any angle.

"I believe he also watches Victoria Park," Chris said blandly.

"That gives sense," Alison said, also blandly.

Mick realized that Alison was showing off. Or maybe sending Chris a message that Chris might as well explain some of the mysteries since Alison was going to figure them out on her own anyway.

If so, it worked. After turning the wagon south, Chris swore Alison to secrecy and told her more or less what she'd told Mick about the Eyes and the Mind.

"You don't seem especially surprised," Chris noted to Alison after finishing her explanation.

Alison shrugged. "When I first came to the Institute, I reported to the dons whenever I spied people pretending to be poorer and more idle than they were, especially if those people seemed to be watching places of interest. I was most vexed when the dons didn't give a fig. Eventually, a don told me that the dons were well aware of those people and unworried by them. No one ever explained to me precisely who those people were, but it wasn't terribly difficult to deduce something like what you've just told me. Or that it was best for me to guard my silence."

"We rats do guard our silence as well as the beefeaters guard the Queen," Chris agreed.

"Is that why Gunner and I are here?" Alison asked. "To see

some Eyes going about their business? To see whether we would see those Eyes and guard our silence?"

"In part," Chris said. "But your services as spotters truly are required, given that the time lightning appears to be spreading."

"And?" Alison prompted.

"And that is all I may say at present," Chris said cheerfully.

They rode on without speaking past Palestine Place and the mulberry trees of Bethnal Green until forced to stop while a locomotive dragging a half dozen train cars chugged and thudded across the road, spitting cinders for dozens of yards. Chris had judged the distance well, and the cinders fell short of the horses and wagon. After quite a bit more patrolling and stopping at outposts, they crossed the Thames at the London Bridge. They worked their way south for a while before stopping at Gaoler's Home Outpost so that Chris could disappear inside to speak to the dons.

By then it was nearly evening, and Mick was struggling to keep alert for alley signs that never appeared, and he'd started to doze off, trusting to Alison's and Chris' superior vigilance. He jolted back awake when Chris started the wagon moving again.

"We're continuing south?" Alison asked in a surprised tone.

Chris said, "I'm to take you to patrol Zoo Cluster and then continue to Demeter."

"Miss North didn't say we were to sleep outside the walls," Alison said. She thought for a moment. "However, she did say that I was to follow your instructions as if they were her own. You too, Gunner."

Chris chuckled. "From the rumors that have touched my ears, I'd say she was telling you to ignore my instructions just as you ignore hers and go gallivanting in pursuit of time phantoms."

Mick snickered.

Alison said dryly, "I rather suspect that was not her meaning."

After an hour and a half of clattering and clunking through the streets in and around the Zoological Gardens, the mares turned onto a lane leading to the Grand Surrey Canal. Mick recognized it as the spot where the younger Mr. Davies had met him and Chris on Mick's first London tour with Chris.

And, indeed, there was the teenage Mr. Davies, sitting on the top rail of the low fence in front of a small building that faced the canal. When the wagon came to a stop, he popped to his feet, nodded politely to Alison and Mick, smiled at Chris, and bestowed pats and apple chunks upon the horses, who nuzzled him affectionately.

After checking the mares' hooves and harnesses, Mr. Davies whispered a few things to Chris, who nodded intently. Mick looked at Alison, who shrugged to indicate she couldn't hear him either. Then Mr. Davies hopped into the driver's seat, taking his leave with a wave of his cap over his shoulder.

Soon, Chris, Mick, and Alison were walking in the shade of the trees and hedges bordering Demeter Farm on either side.

Mick was surprisingly pleased to be back, especially to see Ward, who met them at the entrance to the Scythe.

"Elmer's a sturdy cove, him. All healed up," Ward informed them without any other greeting. "Rosie's much calmed now that he's well again, you can imagine. And her mother and father, naturally."

"Is he here?" Mick asked, hoping to see Elmer in person.

"On the canals," Ward said, shaking his head regretfully.

"And we still haven't any idea why he was attacked?" Mick asked. "Or why the *Baret* was, I mean."

Ward shook his head. "The thieves took some small things, Mrs. Maxwell says, but naught as seems worth hanging or transportation. It's head-scratching, it is."

"Well, the important thing is that Elmer Maxwell is recovered," Alison said.

Ward looked at Alison as if seeing her for the first time. His face was a mix of the usual fretfulness it acquired near fancy people and some other sort of confusion. "Begging your pardon, miss, but have I made your acquaintance? I'm Ward Carlton, from here on the farm."

"Alison March. I don't believe that we've been introduced, Mr. Carlton," Alison said. "But you've likely seen me previously, just as I have seen you. I am a student at the Institute, and I was here this summer."

"That'll be it, miss, no doubt," Ward said, though he sounded pretty doubtful. "Oh, I almost forgot. Chris, Mr. Yardley said you're wanted in the workshop at your earliest convenience. And he said that I'm to show your guests to the schoolhouse for their lodgings."

"Thankee, Ward," Chris said. "Pray tell Mr. Yardley I shall join him and the others shortly. I'd like first to escort Mr. Gunn and Miss March to the schoolhouse. Oh, after that, if you could ask in the kitchen whether they might spare some bread and cheese for my young friends here, I'm certain they would be grateful."

Ward nodded and jogged off.

After detouring to the warehouse to talk to the warehouse workers and to chit-chat with a healthy-looking Elmer as he swabbed the deck of the *Baret*, Chris led them back to Hill

Street but turned left so that they would have to walk a couple extra hundred yards north before turning onto the far side of the drive. As they walked, Chris asked Alison about Lady Penbrook. Eventually, Mick realized Chris was confirming that Lady Penbrook had given Alison the Athena speech.

By the time they reached the intersection of the main drive and the paddock path, Chris seemed satisfied with Alison's answers and said, "I shall now confess that one of my purposes today was to bring you two here so that Lady Penbrook might speak with you."

That sounded ominous, Mick thought.

"There's no call for alarm," Chris said. "I believe that Lady Penbrook simply wishes to ask you some questions about the time lightning. She is an important person in the Project, and important people are accustomed to having their questions answered."

"Surely the dons would—" Alison started.

"I've no doubt that whatever reports Clara North and the Vicar pass along to the Seat have been relayed to Lady Penbrook in one form or another," Chris interrupted. "But she likes to hear about a thing from those who have seen it with their own eyes. Or their own Eyes, which is generally why I have the pleasure of her conversation."

By this point, they had reached the schoolhouse, and Chris took her leave with a jaunty wave.

Before Mick and Alison had reached the door to the school-house, they heard Ward calling to them across the lawn in front of the Manor. They waited at the door while he hustled toward them. He arrived slightly out of breath and carrying something wrapped in a cloth. "Cook was generous," he said, handing the cloth-wrapped item to Mick. "There's bread and cheese and apples and even a quarter chicken."

After Mick and Alison thanked him, Ward said, "If there's naught else, Mrs. Maxwell said I could dine with her and Rosie. They'll be needing some help with the wash, I'm thinking."

"There's nothing else," Alison said. "It's good of you to help your friends."

Ward had been keeping his eyes on Mick's face, but his gaze snapped suddenly to Alison's. "Poppy?" he asked. "'Tis Poppy, isn't it? It *is*."

CHAPTER 10

UNRIPE GRAPES

"Good old Poppy!" Ward continued. "I didn't recognize you looking like such a fine lady, but that was a thing you said to me once, 'It's good to help one's friends,' or words not much different. Different voice, but the same kind face."

"I'm afraid you have me at a disadvantage," Alison said.

Mick admired how calm she looked and sounded. Only a slight stiffness in her face and voice hinted how stunned she was.

Ward shook his head. "I'm sorry. You wouldn't remember me. I was a tiny lad, and my face was mostly blood, I reckon. I was in the Borough—" He paused and looked at Mick. "This was when I was at Orphans, before they let me come back to the farm permanent, y'see. I'd had too much of books and sums and switchings from teachers, and I'd got it in my head to run away. I'd tried to come here but got confused and strayed into the Borough. I got the wrong way of a lobby sneak coming out of a gin palace and, well, he scraped his knuckles on me until Poppy and her friends chased him away. Escorted me all the way back to Orphans, they did, taking turns near carrying me."

Alison's face took on a wondering look. "I do recall," she said slowly. "We were kipping in a dirty boarding house full of thieves and cadgers. We had to do a bunter after some dolly-mops stole our money and we couldn't pay the landlord—" Hearing the coarse words and accent coming out of her mouth, she paused and breathed deeply, returning to her fancy accent. "In any case, I'm glad we were able to come to your aid."

"You might have saved my life," Ward said. "You definitely saved my eye." He tapped a finger just below his right eye. "Nurse said one more fist and I'd have been storing acorns in this socket."

Alison shook her head. "That was mostly the others. I was too small to be of much use."

"Bigger than me. And fast with that razor."

"I'm glad my friends helped you," Alison said. "That lobby sneak was a vicious brute. He came to an evil end, they said. Drowned, probably with some help from bug-hunters."

"But how are you..." Ward trailed off.

Mick assumed Ward was looking for a polite way to ask, "How did you go from street trash to fancy young lady?"

With almost no hesitation, Alison said in her most ladylike tones, "I wasn't born on the streets of London. I had a good family of considerable position. Unfortunate events that I would rather not dwell upon—"

Because they involve time travel, Mick thought.

"—and that do not reflect upon my character or my family's character, left me temporarily without support and protection.

I was forced to live a life to which I was unaccustomed before God restored me to a position appropriate to a person of my breeding." She looked at Ward intently. "I know I can trust you to discuss my … difficulties with no one."

"I'll never breathe a word," Ward said fervently.

Mick could tell Ward meant it. After a few more pleasantries, Ward went to visit the Maxwells, and Alison and Mick took their dinner to the schoolhouse's empty little dining room.

Before they started to eat, Alison lit an oil lamp on the table because the sun had started sliding below the horizon.

"That was really good," Mick said. "What you told Ward." It had felt like an explanation without explaining much.

Alison dug into her portion of the chicken, eating with her fingers. "Miss North made me practice that speech for weeks when I first arrived at the Institute. She knew there was a chance I'd be recognized and need an explanation, you see. But I never did. After so many years, I thought I'd be safe."

"Ward won't say anything," Mick said. "He was smiling at you almost like he smiles at Rosie Maxwell."

Alison nodded, dropping the chicken bones unceremoniously on the table, and turning to the bread and cheese, tearing off big hunks of bread and jamming chunks of cheese into them before cramming the combination into her mouth.

"If you're that hungry, you can have my chicken," Mick offered.

Alison paused her eating and grinned wryly. "I'm not terribly hungry. But Poppy was always hungry. When I remember being Poppy, I eat like her. I do apologize." She resumed eating in her usual ladylike fashion.

Mick smiled. "You should see some of my cousins at a barbecue."

Alison laughed a sincere, merry laugh, and Mick felt like he'd done something useful with the day.

There were only three other boys in Mick's dormitory, teenagers who were studying with the mechanicals. The next morning, they rose with the sun, waking Mick. He lay in bed for a while with his thin, floppy pillow over his eyes, trying to convince himself he could get back to sleep. But eventually, he rose and scrubbed himself clean with a soft, dry cloth, dressed, and went downstairs. Finding the dining hall empty, he went outside to the courtyard, settling onto a bench bathed in a pleasant patch of sunshine. After an interlude of boneless relaxation, he started to notice his hunger. He ignored it until he heard footsteps from the schoolhouse door.

He turned to see Alison walking toward him. She nodded companionably and settled onto the bench beside him.

"There isn't any breakfast in the dining hall, is there?" Mick asked.

She shook her head.

"Drat the luck," Mick said, working on his Victorian vocabulary. "It's great what you and your friends did for Ward."

Alison sighed. "I'm glad we were able to assist him, naturally. It's only, well, it made me think how unusual it was for us to do anything of the kind. We scarcely had the strength and daring to help ourselves, much less others. With Ward, it was my fault, truth be told. Ward looked rather like my brother, in that moment. I may even have believed he was my brother. I simply lost my head and rushed in, and the others had to come to my rescue."

She paused, breathing deeply to calm herself. "From that

time in my life, I can count my good deeds on one hand with fingers to spare. I cannot begin to count the number of times I lied. Or stole food or something I could sell to buy food. Or sweets."

Mick shrugged. "You were just a little kid."

"Yes," Alison said. "I don't blame myself overmuch. Or my friends. Strict honesty would have been the death of us. So would noble bravery. But all the fine ladies and gentlemen who passed us by when we were begging or stealing or starving, they wouldn't have needed to be brave to help us. Or poor Ward. It seems to me that the future, my future, was not so cruel as this place. But then maybe I simply didn't see the cruelty, or see it for what it was."

Mick thought about that. He'd spent a lot of time feeling sorry for himself after his mom died and his dad kept taking assignments far from home. But he'd still had most of his family. He'd had food, a roof, a bed. He'd had school. Heck, he'd had air-conditioning in the summer and radiators in the winter, and that was an impossible luxury now. Maybe that's what happened if you were unhappy—you focused on what you'd lost, not what you had. Maybe that's why everybody with fine clothes and full purses walked right past hungry kids—they were too busy thinking about what they'd lost, what they wanted.

And maybe that included him, he realized. He walked past hungry kids all the time on patrol. For that matter, he mostly walked past the kids at the Institute without really seeing them because he was focused on leaving the Institute, getting back to the life he'd lost. Then again, what was he supposed to do? Just let time kick him in the teeth? Give up his real life?

He was still trying to make sense of that when Ward

appeared at the courtyard gate, carrying a basket full of some very interesting food. "I'm to take you to Lady Penbrook now," he said.

Mick and Alison shook off their gloomy thoughts and rose to follow Ward.

To Mick's surprise, Ward didn't lead them toward the Manor. Instead, he led them north to the paddock path. When Mick asked, Ward confirmed that Lady Penbrook was in the Refuge.

They found Lady Penbrook sitting beneath the watchful eyes of the Nye sisters' portraits, poring over papers spread on a sunlit portion of the table. At the sound of their footsteps on the floorboards, she collected the papers into a fancy leather folder of some kind.

"Mr. Gunn and Miss March, Lady Penbrook," Ward said nervously, keeping his eyes on his feet. He remembered he was holding a basket full of food and held it up. "Mr. Anderson gave me food, my lady. I could try to lay the table, if you wish." He paused, clearly worried. "Only I'm not sure how."

A small smile flickered across Lady Penbrook's face. "That won't be necessary. You may leave the basket on the table."

"Yes, my lady. Thankee." Ward placed the basket carefully on the table and turned back to the door, a relieved look on this face.

"Mr. Gunn, if you will be so kind," Lady Penbrook said, directing her eyes at the basket.

The table and the basket were too tall for Mick to see into, so he lowered the basket onto an empty chair. Once he'd unpacked everything, there were several good-sized Cornish pasties, still slightly warm to the touch, a small bunch of grapes, and a dozen pale petit fours, each stamped with a leafy design.

Lady Penbrook waited patiently while Mick fumbled a bit, putting everything on the thin silver serving platter he found at the bottom of the basket and distributing the similarly light plates and silverware. Once they each had a napkin, Mick carried the empty basket to the opposite end of the table. At Lady Penbrook's request, he filled three wooden glasses from the water pitcher on the table before sitting back down.

"Thank you, Mr. Gunn. Do please serve yourselves and eat," Lady Penbrook said. "We needn't stand on ceremony. Indeed, eating in the Refuge spares me from Mr. Anderson's frowns and sighs when I cannot be bothered to restrict myself to the proper fork."

Mick suspected his face had the same relieved look Ward's had worn on the way out. Mick's table manners weren't great by the twenty-first century standards, as Tía Verónica liked to point out. By Victorian fancy person standards, they were probably bad enough to get him arrested, especially when he was eating with an actual Lady.

They ate in silence for a while. Alison seemed distracted, though maybe she was just being careful not to eat like Poppy.

The food was delicious. A lot of Victorians seemed to think spices were Satan's dandruff, but if you had a cook who was trying and had access to fresh ingredients, the food could be amazing. And it didn't get fresher than a farm. As tasty as the pasties and petit fours were, the best part was the grapes, the first he'd had since dropping in 1853. Grapes were almost impossible to get in Her Majesty's England. But Demeter had a small vineyard in the south fields, and Mick felt lucky to have returned to the farm at the right time to enjoy the grapes.

"I see you share my love of grapes," Lady Penbrook remarked when they had finished eating. "The season has just begun. I remember when it was nothing to bring home bunches of grapes at any time of year, and yet I also suspect I must simply be imagining such a preposterous fancy. It is a difficult thing to remember the future. Either the present feels unreal, or the future does. Or both."

Mick found himself nodding and noticed Alison was too.

"That is why I insisted upon starting my little vineyard as soon as I married my dear husband, the late Viscount. To stave off madness, an alley rat must remember the future. Perhaps one must even create the very future one remembers. Perhaps grapes were so plentiful in England when I was a girl because I planted the seeds as a young woman." She brushed some crumbs into her hand before dropping them onto her plate. "I find the literal seeds to be a goad to planting the figurative ones. A taste or a scent that reminds me of the future pricks me on to build that future. You have met Nurse Peck, I think? And you surely know Dr. Quinn?"

Mick and Alison nodded.

"I repose my well-being in their hands more readily and with greater confidence than in the hairy hands of the most renowned surgeons and physicians in this city. They both began their education at the Institute and continued to Lady Grenville's Academy, as did I. At those schools, young ladies are treated as if they have brains in their heads and even sinews in their arms. After that, as Nurse Peck and Dr. Quinn both had the don for medicine, the Project's societies undertook to provide them with training in no wise inferior to the training given any man. Many other women alley rats are similarly trained in medicine and other useful professions. They must often hide their wisdom and skills, perhaps practicing their professions behind the walls of the Institute or concealing their knowledge beneath the fustian skirts of the country nurse. Still, they have the knowledge. And they build upon it. They are our grapes, if you will forgive the metaphor. I remember a future where women physicians and surgeons were commonplace and would never think to conceal their accomplishments. I like to think the Project's work will help bring about that future."

She paused to look them both in the eyes, first Mick, then Alison.

"The Nye twins," Lady Penbrook said, pointing to the portraits hanging behind, "appear to have come from a place and time capable of terrible cruelty to women, especially dark-hued women, and they dropped in a place that was perhaps slightly better but a time that was vastly worse. Even today, that cruelty persists, here and even more so in what I take to be your nation, Mr. Gunn. So many fortunes built upon and maintained by the lash, the chain, and the bloodhound. The villains will fall, belike, but not tomorrow, and not without watering the vine-yards with the blood of the innocent and the wicked alike."

Mick tried to remember what year Juneteenth started. 1860-something, he thought, once again longing for fifteen minutes with Google.

"Ah, but I have let my hobby-horse gallop pell mell," Lady Penbrook said. "I did not request your presence to discuss grapes or physicians. I wanted to ask you about what we are apparently referring to as 'time lightning.' I am given to under-stand you have both seen it, and I should very much like to know more."

For a half hour or so, Lady Penbrook walked them through where they saw the time lightning, how long it lasted, and whether there had been anybody lurking there at the time, the way Cassandra Halliwell had turned out to be near so many of the fateful fawkes alleys. Alison and Mick took turns describing what they'd seen at the Hungerford Bridge from when the time lightning had appeared until the alley had closed, leaving the dropper baby on the bridge. Alison did most of the talking, making it sound like they'd noticed the time lighting and the alley at the same time, which felt like an insult to Mick's alley sight. He was going to correct her, but he let it go when she shot him a subtle warning look.

After they'd covered the bridge, Mick described the time lightning at the cricket grounds, following Alison's lead by leaving out that he and Gail had seen it way earlier and better than the others. Once Mick had said the lightning was somewhat similar to the lightning on the bridge, Lady Penbrook didn't ask for details about it or the alley that had opened up afterward. She was interested in the adult rats they'd seen in the stands and in Blue and Green.

"A very precise account, Mr. Gunn," Lady Penbrook said after he'd covered everything he could remember. "You paint quite the portrait of Messieurs Green and Blue. I take it you are unable to do the same for the adult alley rats you saw in the stands at Lord's?"

Mick shook his head. "I'm sorry, my lady. They were too far away. None of us could see them very well."

Lady Penbrook smiled cheerfully at him. "Oh, you needn't apologize. The temporal phenomena are what truly matter, and you have both set forth the particulars most admirably."

Mick saw Alison start to ask a question and cut herself off a couple times before she finally asked, diffidently, "Do you make a study of such phenomena, my lady?"

Lady Penbrook waved her hand dismissively. "Oh, once upon a time, I dabbled. But one's alley sight loses its luster, and one's domestic and social obligations grow ever more demanding. At least if one is a woman," she said, her tone a little bitter. She smiled. "But I oughtn't complain. We're not planning to grow sour grapes, are we?"

Mick shook his head since it seemed like the answer Lady Penbrook expected. Alison did too.

"And so, Miss March," Lady Penbrook continued, "I'm merely an enthusiast these days. Still, I'm an enthusiast with considerable property, and so my friends on the boards of the various Project institutions to which I extend my patronage are kind enough to keep me abreast of news and novelties."

They chatted a bit longer, mostly Lady Penbrook asking Alison whether she was contemplating attending Lady Grenville's. Alison surprised Mick by saying she wasn't certain. He was sure she had her heart set on being a don, and dons usually didn't go to Lady Grenville's.

"And you, Mr. Gunn," Lady Penbrook asked. "Have you considered St. George's? As with Lady Grenville's, one must be clever to secure admission, especially if one's skin speaks of the Mediterranean. But you seem sufficiently clever at any hue, and a fine education and valuable social connections can serve as both a shield and a spear."

Mick was a little thrown off by the mention of skin color, so he just said he wasn't really sure. Besides, he wasn't planning to stay in the past long enough to worry about where he would go to school next.

Soon, the conversation drifted to a halt. Lady Penbrook thanked them for their time, asked Mick to put the dishes and silverware in the basket and take it to the Manor kitchens, and then smilingly bid them goodbye without rising.

Once they'd reached the paddock pathway, Alison said, "I'm happy to carry the basket if it's heavy."

It wasn't too bad, and Mick said so.

"That was another test, I think," Alison said.

"Test?" Mick asked.

"Tests, more like," Alison said thoughtfully. "For example, when Lady Penbrook asked you to perform maid duties at the table even though I was right there, a girl not much older than you. You managed not to sulk. Most boys would have pulled a face, at the least."

Mick hadn't thought about it like that. "Maybe she was just testing if I'm good at taking orders since my skin 'speaks of the Mediterranean,' whatever that means."

They skipped over a large puddle in the path, first her, then him.

"Possibly," Alison said. "But if you ever learn to speak properly, I shouldn't think your hue will place obstacles in your path the way it does for Miss Emmet, or even Stephen. Did Miss North ever devise a story for you to hint at when speaking with arrows, possibly that you are the love child of a peer's second son who perished before he could wed your mother, an Italian beauty descended from the Medici who later fled to Canada to mend her heart and hide her shame?"

"That's really specific," Mick said. "And no. No cover story. I didn't know I needed one."

"Doubtless Miss North decided you didn't, and I rather suspect Lady Penbrook would agree. If anything, Lady Penbrook wished to see how you would respond to her remarking upon your skin. And to so many other of her remarks. She was watching our reactions quite closely, much as she did when she talked to me and the others shortly before we left Demeter."

Mick nodded. Lady Penbrook had also looked at him really closely during their conversation in the Refuge.

They passed the henhouse. After a flurry of squawking died down, Mick asked, "Why did we hide how good my alley sight is? If she was testing me, maybe I should have shown off."

Alison frowned. "I'm honestly not sure, Gunner. Perhaps precisely because she was testing you. Us. Until you know people, it's better that they not know the full extent of your abilities."

Mick thought it over as they turned onto the main drive. That made sense, but then Alison had basically spent the day before showing off to Chris, who was a stranger to her. He pointed that out.

Alison nodded. "Miss North spoke quite highly of Chris and told me to be useful. If Miss North trusts her, I trust her."

Mick nodded. He felt bad that Alison spent so much of her life assessing every situation for risks. It had to be exhausting. Then again, it had also kept her alive.

After dropping off the basket at the kitchens, they wandered about the Scythe, looking for Chris. They knocked at cottages and workshops until Mr. Vines, a dirty-faced teenaged mechanical, cracked one of the workshop doors open and acknowledged that Chris was inside. Eventually, he even condescended to fetch her, shutting the door firmly in their faces while he did.

A little while later, Chris slipped outside, carefully closing the door behind herself and joining them on the small, rough stone patio in front of the workshop. Mick heard a bolt snick into place on the inside.

Chris' hands and face were darkened with grease, and she wiped her hands on a dirty pair of trousers. "My apologies to you both. I had intended to meet you in the kitchens, but something arose." She pursed her lips in thought. "I shall be occupied some time longer, and I haven't anything useful for you to do at the moment. I suggest you take your leisure somewhere out of sight of those who might find a chore or ten for you. If I don't find you by, let us say half one, please seek me here."

"Might you *instruct* us to take our leisure?" Alison asked.

Chris chortled. "Sharp as scalpel, Miss March. Yes, you are instructed to take your leisure somewhere that you will not be press-ganged into service, and you must of course treat that instruction as if it came from Clara North herself."

Alison flashed a grin. "Thankee kindly, Miss Biggs."

Alison and Mick had just started back toward the main farm to find an empty schoolroom when they met Ward on the drive. He was struggling under several heavy lunch baskets, which they helped him carry to a couple workshops, including the one Chris was in. At the door to that workshop, Mr. Vines took the basket with a nod, saying, "Florentine graces" before closing and bolting the door.

"Florentine graces?'" Mick asked, as he, Ward, and Alison wandered to stand in the shade of the trees dividing the workshops from the warehouse.

"The mechanicals speak in riddles," Ward said. "Worse than Cockneys, they are. I never understand head nor tail of it."

"The dons do the same when they don't want you to understand," Alison said. She thought for a moment. "I suppose it must mean 'thank you.'"

"You've that right, Po— Miss March," Ward said.

"Alison," she told him.

He nodded but looked skeptical about using her first name. "I only know because I asked Chris. How did you know?"

"Florentines speak one of the Italian dialects," she said, "the Italian for 'thank you' is 'grazie,' and grazie sounds a little like 'graces.'"

Ward looked impressed. After a pause, he said. "If I'm not needed, I should climb up the Crow's Nest. I'm to be on watch until one o'clock."

"Did Chris give you that duty?" Alison asked.

Ward risked raising his eyes for a moment. "Yes, mi—."

"Truly, I'd be grateful if you called me Alison."

Ward nodded. "She did. Chris did, I mean to say." His gaze dropped back down to his shoes.

Alison caught Mick's attention and raised her eyebrows meaningfully. Taking that to mean that the Crow's Nest would be an excellent place to hide from chores, Mick suggested that he and Alison join Ward, who said he'd be glad of their company.

Demeter students weren't usually allowed unsupervised in the Crow's nest, but Mick figured it was probably okay since he and Alison were no longer Demeter students. In any case, nobody objected when they climbed the ladders up to the Crow's Nest. As they climbed up and then settled in, Alison asked Ward apparently idle questions about the chores that Chris told him to do. Mick eventually realized that she was trying to figure out if Chris was training Ward to be an Eye. As far as Mick could tell, the answer was unclear.

They spent a while staring in all directions, except Ward, who had to focus on the canal and the farm, especially for signs of livestock getting out of a paddock and making a break for it. Or eating the crops. Mick wouldn't want to be the one who had to tell Lady Penbrook that cows had eaten her grapes.

Mick mostly gazed north, enjoying the complex, colorful patchwork of London as it appeared from and disappeared behind its shifting layers of smog. Alison had settled herself on one of the rough stools in the middle and disappeared into *Jane Eyre*. His mom had been funny about that novel. She read it once a year, complaining how silly it was but clearly loving it. It was weird to think that the book was basically brand new, not a classic.

When a distant church bell rang one o'clock, Ward left to get lunch and do chores. He offered to fetch them lunch, but that seemed like taking advantage, and anyway they were still full from Lady Penbrook's hamper. Ward said he didn't think anybody would be coming up to the Crow's Nest to take over the watch, so Mick and Alison decided to spend another lazy half hour before going to meet Chris.

Mick was dozing when he woke to the deep voice of Mr. Yardley, the tall mechanical, saying from somewhere below, "I'd almost rather fabricate another than do these cursed repairs."

"We haven't time," said Chris' voice. "Besides, would you truly rather try to grind new glow-glass, especially with the in uzeetatees lenseeum missing?" Her voice grew fainter as she walked away.

"Fair enough," Mr. Yardley admitted, his voice fading also. "Bad enough this month wants it in a week without the slow work of grinding."

Mick's watch said it was nearly half-one, so he and Alison climbed down to catch up with Chris.

They found Chris at the warehouse dock, where she was

just about to board a steam-powered narrowboat that Mick didn't recognize. When she saw them, she turned and walked toward them, meeting them at the open warehouse door.

After warning them in a quiet voice that the narrow boat's crew were arrows, Chris said, "I've been summoned away, I fear. Eliza Richardson, one of the mechanicals, has volunteered to stand in my stead with you this afternoon. The palace has commanded that you patrol the Observatory Cluster. Seems a wild goose chase to me, but it's a lovely day for a stroll."

"Oy, Chris," called one of the narrowboaters impatiently.

"Must dash," Chris said. "You'll doubtless find Eliza taking her lunch in the open air."

Chris turned and jogged back to the boat, which was starting to chug away from the dock as she hopped aboard.

Mick and Alison shrugged at one another and went to find Eliza Richardson, who turned out to be a little blonde woman dressed in a simple grayish cotton dress. She also turned out to swear like a sailor and to have a gift for mimicry, including a hilariously over-the-top impression of Mr. Anderson and a dead-on impression of Lady Penbrook that probably would get her thrown in some sort of Prison for Impertinent Commoners if she ever got caught doing it.

There was a small dons' outpost near the Observatory, but the dons there told them that stirrings were rare and alleys rarer. So, as Chris had predicted, their patrol was a pleasant and uneventful stroll through Greenwich and Deptford. As they went, they often passed cottages, some clustered together in little villages, some scattered lonesomely across meadows and fields. A couple times the quiet gave way to the smoky chugging of a train easing into or out of the Greenwich terminus. After detouring north to see the Thames at its southernmost point in the area, they set their route by picking pleasantly tree-lined lanes, pausing to rest in the shade and to pick wild berries. Sometimes they had to step aside for plodding wagons and, once, not far from the Observatory, for an elegant coach bearing the mark of the Royal Society being drawn at a fast pace by high-shouldered horses.

"Such haste," Miss Richardson remarked, brushing her sleeves free of the dust kicked up by carriage horses. "Perhaps they discovered another planet."

Mick smiled but didn't say anything. A while ago, he'd mentioned something about Mars' moons once during tutorial, and Mr. Victor had chewed him out afterward for mentioning moons that hadn't been discovered yet.

After another couple hours of wandering, more to savor sunshine and summer breezes than with the hope of spotting alley phenomena, they turned back to Demeter. Alison and Mick enjoyed a quiet evening on the schoolhouse patio, eating chicken sandwiches before Alison read to Mick from *Jane Eyre* by the light of an oil lamp.

The next morning, Alison and Mick ate breakfast with Ward on the warehouse dock before one of the mechanicals dropped by to inform them that a cab was waiting for them on the Manor drive.

Neither knew what to make of that, and they didn't get much explanation from the dons waiting for them in the cab. Mick recognized them both as dons who had kept watch over Cassandra Halliwell after she'd been captured, but he didn't know their names until they introduced themselves as Matilda Jennings and Harold Bateson. Both looked to be in their early twenties, and both were tall and broad-featured, though Miss Jennings was pale and blonde and Mr. Bateson was olive-skinned with jet-black hair. He looked a lot like Mick's cousin Mateo, except for having bigger shoulders.

The two dons looked worried but talked in cheerful tones about the weather, cricket results, and the blander bits of news plucked from the broadsheets. Mick tried not to worry about what they weren't saying. Somebody would tell him something when he got back to the Institute. And he'd probably end up wishing they hadn't.

CHAPTER 11

COUNT EVERY SECOND

M ick and Alison soon ended up in the solarium for a discussion with worried adults and a bruised Gail Atkinson.

Miss North, Mr. Victor, and Miss Emmet were seated on the sofa near the dormant fireplace, with the Vicar standing behind the sofa. Mick and Alison were in arm chairs, as was Gail, her wry expression partly distorted by swelling.

Gail and Stephen had been attacked and kidnapped the previous morning. For Mick's and Alison's benefit, Miss North was sketching out a story that Gail was clearly tired of telling and hearing. Gail and the Snobs had been patrolling south of the river near the railway terminus when there had been almost a quarter hour of time lightning right before a horse kick Seven started to open on Belvedere Road.

"A horse kick?" Mick asked. Horse kick alleys were the only kind of alley with almost no light show. According to *Broome's*, the only visible light was faint haze with a dull frame. And just before they closed, they sent out a shockwave, as if from an explosion, that only affected alley rats. They were also rare. He'd never seen one in person, and he wasn't even sure one had opened during his time in 1853.

"They truly do kick," Gail said. "We kept a distance of fifty feet, in accordance with *Broome's*, and it still pushed us back a foot or so. Only us, mind. There were some laborers, from the timber yard, I believe, who were only a few feet away from it when it kicked, and they clearly felt nothing."

Miss North resumed the story. Gail and the Snobs were checking on the dropper who had come out of the aperture when Gail spotted a small group of people on the Waterloo Bridge who also seemed to be watching the aperture. Daniel and Flora stayed with the toddler, and Gail and Stephen took off running toward the bridge. The people on the bridge fumbled about a bit before running away. Gail and Stephen didn't even get to the bridge because they ran into Blue and Green, who were with a couple bigger, older men. The older men grabbed Gail and Stephen, and Blue said, "That's her."

After that, Gail and Stephen both ended up on some sort of little boat with hoods over their heads. They tried to ask questions or call out and got smacked hard in the head until they stopped. Then they bounced about in what had felt like a small cart or large barrow before being carried up some stairs and left in a room, still hooded, with their wrists and feet bound to a post.

Fortunately, the Eyes at the Waterloo Bridge lookout had seen Gail and Stephen getting shoved into a rowboat. One of the Eyes ran along the Thames, tracking the rowboat and alerting the Eyes at the bridge lookouts along the way. The rowboat tied off at the Pickle Herring stairs just long enough to unload Gail and Stephen into a waiting hay cart. Then one of the men and either Green or Blue rode with them to a nearby abandoned warehouse.

"And none of your abductors said anything beyond threatening you with violence if you cried out?" the Vicar asked.

"Not so far as I remember," Gail said. "But my memories of what took place after I was struck on the head are a muddle until Mr. Burton and I were tied up and left alone. I had the most miserable headache until Chris Biggs and the dons from Gaoler's Home removed our hoods and untied us."

"Are you all right?" Mick asked. "Is Stephen?"

Gail waved her hand. "I shall be shipshape and Bristol fashion soon enough, I'd imagine."

Miss Emmet said, "Miss North, I believe that Dr. Quinn said that Mr. Burton also was recovering well, did she not?"

Miss North nodded. "You may visit him when we finish our discussion," she told the kids.

Mr. Victor had been staring into space for a while. He turned his attention to Gail. "And you couldn't make out what the group on the bridge was doing? The people who hurried away when you caught sight of them?"

Gail closed her eyes in thought. "No. There were four of them, I believe. Directly after they seemed to notice that I had spied them, one or two of them disappeared for a moment, as if stooping down and then straightening back up. But then they simply turned and bustled off."

"And you recognized none of them?" the Vicar asked.

Gail shook her head. "They were too far away, I'm afraid. Perhaps Mr. Burton ..."

"As yet, he remembers less than you," Miss North said.

"If we have concluded...?" the Vicar asked, looking at the professors, who nodded. "Very well, then. Miss March, Mr. Gunn, we summoned you here so that you could learn what there is to learn of the facts of this matter, but even more so that you could learn of its seriousness. We have already informed Miss Atkinson that her team's patrols will be more sparingly undertaken and that they will be accompanied by a pair of dons at all times."

"And likely one or two of Miss Biggs' nosy urchins," Miss Emmet added.

"Indeed," the Vicar said. "And Mr. Gunn will receive a similar retinue for protection."

"This youth—Blue—clearly recognized Miss Atkinson," Miss North explained. "There are countless reasons why that might be, but the simplest is that he recognized her from the day of the cricket match. I'm sure you'll see why."

Mick looked to Alison for help. She frowned for a moment before saying, "It seems likely that either Blue recognized Miss Atkinson as one of the people whom he and Green were following that day after the cricket match or as one of the people who saw the time lightning at the cricket match. Or both. And if Blue recognized Miss Atkinson from that day, he and Green might well recognize Mr. Gunn. Especially if it's to do with time lightning. Or anything to do with alley phenomena, really." She paused. "And it's likely the time lightning."

Miss North shot Mr. Victor a look that Mick couldn't interpret. "How so, Miss March?" she asked.

"After the cricket match, Blue followed Miss Atkinson and Mr. Burton both, did he not?" Alison asked.

Mick nodded.

"And," Alison said, pausing to check her logic, "at the

Waterloo Bridge, Blue said, 'That's *her*,' correct? Not 'that's *they*.'"

Gail nodded.

"Though I feel morally certain he would have said, 'That's them,'" Miss Emmet said. "Ruffians do struggle terribly with the nominative case."

Miss North gave Miss Emmet the same look Tía Verónica had always given his mom when his mom told a dumb joke. Miss Emmet flashed a tiny grin.

"Your conclusion being, Miss March?" Mr. Victor asked.

"Well, I can scarcely say it's a certainty," Alison answered, "but it does rather seem that Blue must have recognized *both* Miss Atkinson and Mr. Burton. He did follow them both that day, after all. But for some reason, he singled out Miss Atkinson, suggesting that whatever he found important about her was not that he followed her that day, or at least not *only* that he followed her."

The adults were good at keeping their faces unreadable, but Mick was pretty sure they were impressed. He knew he was. He patted Alison's elbow approvingly.

"Quite possibly it is just as Miss March so ably deduces," the Vicar said. "Though many things remain shrouded and confused. In any event, you children may go, with our thanks."

"And with our request that you take seriously the potential danger facing you," Mr. Victor said.

"I take it quite seriously, Mr. Victor," Gail said as she rose gingerly to her feet. "If these two don't, I shall quite willingly beat them about the head and truss them in the cellars until they do."

"I shall hold you to that, Miss Atkinson," Mr. Victor said.

Was that a joke? Mick asked himself. Had Mr. Victor just

told a joke? Weirdly, that seemed like another reason to take the situation seriously. Whatever the situation was.

Afterward, they visited Stephen in the infirmary, where they found him chatting with Owl while Dr. Quinn's apprentice Ellen Weathers alternated between examining Stephen's head and grumpily flipping through a massive tome that Mick recognized as the *Compleat Compendium of the Maladies of the Head and Skull*. Mick grinned slightly to see it. In a way, it had once saved his life, though as a weapon rather than as a medical book.

Stephen was slightly more battered than Gail but seemed alert and happy to see them. Miss Weathers said he should recover fully, which everybody found deeply reassuring. Miss Weathers had a calm, blunt competence that almost all the kids found soothing when they were ill or injured. She was going to be an awesome doctor, Mick figured, even if it would be a battle to get Victorians to take her seriously outside the Institute. Mick thought about Lady Penbrook and her grapes, and it sank in a little bit how important that sort of thing was.

After Miss Weathers went back to watching the nursery, the rest of them stayed and joked with Stephen for a bit to keep up his spirits. Gail asked him about the attack, but he didn't remember anything that Gail hadn't already covered with the professors.

Eventually, Miss Weathers returned and shooed them out so that Stephen could rest. "And you should take your rest as well, Miss Atkinson," she told Gail. "You can wait until tomorrow to sharpen your daggers and plot your vengeance."

Gail grinned at her. "I shall have you know, Miss Weathers, that I find sharpening my daggers ever so restful."

. . .

The next little while was surprisingly lazy for Mick. He seldom left the Institute because he had to be accompanied by dons whenever he did, and the dons had more important things to do than babysit him. The same was true for Gail, so they both had extra time for concentration and course. Within a couple days, Gail had shrugged off any physical issues from the attack. If she had psychological issues, she didn't discuss them with Mick, even though he asked how she felt a few times. She seemed to like keeping busy, including spending a lot of time helping Miss Mitchell and the other dons study time lightning. Mick occasionally listened to their discussions, but he mostly couldn't understand.

Like Gail and Mick, Stephen was also pulled out of patrol rotation. At first, he was shaken up by it all, but he gradually returned to normal, at least as far as Mick could tell from the occasional chats they had when they ran into each other around the Institute.

Of course, despite the danger, Mick and Gail might have gone patrolling more if the time lightning had kept ramping up. But, as far as anybody could tell, the time lightning was on vacation, and the normal time alleys seemed to be behaving themselves. Hearing Alison, Leech, and Dolly talk, it sounded like they mostly spent patrol going to street vendors for baked potatoes and coffee, buttering up Constable Archer and the other neighborhood cops, and noting the occasional stirring, which was always doing normal stirring things. Well, as normal as time travel got, anyway.

Mick made sure to spend as much time as possible exercising, relaxing, sleeping, eating, ducking chores, and dodging homework. Gail complained about being stuck in the Institute, but Mick thought it was great. And he knew it was too good to last.

Mick was right. If the time lightning had been on vacation, it came back rested and ready to put in some overtime. There were three sightings in five days, all south of the river. Then there was nothing for two days. After that two-day lull, Mr. Victor found Mick eating lunch with Owl and Dolly and told him to get dressed and meet him in the warden's office. "Posthaste, Mr. Gunn. Posthaste."

Mick arrived at the warden's office at the same time as Miss Jennings, who was wearing a light blue lawyer's daughter's dress and matching bonnet. Or a lawyer's wife's dress, he supposed. Victorians got married creepily young, especially the women.

Mr. Victor was telling the warden that the three of them would be going to the Society for Chronal Fancy for a few hours. That surprised Mick. The Society for Chronal Fancy was basically just a three-dimensional cover story. The Institute, and probably a few other parts of the Project, needed books about alley phenomena, everything from go-to guides like *Broome's* to ten-pound tomes packed with gibberish so boring that even Alison disliked them. To avoid connans—and to avoid getting locked in the madhouse—nobody was allowed to take those books outside of approved Project locations like the Institute, at least not without high-level permission. But just in case a book about time alleys did get loose, all the books printed in the last few decades included the Disclaimer, a short paragraph near the front saying the book was a publication of the Society for Chronal Fancy, whose members enjoyed publishing works of fiction about time travel. The Society also published actual works of fiction about time travel, which Leech said were designed to be too dumb to take seriously and too boring to finish. Mick had tried to read a couple and had to agree.

After leaving the Institute and walking briskly in silence for a few moments, they passed the rear of the British Museum. Miss Jennings said, "Do tell me we aren't obliged to attend Mr. Billbane's lecture."

Mr. Victor smiled tightly. "We are not."

"Thank the heavens," she said. She turned her attention to Mick, who was half-jogging to keep up with them. "Is this your first visit to the Society for Knotty-Pated Numbskulls?"

Mick nodded.

"Lucky chap. Try not to laugh, no matter how you are provoked. There are always dons and members of the Institute faculty in attendance at the Society's lectures, and they aren't permitted to laugh either."

As they walked past the south edge of Russell Square, she added, "I do hope this goes without saying, but conquer the urge to say things such as 'That's not how it really is in the future. I know because I hail from the future.'"

It did go without saying, so Mick just nodded slightly.

A few minutes later, they had reached an elegant maze of tall gray buildings. One of them was the Society for Chronal Fancy. They turned onto a narrow lane and entered the Society through a side door so low that Mr. Victor and Miss Jennings had to stoop to enter. After clomping along a cramped hallway, they reached a door that led to an office full of activity, loose papers, and stressed-out dons. Mr. Victor told Mick to wait in the corridor, and then he and Miss Jennings went in, closing the door behind themselves.

Mick studied the empty, dim hallway. Based on the murmur of a dozen or so voices coming through a nearby open doorway, the main salon was nearby and the lecture hadn't started. Mick could hear most of a conversation among two Englishmen and a Frenchman. One of the Englishmen was interpreting to and from French. The Frenchman was trying to explain a story he'd written about a guy whose balloon got hijacked, but the non-translating Englishman kept interrupting to ask if Parisian women were good-looking and liked to drink wine. It was sort of funny because polite Victorian gentlemen weren't allowed to say, "Shut your piehole, Chester," but the translating Englishman was obviously thinking it.

Eventually, Miss Jennings opened the door to the office to wave Mick inside. There were six dons there, including Miss Jennings and Mr. Bateson. Mick knew a couple of the others by sight but not their names. They and Mr. Victor were clustered around a battered oak table not quite big enough for everyone. There were a couple desks covered in paper but no extra chairs, so Mick just stood awkwardly near the door.

Mr. Victor told Mick, "Two separate greet teams reported stirrings that suggested a glow-orb Seven or Eight would be opening near Furnival's Inn an hour or two hence. The stirrings suggested there would also be time lighting."

Time lightning didn't seem to have its own stirrings separate from the alleys it preceded. But apparently if you were really good at sensing alley stirrings, they felt different when there was going to be time lightning. Mick hadn't ever been at an aperture site early enough to sense a stirring for an alley with time lightning, so he didn't know whether he could have sensed it, but he suspected he couldn't have. He bet Leech could, though.

"So I'm supposed to spot the time lightning?" Mick asked.

"You were," Miss Jennings said. She held up a small scrap of paper and raised her eyebrows at Mr. Victor, who nodded his approval. Miss Jennings handed the scrap to Mick.

On the scrap, small, neat penciling gave the date and a time 10 minutes earlier. Beneath that, it said, "S REPORT TL NOT EARLY HYPNOTIC TRANCE BIRD TIMELY."

"Well, naturally," Mick said.

Everyone chuckled except Mr. Victor, who looked carefully at Mick. "This is a message, Mr. Gunn. Try to deduce its meaning. As a hint, I shall inform you that one of the dons' mottoes is 'Count Every Second. Consider Every Instant.'"

Mick recognized the phrase from the door in the dons' lounge. He eventually figured out that "Count Every Second" meant he should read every second word. With nudging, he skipped the "S" and got "TL EARLY TRANCE TIMELY." Given why he was there, he figured out that "TL" meant "time lightning," but Mr. Victor had to tell him that "trance" was an old-fashioned way of saying "alley." Too late, Mick remembered that Alison had once told him that. So the message was "Time lightning early. Alley timely."

"So the time lightning already happened?" Mick asked. "But the alley will be at its regular time?"

"Correct," Mr. Victor said.

Mick nodded. He thought for a moment. "I don't wish to seem rude," he said, pleased with that bit of properly Victorian phrasing, "but isn't that, well, an easy code? I mean, I needed help, but I'm just a kid, and it only took like two minutes."

"The message in your hand," Mr. Victor said, "had already

been largely stripped of its ciphering. What you puzzled out was merely the, let us say, temperamental ciphering."

There was a knock at the door, which opened as far as the heel of Mick's shoe. Mick moved as far forward as he could without climbing onto the shoulders of the don sitting in front of him.

A pale young man with wavy red hair leaned through the half-open door. "Mr. Victor, Lord Harrowgrave's carriage has pulled into the drive."

Jostling and sidling, the dons cleared a path for Mr. Victor and Miss Jennings to join Mick and the redheaded man in the corridor. Mr. Victor rapped at the door and was answered with the click of a bolt being pushed home.

"Thank you, Mr. Evans," Mr. Victor said in polite dismissal. Mr. Evans nodded before backing up a few steps and turning into the salon.

"Miss Jennings," Mr. Victor said. "I shall speak with his lordship. Pray meet me here afterward. And do try to conceal Mr. Gunn from the excitement that so often finds him."

Miss Jennings nodded soberly before Mr. Victor followed Mr. Evans' footsteps into the salon.

Miss Jennings looked at Mick for a moment and then started walking toward the far end of the hallway. Mick followed. Hidden in the unlit gloom at the end of the hallway was a narrow, uneven wooden stairway. Miss Jennings hiked up her dress and glided silently up. Mick followed behind, each footfall causing a symphony of squeaks like a cat mauling an accordion. At the top of the stairway, Miss Jennings led him down another dimly lit hallway before opening a door. Following her through the door, Mick found himself in a long, narrow room with a half-dozen padded benches rising upward like bleachers. They were the only people there.

Miss Jennings whispered that he should be silent and led him to the front of the room, where there was an elaborate banister but no wall. Below was the salon. The crowd had grown a bit since they had arrived. There were about twenty people, standing mostly in clumps of two to four. The salon was lit by large, high windows, so it was easy to spot Mr. Victor's close-cropped hair and stiff bearing. He was standing near a window, apparently waiting to speak with a fine gentleman who was talking to a brightly dressed woman. The man was a few inches shorter than Mr. Victor but just as broad in the shoulders and had dense, perfectly trimmed facial hair. Mick eventually recognized him as the man he'd seen coming out of the Seat the day he and Chris had gone there. So he must be—

"Lord Harrowgrave," Miss Jennings whispered. "I'm not sure with whom he is conversing. And I believe you know Mr. Phillips."

Mick spotted the Institute's cherubic young music professor, who was chatting cheerfully with Mr. Evans and a short, gray-haired Institute professor whose name Mick didn't know, though he seemed to remember that she taught some sort of torture math that only a few dons dared to study each term.

"Mrs. Cutter," Miss Jennings whispered. "She told me once she met her late husband here, which makes her more forgiving of this asylum than I suspect she would otherwise be."

Mr. Evans escorted the unknown woman with Lord Harrowgrave to the punchbowl, allowing Mr. Victor to engage Lord Harrowgrave in conversation. Miss Jennings stared intently at the conversation, which mostly involved Lord Harrowgrave talking and Mr. Victor nodding slightly. Lord

Harrowgrave seemed to be sneering during the entire conversation, but Mick tried to be generous. Lord Harrowgrave might be a friendly, down-to-earth guy who was cursed with resting snob face. After a few minutes, Mick tried to ask Miss Jennings a question, but she waved him silent. Not long after that, Mr. Victor gave Lord Harrowgrave a polite bow, and Lord Harrowgrave nodded before striding to the front door so briskly that the butler almost couldn't open it in time.

Without a word, Miss Jennings turned to leave. Mick followed her back to where Mr. Victor had told them to meet him. Mr. Victor appeared shortly, coming not from the salon but from the crowded office. Nodding slightly, he walked toward the side door they'd used to enter the Society.

Back in the bright afternoon sunlight, they walked in silence. Mick assumed they were headed to Furnival's Inn for the glow-orb that was supposed to open soon.

"Such a pity to miss Mr. Billbane's lecture," Miss Jennings remarked. "I believe the theme is the inevitable colonization of the ocean floor, is it not?"

Mr. Victor smiled slightly. "Alas, Miss Jennings, the Society for Chronal Fancy is hardly the Royal Society."

"Of which I am an officer, as it happens," Miss Jennings said in a plummy aristocratic accent. Mick assumed she was imitating Lord Harrowgrave. "Does he say that every time he visits the Numbskulls, I wonder."

"My familiarity with Lord Harrowgrave's visits to the Society is not so extensive as to permit me to answer."

Miss Jennings laughed merrily. "He does understand that the purpose of the Society is precisely to be a passel of gormless chitchatters, does he not?"

"His lordship has a very keen understanding of matters

relating to the Project," Mr. Victor said. "His supply of under-standing far exceeds his supply of patience."

"There I can sympathize," Miss Jennings said. "His lordship wishes be kept immediately and fully abreast of any develop-ments relating to time lightning. Was there anything else? I find his lordship's beard an obstacle, I fear."

Mick realized that Miss Jennings hadn't simply been guessing at the content of Mr. Victor's chat with Lord Harrow-grave. She'd been reading their lips.

Mr. Victor said, "We are to advise him of any changes in the alleys as well."

"Beyond the fact that the time lightning may now be happening hours before its alleys?" Miss Jennings asked.

"His lordship was already so informed," Mr. Victor noted.

They arrived at Furnival's Inn in time to consult with the greet team and then to watch a beautiful green-gray glow-orb Eight open half a block away, singing its siren song to Mick, who tried to ignore its summons. In due time and without surprises, a dropper not much younger than Mick appeared, apparently healthy, although heartily confused by where she was and why her clothes were in tatters. The greet team smoothly covered her in a cloak and ushered her to the Insti-tute's carriage, which awaited out of sight around the corner.

After inspecting the aperture site and finding nothing unusual, Mr. Victor, Miss Jennings, and Mick began walking back to the Institute. Speaking quietly, they compared notes on the aperture. As usual, Mick had seen it the most clearly, but his observations matched theirs. Miss Jennings explained a bit more about how to understand the kind of half-decoded message he'd looked at earlier, and then they chatted about the weather.

It was all calm and routine. Except that something was happening that was worrying lords and getting spotters kidnapped. Suddenly, the sunny afternoon seemed ominous, and it occurred to Mick that lightning usually led to thunder. They already had time lightning, so was time thunder headed their direction? He spent the walk back to the Institute silent and tense, bracing himself against time thunder, whatever it might turn out to be.

CHAPTER 12

HIDDEN THORNS

For a while, Mick still wasn't allowed to go on regular patrol, and generally neither was Gail. But there were several reports of time lightning each day, and some of them were even accurate, so he and Gail usually left the Institute at least once a day to investigate those reports. Mostly, they went separately, and Mick often found himself in far-flung parts of the city that he'd never seen. Usually, Mr. Victor or Miss Jennings was with him, along with another don, though a couple times Chris or Miss North was in charge. Miss Emmet said that Miss North was mostly busy with some sort of super-secret Project business. And Chris was busy doing whatever she did with mysterious mechanicals and the Eyes.

Mick usually went by cab or carriage, but if he went on foot, a pair of Eyes would shadow him from a discreet distance. If circumstances permitted, one of the Eyes would sidle up to Mick and his protectors early on to identify himself or herself and to point out the other Eye. They would then fade into the background. Mick got pretty good at spotting them and even began to recognize a few of them. But they rotated a lot, so he never really got to know them.

As September began to slide into fall, warm weather became precious. So when a fine Sunday afternoon presented itself, Mick, Leech, and Dolly climbed to the roof and sat on one of the cistern braces, which gave them a very pretty view of the city. Alison and Owl had hitched a ride to Orphans with Miss Emmet, so Mick didn't have to listen to Leech and Owl bicker, and none of them got updates on Alison's research into time lightning.

Although Alison continued to devour huge books at an impressive rate because it offended her to confront a problem she couldn't solve with research, she wasn't discovering much that differed from what Mick occasionally learned from Gail or the dons. Unless sworn to secrecy, Mick always relayed what he learned to Alison, and he even helped her chip away at her research, in part because she was his friend and in part because it was starting to seem like whatever was happening might eventually allow alley rats to shuttle the alleys again. And if there was really a way to go back in time and then go forward again, then maybe there was some way to skip going back and just go forward. And that might give Mick a shot at going home, so he needed to learn all he could.

The current theory was that time lightning was a side effect of some phenomenon—or possibly some person—"anchoring" the "threads" of the alleys tied to the time lightning. At the Institute, everybody always described time alleys as basically being trains from the future to the past. Of course, a time alley wasn't a reliable train, and it might not travel in a straight line. It might do lunatic loop-the-loops that would get a real train shut down by safety inspectors because passengers kept getting thrown off. But if you managed to cling onto the time train from start to finish and then get off, your trip was over. The train, the tracks, and the stations all magically disappeared, and the only way back to the future was to walk forward at the plodding pace of normal time. But it turned out that, even though the train and the stations disappeared, the tracks didn't, at least not completely. And there were a lot of junctions, places where one track touched—or could be made to touch—another track. So if you could get into one alley and dodge the trains and whatever other deadly dangers swirled around metaphorical train tracks, you could shuttle the alleys. Those metaphorical tracks were called "threads," and apparently it was easier to travel on them if you could move their drop points so that they touched the same "place" in time, a process called "anchoring."

"Oy, you rule-breaking ruffians," called a gruff voice through the open window to Mick and Leech's room.

Mick panicked for a second. As did several kids from Tory Five a couple dozen yards away, who immediately slithered back down to their rooms.

Mick, Leech, and Dolly exchanged nervous glances. Technically, they were breaking the rules by being on the roof without a professor. But they relaxed when Chris slid gracefully through Mick and Leech's window, followed with almost equal grace by Miss Mitchell and with a few quiet grunts from Miss Jennings.

Chris grinned at them and beckoned them to clamber down from the cistern.

"It's all right," Mick told Dolly and Leech as his feet hit the rooftop's fine gravel. Leech looked intrigued. Dolly looked nervous.

"You've been summoned to the Turret," Miss Mitchell said.

Mick knew from the expression on Dolly's face and her intake of breath that she was about to ask if that included her and Leech, just like he knew that Leech's warning glance at her meant that she should keep quiet.

Chris flashed her easy grin. "Yes, all three of you."

They trudged toward the Turret, which was on the roof above the professors' wing. It wasn't a real turret, of course. It was a walled rooftop deck that looked a bit like a turret. Mick had never seen inside it until they stepped through an arched door on a wall facing away from the students' wing. It turned out to be a large area furnished with teak and wrought iron furniture and decorated with a surprising number of plants in elevated planters.

The furnishings included a pair of good-sized round tables with decorative tile tops. Mr. Yardley and Miss Richardson, the mechanicals, were sitting at one of tables with Gail and the gray-haired torture math professor. Chris and the dons settled in amongst them. After being told to sit, Mick and his friends settled in too.

Sitting down, at least, the torture math professor didn't look a whole lot taller than Mick, but she had the same oversized presence that Miss North and Mr. Victor had. She also had surprisingly bright alley rat eyes.

"This is the boy with the magic eyes?" she asked, looking at Mick.

"The very same," Chris said.

"That must make these two"—her eyes flickered to Dolly and then Leech—"the girl with the field marshal's baton and the boy blessed by the blarney stone."

Mick knew that Leech was blarney boy, but he'd have to ask somebody about Dolly and the baton later.

"I'm Mrs. Cutter," she continued. "I teach the mathematics that only the bravest dare study. Mr. Yardley and Miss Richardson were once my pupils, and Miss Jennings now bears that cross. Miss Mitchell continues to evade my snares."

Miss Mitchell laughed. A little nervously, Mick thought.

"Mr. Gunn," Mrs. Cutter said, "are you familiar with our hypotheses about the nature of time lightning?"

"I've heard the version without math. Mathematics," he said. "But I don't really understand it."

"Do tell, Mr. Gunn," she said.

He did his best to explain about trains and threads and the rest.

"You understand it rather well for somebody who doesn't understand it," Mrs. Cutter said. "But the sad truth is that we may none of us understand it. We have hypotheses, some of them quite compelling, but it is urgent that we test them to know whether they come anywhere near the truth. The delay between lightning and alley is growing daily. We had an aperture open this morning twenty-seven hours after its lightning."

Mick stopped himself from saying "wow" out loud, but his lips formed the word.

"It appears that the longer the delay," Mrs. Cutter said, "the closer the anchoring comes to completion. And the delay is accelerating. If our equations are correct as well as beautiful, when the delay is roughly five days, the anchoring will be complete."

She looked around the table. "You all have roles to play in this, as do many others who are not here, naturally. I thought it important that you see that you are part of a larger endeavor and to know that the matter is urgent."

"Mrs. Cutter?" Dolly asked softly.

Dolly hated to draw attention to herself, so Mick knew whatever she was about to ask had to be important.

"Yes, child?" Mrs. Cutter replied.

"Is it necessarily something bad? Whatever is happening with the alleys? Mightn't it be a good thing to be able to shuttle the alleys again?"

Exactly, Mick thought. Especially if it turned out that everybody who had said that something like the Realignment was impossible *also* turned out to be wrong about returning to the future.

"A good question, child," Mrs. Cutter said. "And an important one. The answer is that we do not know. But alleys are tricky, fickle, and sometimes fatal. The anchoring might kill people. And to travel in time deliberately is to have power— real, terrifying power. Before the Collapse, people killed for such power, and surely would do so again. And what if the time lightning is not the act of chance or of the gods, not a whim flung from the hand of immortal Zeus? What if it is the work of human hands? Then we must ask ourselves what sort of people would undertake such a dangerous project in secrecy and in defiance of every principle of the Project. And for that matter, what sort *could*? Powerful people, surely, and, I'd wager, almost certainly not people who mean us well."

They sat somberly for a while. Mick tried to sort out his thoughts. Obviously, he didn't want to help bad people do bad things, even if he thought there might be a way for him to get back home by doing so. But maybe there was a way to turn what they were doing into something good. Or maybe he could use it to go back home before the good guys shut down whatever it was. It's not like he was trying to seize power or ruin people's lives. He just wanted to dangle Swaggy Bear over Emilia in her crib and complain to Tía Verónica about Uncle Dan's Netflix choices.

Eventually, the mood lightened a little, and the conversation turned to practicalities. It confirmed what Mick had suspected, that his role would be to show up at time lightning or the associated alleys and describe everything he saw to people who might actually understand what was happening. He had mixed feelings about that. He was happy to be useful. But he felt like a bomb-sniffing dog. The dons and professors put on his leash and trotted him over to an alley. He used his super-sensitive time-nose to sniff out possible time-bombs. Then they patted him on the head and sent him back to his kennel. He had no role on the bomb squad itself, no place among people who would have to figure out if there really were bombs and, if so, how to defuse them.

Days later, Miss Jennings, Mr. Bateson, and Miss Mitchell were escorting Mick, Gail, and the Snobs to an anticipated time alley near Chesterfield House. About a day earlier, there apparently had been truly spectacular time lightning at the site, and a fairy path was predicted to open there soon. The professors had apparently decided that both Mick and Gail needed to be on hand. So Mick and Gail were walking side by side, surrounded by the others. Plus, of course, unseen Eyes were orbiting the group like the undiscovered moons of Mars. All the protection seemed a little ridiculous to Mick. It was like when the President's kid had ten Secret Service agents guarding him at a kiddie soccer game.

Just as the very bright but otherwise unremarkable fairy path Ten closed without a dropper, Gail said, "Isn't that …? From Lord's?" She pointed to a nearby carriage drawn by two tired-looking horses, one chestnut, the other black. Through the sooty glass of the cab's window, Mick could see the silhouette of a man. The silhouette did look familiar, somehow.

Gail and Miss Jennings both started forward, but Gail only made it a couple steps before Miss Mitchell grabbed her wrist. The scruffy carriage driver turned his head at the movement and slapped the side of the coach, which rocked slightly as someone climbed in on the far side. The unseen carriage door slammed shut, and the carriage started to roll forward.

Miss Jennings was approaching the carriage, moving faster and smoother than should have been possible for someone wearing such a big dress. She was about to close the gap to the slowly accelerating carriage when she was nearly tackled from the side.

She stopped abruptly, and her would-be tackler missed her and tripped over the leg she swung into his path. He fell heavily to the ground, and stayed there as Miss Jennings dropped a knee into the small of his back and settled her weight upon him. Mr. Bateson rushed over to help Miss Jennings and to say things in a deep voice to a rotund gentleman in an old-fashioned waistcoat who was spluttering peevishly at Miss Jennings. Miss Mitchell caught the attention of one of the Eyes and flicked her fingers at the girl, who took off running.

Miss Mitchell called Stephen, Flora, and Daniel over, whispering to Flora and Daniel to find someplace in sight of Miss

Jennings and Mr. Bateson to wait for help to arrive from the Institute. Still whispering, Miss Mitchell said, "Miss Atkinson, Mr. Gunn, Mr. Burton with me, if you please." Keeping them all in front of her as they all began to walk, she added, "Hidden Thorns."

"What's Hidden Thorns?" Mick asked Gail quietly.

"A nickname for the Ladies Society," Gail replied.

Mick tried to remember what he'd seen. "Was that Green?" he asked. "Who tried to tackle Miss Jennings?"

"I believe so," Gail said. "Though I only caught a glimpse of his face."

A couple blocks later, they reached the entrance to the Ladies Society. As they entered the lobby, a young woman in a sober brown dress standing at a lectern near the door looked up from a ledger book and asked, "Are you members of the Soc — Oh, Miss Mitchell." She said doubtfully, "The lecture must be very nearly concluded, but perhaps—"

"That's most kind, Miss Nash, but not necessary. We're looking for Miss Biggs."

Miss Nash pursed her lips in thought. "I believe she's attending the lecture. It's quite well-subscribed. Improving Deportment in the Laboring Classes." Her tone of voice was neutral, but a quick eye roll suggested her opinion of the topic.

Miss Mitchell nodded slightly. "Is there to be a reception?"

"In the blue room." Miss Nash glanced over her shoulder at the ornate clock hanging on the marble wall. "The doors should be opening momentarily." She looked at Mick. "Regrettably, children are not permitted in the Society rooms."

"But he's so very nearly trained to house," Miss Mitchell said, deadpan.

Miss Nash tittered.

Miss Mitchell led them to a bench in an alcove that offered a good view of the blue room. From there, Mick looked around the lobby. It felt a lot like the Institute's lobby—tall, airy, lit by high windows and a skylight. But the marble floor was more gray than white, and instead of a switchbacking stairway going all the way to the top floor, two stairways with widely separated bases curved upward to meet at the floor above. A mural covered much of the nearest wall. Mick realized that there were several huge rose bushes that showed no sign of thorns. "Why is it 'Hidden Thorns'?" he asked. "Not 'Missing Thorns'?"

"A matter of temperament, I suppose," Miss Mitchell said. "Some of us prefer to think that even if we must go about dressed like flowers"—she pointed to her dress and Gail's—"we nonetheless have thorns. After all, Athena," she said, pointing to a helmeted woman in a toga and helmet at the center of the mural, "has her spear."

Miss Mitchell sat thoughtfully for a moment. Then, in a soft but emphatic voice, she said, "In the Project, there are many who think women, or 'dusky hued' people, or the Irish, or the Welsh, or Jews, or Moslems, or, well, almost everybody ought to be grateful that they are permitted to live in a country governed by so many superior English men. Many of them probably believe in their secret hearts that even Her Majesty is simply a doting godmother put on this Earth to tell them how valiant and dashing they are. Many people are willing to agree with them, to attend lectures about how to tell the laundress to stand up straight and speak better. Though not too straight or too much better, or we shall accuse her of putting on airs above her station. But some of us think that we deserve more than we are permitted and that we can offer rather more than is expected. Some of us would rather be Athena than Hestia."

Gail and Stephen were nodding firmly. Mick got the gist and agreed too.

Miss Mitchell seemed to be considering whether to say more when the doors to the blue room opened. Seconds later, the doors to a room across the lobby also opened, and prosperously dressed people, mostly women, began streaming out toward the blue room. Miss Mitchell stood to survey the passing crowd. Mick spotted Lady Penbrook in the company of several women about her age, all dressed in similarly expensive clothes. A minute or so later, Lord Harrowgrave walked by, discussing something with a distinguished-looking gentleman in an elegant suit. Lord Harrowgrave still had a haughty expression, and Mick still didn't like him.

A group of young men and women passed by, including a young woman in bright green dress twirling her fingers in her long sandy hair who reminded Mick of somebody.

Gail snorted with laughter.

"What?" Mick asked.

"Chris," Gail said gleefully. "Speaking of going about dressed like a flower."

Mick looked around the lobby in confusion, not seeing Chris.

"In the green dress," Gail said

Mick stared as the woman passed. Huh. Gail was right. "But…"

"It's a wig," Gail explained patiently. "Quite a fine one."

Well, as disguises went, it was as effective as being a dirt-faced pauper, though all that make-up might be harder to wash off than dirt.

Once the flow of lecture-goers had slowed to a trickle, Miss Mitchell said, "Miss Atkinson, Mr. Burton, please remain in the lobby with Mr. Gunn. I shan't be long."

Miss Mitchell joined the remaining lecturer-goers entering the blue room and disappeared from sight.

Gail and Mick looked at each other. "She did say, 'in the lobby,'" Gail pointed out.

Mick knew she meant that Miss Mitchell hadn't actually said they had to stay on the bench. "True," he said.

"So if we just make our way near the door..." Gail said.

"And stand just so..." Mick added.

Stephen looked back and forth between them and grinned.

They positioned themselves several yards from the door to the blue room and treated the reception like a time alley—watching it closely while pretending to look elsewhere.

Lady Penbrook and Lord Harrowgrave were talking to one another near the doors and were visible except when people crossed in front of them. Although Lady Penbrook's eyes had a brighter alley rat glow than Lord Harrowgrave's, they both had a similar probing quality to their gaze. When a couple taller gentlemen moved out of the way, Mick realized that Chris was with Lord Harrowgrave and Lady Penbrook, smiling a brainless smile that Mick had never seen on her face. Miss Mitchell sidled up to Chris, who introduced her to the lord and lady. Miss Mitchell gave a small curtsy to each, and Lord Harrow-grave's face curled into a sneer that took a while to unclench.

At that point, Captain Britain appeared with a woman who seemed familiar and might even have been the woman in Lord Harrowgrave's carriage that day at the Seat. It was hard for Mick to tell because she mostly had her back to him and was wearing a stylish veil that fell nearly to her mouth. Captain Britain and the veiled woman bowed and curtsied to Lady Penbrook, but the veiled woman soon took her leave, walking gracefully past Mick, Gail, and Stephen on her way to the exit.

After that, the crowd gradually shifted so that Mick could no longer see any of the people he was trying to watch, except for Captain Britain's forehead and wavy blond hair.

Fortunately, Mick didn't have to stare at the man's super-hero hair too much longer. Lady Penbrook, Chris, and Miss Mitchell emerged from the blue room and headed toward the front doors. Miss Mitchell beckoned to Mick, Gail, and Stephen, who joined the party.

As they stepped into an overcast but pleasant evening, Lady Penbrook greeted them all by name, which made Stephen grin like a goofball. "Pray inform me," Lady Penbrook said, "of the nature of the emergency that blessedly cut short my conversation with that boor Harrowgrave. I assume there *is* an emergency?"

"An urgency, at least, my lady," Miss Mitchell replied. "A ruffian attacked one of the dons at an aperture just now. She is uninjured, fortunately."

"Attacked a young lady?" Lady Penbrook said, sounding shocked. "Appalling. I'm relieved to hear no harm befell her."

"Quite, my lady," Miss Mitchell said.

"And the ruffian?" Lady Penbrook asked. "What became of him?"

"I believe he was apprehended, my lady," Miss Mitchell said.

"And you desire Miss Biggs to investigate the assault?" Lady Penbrook asked.

"Indeed, my lady," Miss Mitchell said.

"And how did you all come to gather at this aperture?" Lady Penbrook asked, surveying them. "An unusual, and rather large, assortment of alley rats, I should venture to say."

Mick was watching Miss Mitchell's face as she decided how to reply when Stephen piped up, "There had been time lightning, my lady. Yesterday, that is to say. And the professors wanted the alley carefully observed."

"Ah, quite," Lady Penbrook said, appearing to lose interest. "Wise of them."

They continued walking through a neighborhood so fancy that Mick wasn't sure he was even allowed to use the sidewalks. Even the paving seemed to be some sort of special macadam that muffled the wheels of the elegant carriages gliding past. After a few moments' chitchat, they found their way into the Adam's Mews near Grosvenor Square. "My townhouse, you see," Lady Penbrook said. "I shall take my leave of you here. Miss Biggs, I hope you'll agree that the dress is quite becoming."

"Oh, indeed, my lady," Chris said, with her usual roguish smile. "As is the wig, though it's rather like wearing an overfed cat upon my head."

"No cat was ever so obedient, or helpful, as a good wig," Lady Penbrook said.

"Indeed not, my lady," Chris said with a chuckle.

Everyone bowed or curtsied to Lady Penbrook, even Mick, who tried to imitate Stephen. Lady Penbrook acknowledged them all with a genial nod. As she raised her skirts and turned to climb the short stairway to her townhome, the front door opened to reveal a foyer and butler so fancy that Mr. Anderson would have wept with envy. They watched until the door closed behind her.

"That dress *is* ever so becoming, Miss Biggs," Miss Mitchell said in a mildly teasing tone.

"It's becoming a pain in my arse, is what it is," Chris said. "And this wig too." After a pause, Chris said to the full group. "Right-o, you all may have the privilege of escorting me to Lady Grenville's, where I can prise this grimalkin's claws out of my scalp."

A couple days later, Mick found himself perched on a tall stool in a back room of the grubby barristers' offices that served as the public face of the Gaoler's Home Outpost.

Mick, along with Mr. Victor and Miss Jennings, were in the offices rather than out on the street watching for the whirlpool Six that was due to open soon because the whirlpool was halfway between the Queen's Bench Prison and the County Gaol, a rough neighborhood populated by grim-faced locals who looked like they had spent time in at least one of those places. Mr. Victor was sitting behind a battered desk reading over the outpost's coded log book, and Miss Jennings was watching the street through a sooty window. You couldn't quite see the whirlpool from the window, but you could see the Eye stationed on the street below who would signal when the dons watching the whirlpool decided that Mick and the others needed to come down.

Mick, Mr. Victor, and Miss Jennings were wearing shabby but respectable clothes, trying to look like the "honest poor," possibly come from the countryside to consult a barrister about a relative facing trial. Mick's cheap clothes were weirdly comfortable. They were thin and soft, which meant that he wasn't constricted by a heavy woolen layer of respectability. He sort of wished he hadn't put them on because he'd finally managed to forget that his normal Institute clothes were uncomfortable. Then he reminded himself he should *want* to remember that his Institute clothes were uncomfortable. They weren't his real clothes, and this wasn't his real life.

"It's time," Miss Jennings said.

After Mr. Victor returned the log book to the don on duty, Miss Jennings led them down the back stairway and locked the rear door. Mr. Victor took up position on Mick's left, and Miss Jennings positioned herself on Mick's right, escorting him around the building and a hundred yards up a narrow street leading to the Blind School.

There, they were met by one of the dons, a sturdy, slope-shouldered young man who looked for all the world like an impoverished clerk sneaking away from work to smoke a pipeful of cheap tobacco. Miss Jennings whispered to Mick that his name was Mr. Cooper.

Hardly moving his lips from their seal around the clay stem of his pipe, Mr. Cooper said, "Whirlpool behind me."

The whirlpool was twenty yards into a vacant lot, and Mick and the others avoided staring at it. Even from the corner of his eye, Mick could tell that it was starting to take form and would soon be developing a ring. It was an uncommon blend of yellow and orange but otherwise not unusual.

"Mr. Huxley and I are fairly certain that someone is watching the alley from the second floor of the red brick building," Mr. Cooper said. "The room with the white curtains."

Mick looked around for the other don and spotted him leaning against a building on a nearby side street.

Mr. Cooper added, "Mr. Huxley thinks it's two men, one tall, one short. I'm too short-sighted to say. But there's someone there, and that's the first soul I've seen at that window in the months I've been at Gaolers."

A quick glance told Mick there might have been someone at the window with the white curtains, but he wasn't sure, and he knew better than to stare.

Mr. Victor, Miss Jennings, and Mr. Cooper kept watch while Mick quietly narrated what the whirlpool was doing— swirling, pausing, swirling the other direction, developing a clear, purplish ring so dark it bordered on black. Nobody took notes because it would have been too conspicuous in that neighborhood. When the whirlpool's speed maxed out, Mick closed his eyes against the inevitable blaze of alley light that would come when the alley opened.

Almost the instant he opened his eyes back up, the world shook and spun. He hit the sidewalk hard and managed to roll out of the way before a heavy shoe could stomp his head. He rolled a couple more times until his face brushed the weeds of the vacant lot. He got to one knee and tried to make sense of what was happening.

It was a melee. There were three big men and a teenager attacking Mr. Victor, Mr. Cooper, and Miss Jennings, who were holding their own pretty well. Mr. Victor smoothly dodged a couple wild swings from one of the big men, stepped in, kicked the man's knee, and hit him with two blurring punches that dropped the man heavily. Miss Jennings did some sort of jiu-jitsu-looking move that sent the teenager flying to land not too far from Mick. The teenager—whom Mick recognized as Blue —scrambled to his feet and took off running. The other two big men had Mr. Cooper in trouble until Mr. Victor, Miss Jennings, and then—arriving at a run—Mr. Huxley squared off with them. The big men looked at their opponents, glanced at the unconscious form of their comrade, and took off with surprising speed in the opposite direction from Blue.

"Mr. Cooper, Mr. Huxley," said Mr. Victor, "see if you can gain admittance to that room with the white curtains, or at least can spy someone leaving. After that, please have the peelers sent to the county court. Sergeant Monks, if he's available." The two dons took off running.

"Miss Jennings, pray assist me in lifting our friend into his barrow."

Mick realized that the barrow was how Blue and the big men had gotten so close. As best he could remember, the men had been casually pushing the barrow, and Blue had been walking mostly out of sight behind them. Mick had spotted the big men as soon as they'd turned onto the street, but they'd looked so much like they'd belonged that he hadn't paid them much attention. Apparently, the others hadn't either.

By the time Mick had sorted that out, Mr. Victor and Miss Jennings had bound the man's hands with a length of cord that materialized from somewhere in Miss Jennings' skirts and loaded the man ungently into the barrow. A few passersby watched with interest but didn't say anything. It was the sort of neighborhood where people didn't talk about other people's business, at least not in public.

"There wasn't a dropper, was there?" Mick asked.

Miss Jennings shook her head. "I was watching carefully for a dropper. Apparently at the expense of watching for an ambush."

"We were all remiss," Mr. Victor said as he started wheeling the barrow back toward the outpost. Miss Jennings walked a few paces behind, keeping watch. Mick stayed between them.

A while later, Mr. Victor grunted as he strained the barrow

over a bump in the road and then paused, setting down its back legs. He stepped several paces away from the barrow. Miss Jennings and Mick joined him.

Mr. Victor whispered, "I believe he truly is unconscious, but speak softly in case he is counterfeiting." After they nodded, Mr. Victor continued, "I cannot contrive a way to get him into the outpost without every spy and gossipy purlman in the neighborhood taking notice."

"Nor I," admitted Miss Jennings.

"Then my plan, flawed though it is, is to push this gentleman to the court and stand outside denouncing him angrily. 'I want this man here to swing for the attempted murder of my wife and innocent child not ten minutes previous,'" he said in some countryside accent, "'and this is why decent, law-abiding Christians ought never come to this Sodom as calls itself London, we ought not, indeed.' Once he is in the custody of the authorities, we can arrange his questioning. That is why I asked Mr. Huxley and Mr. Cooper to bring the police to the courthouse."

"Will your wife and innocent child accompany you?" Miss Jennings asked.

"I think not," Mr. Victor said. "When we pass the outpost, take Mr. Gunn within and look to his safety."

"Will that not be conspicuous, if indeed the gossips and spies are watching?" Miss Jennings asked.

"Quite possibly," Mr. Victor acknowledged. "But in this instance, Mr. Gunn's safety is paramount. I believe he was the intended victim just now, and I would have him off the street immediately. Telegraph Miss North and Miss Emmet to tell them what has happened, including any information Messrs. Cooper and Huxley can offer you. If Sergeant Monks is able to meet me there, I shall be able to extricate myself quickly and return to the outpost. If not, I may be obliged to play the indignant Kentishman until finding a suitable moment to abscond. If I do not return by quarter past five, take a cab to Demeter."

When Miss Jennings and Mick reached the outpost, Mr. Cooper was probably still speaking to the police, and Mr. Huxley had little to report, except that he and Mr. Cooper had arrived in time to see a tallish man step into a cab from the building they had been watching. They couldn't say whether he was one of the men they had seen at the window with white curtains or whether his comrade had already been in the cab, if there had been a comrade at all.

Five-fifteen came and went, so Miss Jennings arranged for a cab to take them to Demeter. Chris met them at the entryway to the Scythe and showed them to an empty cottage. She said the mechanicals who lived there were at the Institute, helping Mrs. Cutter do torture math, so Mick and Miss Jennings were welcome to sleep there.

"It's a great privilege to sleep in this cottage, Mr. Gunn," Miss Jennings told him.

Mick looked skeptically around the small, plain cottage.

"Oh, 'tisn't much to look at, I'll grant you," she said. "But from the knee down, this is the very first mechanicals' workshop. Built in 1771, see?" She pointed to a big stone near ground level, near the door frame.

Mick squinted in the dim light. There, in large font, was 1771 carved in Roman numerals (MDCCLXXI), with "v.v." in front of it.

"'v.v.' is May 5?" Mick asked.

"Indeed," she said.

"Why from the knee down?" he asked.

"I believe from the knee down, the workshop was stone, and

from the knee up, it was wood. And the mechanicals burnt it down, as they tend to do when they tamper with hideous and unnatural forces."

There were a bunch of other symbols on a stone on the opposite side of the door that looked like they'd been there just as long as the 1771 carving: words, numbers, Roman numerals, and even what might have been eyeball emojis. Mick stopped trying to make sense of it when Ward brought sandwiches for dinner.

Mick could tell that Ward sensed something bad had happened. But Mick couldn't say anything about it, so he just sat on his cot and tried to look cheerful while he scarfed his sandwich. Miss Jennings did the same on her cot.

After Ward left to eat dinner with the Maxwells, Miss Jennings closed and barred the cottage's only door.

Miss Jennings and Mick sat on their cots in awkward silence until Mick said, "You and Mr. Victor are good at fighting."

"More he than I," she said. "But one does learn to defend oneself."

"Mr. Victor knocked that guy out cold," Mick said. "Was he a boxer or something?"

"Not in any official capacity," Miss Jennings said with a smile. "And I believe most pugilists frown upon the use of knuckle-dusters."

"Knuckle-dusters?"

"Perhaps you know them as brass knuckles."

"Mr. Victor uses brass knuckles?" Mick asked. For some reason that really surprised him.

"Mr. Victor is an eminently practical gentleman," Miss Jennings said. "That's why I married him."

"Wait— not...?"

Miss Jennings laughed merrily. "Oh, goodness, not really. I'm many things, but a Kentish farm wife isn't one."

Mick realized how dumb he was being and laughed. When he stopped, he gathered his courage to ask, "Why did Mr. Victor say I was supposed to be the victim?"

Miss Jennings pursed her lips. "I can think of two reasons. First, the ruffian whom Mr. Victor carted to the court. He seemed to go straight for you. He would have had you if Mr. Victor hadn't pushed you aside."

"Mr. Victor pushed me?"

"You didn't see?" she asked in surprise.

"I had my eyes shut. The flare right before an aperture opens usually hurts my eyes if I don't close them."

She looked at him and shook her head slightly. "Your alley sight truly is remarkable."

"What's the second reason why that guy—that man was after me?"

"That remarkable alley sight, Mr. Gunn. First Miss Atkinson. Then you."

Mick decided that made sense. "With Gail it was Blue, Green, and two big guys by the Waterloo Bridge," Mick said.

"Blue and Green?"

"From the cricket match. You tackled Green, just before the Ladies Society."

"I'm afraid you've lost me, Mr. Gunn."

Mick reminded himself that just because he knew about something didn't mean everybody else did too. He explained briefly about Blue and Green. As he did, he realized something: "I forgot to tell you that the younger one who ran away, today at the whirlpool, that was Blue. Or did I mention that?"

"You assuredly did not." She sighed and stood up. "Stay here and bar the door behind me. Don't open to anyone but me, and only if I say—" She paused and chuckled. "Only if I say, 'The cow's in the corn.'"

"Where are—"

"I have to send a telegraph to tell the others about your little boy Blue. It might prove important."

Chapter 13

Consider Every Instant

The next morning, Mick woke early to knocking at the door. A few cots away, Miss Jennings also awoke. She wiped some sleep drool from her mouth and staggered to the door, standing with her hand on the bar but not moving it. She raised her other hand and, staring at Mick, put a finger to her lips.

"It is I, sweet, angelic Chris Biggs," said Chris' cheerful voice through the door.

"I don't know any sweet, angelic Chris Biggs," Miss Jennings said, her shoulders relaxing. "I know a cross covess by that name who skulks in dark corners. Might you mean that Chris Biggs?"

"Matilda Jennings, I am wounded to the quick," Chris said, laughing.

Miss Jennings lifted the bar and opened the door, allowing Chris and a pleasantly cool breeze to enter the cottage. The two women hugged briefly. Mick was reassured to see Chris back in her scruffy men's clothes. The fine lady in the elegant gown at the Ladies Society had seemed like a stranger.

Chris looked at both of them. "You've not broken fast, I expect."

Mick and Miss Jennings shook their heads.

"Well," Chris said, "as luck would have it, I've some victuals with me. Pasties." She pointed to a basket beside the cottage door. "They come at a price. You'll have to listen to me tell you the news of the world." Her tone was casual, but something in her expression suggested that it was important news, and not necessarily good.

Miss Jennings gave Chris a careful look. "Well, 'tis rather a high price," she said in a casual tone matching Chris'. "Still, I am peckish."

Mick nodded to show he was in. Chris led them into the warehouse and up to the Crow's Nest. Miss Jennings managed to make it up the ladder despite her dress, and Chris moved with ease despite the food basket dangling from her shoulder.

Once they were all in the Crow's Nest, Chris closed the trap door. "We may speak freely here," she said. "But quietly, I think."

Mick and Miss Jennings nodded. They all stood at the north railing. The city was smoky to in that direction, especially to the northeast, where a haze spread from the Isle of Dogs, half-shrouding the West India docks and the Royal Observatory in Greenwich Park.

"The princes of the palace," Chris said, "are closer to understanding time lightning. They are ever more certain that it involves threads and anchors, and that it is the result of a human hand. Or many hands. They are calling it the 'Realignment,' if I deciphered the telegram correctly. I don't profess to understand it, but they seemed to think that you two might."

Mick didn't, but Miss Jennings nodded and looked worried. The part about people causing the time lightning was a little scary. Maybe more than a little.

Chris continued, "They also say that they have discovered a new alley cluster."

Miss Jennings raised her eyebrows. "The professors are always arguing about whether something is a cluster unto itself or simply part of another cluster."

"There seems to be rather little argument about this one," Chris said. "Of late, there have been many temporal phenomena on and near the Thames by the Hungerford Bridge."

Miss Jennings frowned. "*On* the Thames?"

That surprised Mick too. Alleys almost always opened outdoors, and always on solid ground. Or solid enough, anyway —maybe on a bridge, maybe on a street running above the London sewers, but always on a hard surface. Not a thousand feet in the air. And not on a river.

Wait, though, he thought. Those were all the alleys he'd read about or seen as a spotter. But in his own alley, he'd gone through countless way-worlds, and some of them had dropped him in water. Most alley rats never went through a way-world. and those who did usually stopped in only one or two. Mick had gone through dozens, maybe hundreds, each stop briefer than the last until they blurred by too fast for him to be sure they were happening at all. But he'd dropped into water a few times. Maybe it had just been puddles or shallow little streams. Nobody really knew what way-worlds were, or even if they were part of the real world. So maybe it hadn't actually happened at all. But it had felt real. And some of those drops might have been rivers. Maybe even the Thames.

"But we never find droppers in the Tham—" Miss Jennings

stopped herself, and her face took on a horrified expression. "You don't think…"

That alley rats have been drowning in the Thames? That was an awful thought. But not a crazy one. Mick stared at the Thames as it sparkled in the west and lurked in the smoke to the east. The Thames regularly claimed victims among Londoners, people who all knew it was there and who weren't getting dumped into it from a century in the future. It was amazing to Mick how many people in 1853 didn't know how to swim. Apparently even a lot of sailors in the British Navy didn't know, which just seemed crazy. Of course, alley rats came from the future, so maybe they could swim. Maybe they just dropped in the river and swam to one of the stairways or got picked up by kindly wherrymen. Maybe they went to the streets like Alison or to Orphans or to the workhouses. That would still be bad, but better than drowning.

They stood silently for a while, staring at the river. Chris and Miss Jennings looked as grossed out as Mick felt.

From below, there came the creaking of somebody on the ladder. Chris opened the trapdoor and looked down. "Ho, Oliver," she called down.

"Ho, Chris," Mr. Yardley replied from a couple of stories below.

They waited silently as he clambered up. After shutting the trapdoor behind him, they arranged themselves in an approximate square, facing one another. Mr. Yardley pulled a scrap of paper from his breast pocket and handed it to Chris. She unfolded it, read it, and passed it to Miss Jennings, who read it and passed it to Mick.

Mr. Yardley looked like he was about to protest, but Miss

Jennings said, "Mr. Victor wishes Mr. Gunn to learn the rudiments of deciphering."

Mick read the penciling on the scrap of paper. "D TL PRINCES NO FIRST TO BE PRESENT AVERAGE TIME VERDANT CHANTRESS SIGHT." He sighed. One of those.

They made him guess at it, giving him hints as he struggled. He'd already learned that "S" meant "sinister" and "D" meant "dexter," which were Latin for "left" and "right," and that he was supposed to picture the dons' motto written out on one line:

Count Every Second. Consider Every Instant.

So "S" meant to use the part on the left side: "Count Every Second." And "D" meant to use the part on the right side: "Consider Every Instant." He already knew that "Count Every Second" meant use every other word. "Consider Every Instant" just meant to use every word.

Okay. He already knew "TL" meant "time lightning." Next, he should probably break up the message into chunks and try to decipher each chunk. So was the next chunk "princes," "princes no," "princes no first," or something else?

After he'd been silent for a moment, Miss Jennings said, "It may help you to remember that His Royal Highness' native tongue is a German language."

Right. The Queen of England's husband wasn't English. Victorians had jokes about that, though usually quiet ones. And if it was *the* Prince, then it was actually "Prince's," not "princes," which meant the Prince had to have something. So—"Prince's no?" What was "no" in German? Nightcrawler was German. What did he say? *Nyet?* No, that was Colossus. But it started with an *n. Naan.* Nope, that was bread. Wait …

"*Nein*," he said. "Is the first part 'time lightning *nein*'?"

"Well done, Gunner," Chris said. "The next bit is 'first to be present.'"

"Winner?" Mick guessed. "Early?"

"Focus on 'to be,'" Miss Jennings said.

"In German?" Mick asked. If this was a German test, he was going to flunk.

"English," Chris said.

Mick only knew grammar from studying Spanish, but he knew that first person was "yo," "nosotros," and "nosotras," which were "I" and "we" in English. And apparently he was looking for "to be" in the present tense. "Am? Are?" he asked.

"Am," Miss Jennings said.

"Time lightning *nein* am?" Mick asked skeptically. "No, 'time lightning nine a.m.'"

"Indeed," Chris said. "Well done."

Unfortunately, that was where Mick peaked. Even after Chris told him that the next chunk was "average time" and he should only worry about "average," he went off the rails. Their faces told him that it definitely wasn't "normal," "basic," "mediocre," "mid," or "meh."

Soon, Chris took pity on him and revealed that the full message was "Time lightning nine a.m. Greenwich Observatory."

Mick rolled his eyes.

Chris chuckled. "It is, in essence, an inside joke, Gunner. And it worked to protect the message from you, did it not? So even if some clever person breaks the Project's true ciphers or steals one of these deciphered scraps, they will have to understand our inside jokes, which can be quite difficult."

When she put it that way, it made sense. Maybe Mick just

didn't like inside jokes. At least not ones that left him on the outside.

Wait— He checked his pocket watch. It was 8:55. "Nine o'clock *today?*" he asked.

"Indeed."

"Then why—"

"Because I only just now got the telegram," Mr. Yardley said. "I came straight away."

Mick looked at Chris. "But instead of going there, we played crossword puzzles."

"Tut, tut, Mr. Gunn. Connans," Chris said with a wink. "Don't look so ill-used. We would never have made it to the observatory in time," Chris said. "Besides, I'd already had a very stern telegram from Miss North saying that you are not to leave the farm. And another from Mr. Victor saying the same thing."

"So what am I supposed to do?" Mick asked.

"I'm assuming you brought it?" Chris asked Mr. Yardley.

He nodded.

"Scientific method?" she asked.

When Mr. Yardley nodded again, Chris pointed to the brass telescope. She unfastened it from its mount inside the north rail and fastened it to an identical mount on the east rail. She opened the nearest window and swiveled the telescope to face the Greenwich Observatory.

"You can see time alleys through a telescope?" Mick asked.

"Well, *I* certainly can't," Chris said. "But I'd expect you can."

"One can see them through a window, after all," Mr. Yardley said. "Either way, it's simply glass."

Mick couldn't argue with that. But it seemed weird to use a no-nonsense scientific instrument like a telescope to observe a maybe-magical time alley. In any case, he was pretty sure he wouldn't be able to hear or feel the alley song from so far away.

Chris checked her watch. "It's a few minutes to the hour. Perhaps Mr. Gunn should have a look."

Mick checked the telescope, figuring out how to focus and move it so that he could scan the buildings of the Observatory itself as well as the surrounding gardens and woods. They were a long way away, so the telescope had to be zoomed in really tight, which meant that even the lightest jostling made the image bounce or lose focus.

Even after he mostly got the hang of using the telescope, he couldn't see anything that looked like time lightning. They weren't sure what that meant. It might have meant that the lightning was behind one of the onion-topped telescope buildings or even behind the hill on which the observatory sat. Or that there was no time lightning. Or that there was time lightning, but it was disappearing into the light from a sun that still hung low in the sky in pretty much the same direction as the Observatory.

At Chris' request, Mick kept looking for a while, pausing only to stretch his neck a couple times. Still nothing.

At about 9:15, Chris was saying, "Well, Oliver, perhaps we ought to try the other—" when Mick spotted something.

"I think…" Mick said. He paused. It was hard to be sure, but … *yes*. There, faintly flickering threads of white light on one of the large lawns sloping away from the Observatory buildings. It looked like it ought to be shocking a group of ladies wearing hats like flying saucers.

"Time lightning," Mick said.

Miss Jennings and Mr. Yardley both looked through the

telescope but saw nothing. Chris simply laughed when Miss Jennings offered her a turn.

When Mick looked again, it was still fuzzy, which might have been the lightning or the telescope.

Mr. Yardley removed his grease-stained jacket and leaned over the railing, holding the jacket so it blocked some of the sunlight. That helped a bit, but the image was still fuzzy and small.

Mr. Yardley worked to find a way to tie his jacket in place to shade the telescope while Miss Jennings took notes as Mick described what he saw. Mick did his best, but it was frustrating to be able to see the time lightning but not be able to give many useful details. He wasn't even sure if the faint hints of yellow he was seeing were from the time lightning or were just extra sunshine sneaking through Mr. Yardley's jacket.

After about twenty minutes, Chris asked how much longer Mick thought the time lightning would last. He sighed in frustration and said maybe twenty to thirty minutes, but he really couldn't tell.

A minute or so later, someone politely tapped his shoulder, and he looked up from the telescope. "If you'll permit me," Mr. Yardley said, quickly unfastening the telescope from its mount and setting it on the floor. He took a velvet bag from inside his satchel, extracting something from the cotton wool packed inside the bag. It turned out to be a cap of some sort with a lens at the center. He fitted the cap over the wide end of the telescope and fastened it in place by gently turning a set of threaded clamps. Next, he placed a thick black velvet sleeve where the cap met the telescope and clamped it in place with a pair of rings at the sleeve's top and bottom. Then he lifted the telescope back up and fastened it to its mount.

That done, he gestured to Mick to resume looking through the telescope.

Mick pressed his eye to the eyepiece. *Wow.*

He pulled his head back and stared at the Observatory with just his own eyes. It all looked normal.

Chis and Oliver laughed delightedly. Miss Jennings looked puzzled but intrigued.

Mick put his eye back to the eyepiece. *There* was the time lightning in all its glory. There was the core "storm cloud," a seething blur of white flashes tinged with yellow and the occasional pink flash. It spread outward from there, mostly flowing down the grassy hill like whitewater cascading through the rapids and then surging back up as if gravity had reversed. Mick tried to describe everything he saw, talking faster as things got busier. Purple flares emerged, quickly becoming purple pulses easing downhill and then back up, much like they had gone back and forth on the Hungerford Bridge. Then the yellow-tinged white lightning crackled as shimmering pink strands wove through it while the purple blobs began to race both directions, passing through each other without slowing.

When Mick was pretty sure the lightning was about to explode before going dead, he closed the eye pressed to the telescope. Not long later, there was a flare of light that turned his eyelid peach and pink. When it went back to normal, Mick risked opening his eye and saw nothing but grass, trees, and ladies with flying saucer hats.

Miss Jennings handed her notes to Chris, who confirmed a few points with her and Mick before tucking the notes into a pocket, opening the trapdoor, and descending the ladder in a speedy half-slide.

Mr. Yardley had a big grin on his face as he unfastened the

telescope from its mount and then gingerly removed the cap and sleeve from the telescope.

"What on earth is that device, Mr. Yardley?" Miss Jennings asked.

Mr. Yardley paused to think. "Please don't discuss it with others just yet. But I suppose the cat's out of the bag for you two. It's a special lens made out of glow-glass."

Mick felt like he'd heard of glow-glass but couldn't remember where.

"What's glow-glass?" Miss Jennings asked.

Mr. Yardley smiled and then grimaced. "It's a damned nuisance, mostly," he said as he fastened the telescope back to its mount. "Very hard to make, very easy to mar. But, if one actually manages to mix the frit properly and a hundred other finicking things go right, well, one has a sort of filter that makes the light associated with temporal phenomena easier to see. Only, not for everybody. Glow-glass is rather exclusive, I'm afraid. Only those with extraordinary alley sight find it useful, it would seem. It has little or no benefit for most of us."

He sighed and looked at Mick wistfully. "Would you say you saw things more clearly than you would have in person?"

Mick shrugged. "I don't know. It looked basically like the time lightning I saw up close. But, I mean, I wasn't up close, was I?"

"You were not. And you were fighting the sun."

"Not after you put that on," Mick said, pointing at the satchel where Mr. Yardley had carefully stowed the glow-glass cap.

Mr. Yardley smiled proudly. "This is the first trial we've been able to make with a telescope. We had been working so hard on repairing— on another project. I'd say it was a very successful trial, indeed. Thank you, Mr. Gunn," Mr. Yardley said, staring east toward the Observatory and resting a hand on the telescope. He laughed cheerfully.

"What is it, Mr. Yardley?" Miss Jennings asked.

"It just struck me," he said, patting the telescope. "With our little glow-glass cap and this small telescope, we just saw something that all of the enormous telescopes at the Observatory could never see, even though it was in their own garden."

Miss Jennings chuckled. "I suppose even the Royal Observatory must have blind spots."

The words *"punctum caecum"* flashed into Mick's mind. It took him a second to remember his conversation with Chris in Cavendish Square about blind spots and how sometimes the thing that let you see also was also the thing that created your blind spot.

He looked at Mr. Yardley and Miss Jennings and then at London and beyond. No doubt the Institute and the Project had blind spots in general. They had to have them for time lightning too. He wondered what they might be, hoping that he and his friends wouldn't find out in a painful way.

The rest of the day passed idly for Mick. Since he wasn't allowed to leave the Scythe, he remained in the Crow's Nest. With the windows open, he had a cool breeze on a warm day, which made it a pleasure to spy on London, eat pasties, and lie on the rough wooden floor for the occasional nap.

He was alone the rest of the morning, leaving the Crow's Nest only to pee. In the afternoon, Ward spent a while with him on watch. As far as Mick could tell, Ward was the only person who regularly kept watch from the Crow's Nest, which meant it was empty a lot of the time. Mick wondered if Chris had made up the chore just so Ward would get some breaks from running everybody's errands.

Chris, Mr. Yardley, and Miss Jennings returned late that afternoon. Chris hollered Mick down from the Crow's Nest, and they gathered in the shade of an oak tree near the canal, not far from the warehouse dock. Chris, Mr. Yardley, and Miss Jennings were dusty but triumphant.

They took turns explaining that they had visited the Observatory Outpost, and the dons there reported having seen a team of surveyors at work on the same part of the lawn where the time lightning had appeared that morning. They had appeared a half hour before the time lightning and started packing up to leave as soon as it had stopped. There had also been a team of surveyors, possibly the same ones, at the same spot the day before. "One of them was a woman," Miss Jennings remarked. "Apparently of obvious breeding."

"'A splendid beauty' were Mr. Thompson's words, if I remember correctly," Chris said.

"If only Mr. Thompson were half so able to describe the time lightning as our lady surveyor's swan-like neck," Miss Jennings said.

The surveyors returned the very next morning to the bottom of the hill where the time lightning had appeared. Perhaps distracted by trying to avoid drawing attention to themselves for appearing to work on a Sunday, they apparently did not notice being secretly photographed by Eyes with a calotype camera hidden in a picnic basket.

Chris brought the developed photos to the dons' cottage where Mick and Miss Jennings were staying. The three of them gathered at a small table near the window. One after another,

Chris laid out the photos. In the first three, the people were vague smudges. Chris explained that usually happened with calotype photos if the subject of the photograph didn't stay motionless for at least sixty seconds. But the last photo had a useful image. A tall, light-haired, broad-shouldered man stood behind some sort of complicated device that looked a little like a telescope that had been smushed so that it was taller than it was long. An elegantly dressed woman was peering into its eyepiece. She wore no hat, and her dark hair was pulled back from her face. The man's face was blurred, but the woman's was crisp. And very familiar.

"That's the woman from the carriage at the Seat," Mick said. "And from the Ladies Society too, I bet. And the guy. Is that Captain Britain? I mean, whatsisname, the one who was with her at the Seat. And the Society."

"August Blake," Chris said. "Yes, he and the gentleman in the photograph could be one and the same. I believe the lady is an alley rat named Catherine Collins. And I fear I recognize the theodolite."

"That's the thing she's looking through?" Mick asked.

"Indeed," Chris said. She looked troubled. Grim, even. Mick had never seen her look grim.

Miss Jennings spotted it too. "What's amiss?"

"A girl who is not yet wed," Chris said automatically, her mouth smiling, her eyes distracted.

That dumb joke made Mick think about other dumb jokes he'd heard recently. The ones in the coded telegrams. "Captain Britain is named August?" he asked.

"August Blake," Chris said distractedly.

"So ..." Mick paused to gather his thoughts. "Mr. Yardley made that thing, didn't he? The troglodyte."

Chris turned her gaze to Mick. "Theodolite. How did you reach that conclusion?"

"I was in the Crow's Nest, and you and him were talking, on the ground. He said something about repairing something, and you said something about glow-glass. And then he said something weird. Back then, I thought I'd heard wrong because his voice was fading out." Mick tried to remember. "It was something like 'this month wants it for—' no, 'in.' 'This month wants it in a week.'"

Chris chuckled mirthlessly. "And I try to be so circumspect."

"'This month' was a little inside joke for 'August,' wasn't it?" Mick asked. "August Blake wanted it in a week."

"Oh dear," Miss Jennings said.

"You're realizing it, are you not?" Chris asked her.

Miss Jennings nodded.

"Realizing what?" Mick asked.

Miss Jennings looked at Chris, who shrugged and said, "He's figured most of it out. Better to explain it so he'll know why he needs to be silent."

"Mr. Blake is in Lord Harrowgrave's employ," Miss Jennings said. "One of his secretaries. Most things he does are done at his lordship's bidding."

"And the theodododil— And the thingummy, that was for Lord Harrowgrave?" Mick asked.

Chris nodded.

Miss Jennings said, "So if Mr. Blake and the young lady are involved with the time lightning, we may be assured that it is at Lord Harrowgrave's direction."

Chris nodded again.

"And so," Miss Jennings continued, "Lord Harrowgrave's

insistence that he be kept abreast of what we learn about time lightning isn't—"

"—isn't an interest in the time lighting," Chris said, "but rather in whether we realize that his lordship is involved."

"Indeed," Miss Jennings said. "Chris, are you able to tell us what the glow-glass theodolite does?"

Chris shook her head. "If anybody knows, it would be Oliver," she said. "A normal theodolite is a surveyor's tool for measuring, so presumably a glow-glass theodolite measures time alleys. Or time lightning."

"Do you remember our respite from the time lightning?" Miss Jennings asked. "It lasted about a week, didn't it?"

Chris nodded, looking distressed.

"I'll wager that was the very same time when Mr. Yardley was repairing the glow-glass theodolite, was it not?"

Chris and Mick both nodded.

"And I'll wager the time lightning didn't begin in the first instance until after you delivered the theodolite to Mr. Blake," Miss Jennings said to Chris.

"Perhaps not," Chris said. "Perhaps not."

"So Mr. Blake and Miss Collins must be doing something to cause the time lightning, mustn't they?" Miss Jennings asked. "Almost certainly at Lord Harrowgrave's instruction."

"Apparently so," Chris said.

The two women were silent for a moment. "What must we do?" Miss Jennings asked.

"We must," Chris said with a deep sigh, "reflect carefully upon whom we can trust."

CHAPTER 14

THE ATHENA UNDERTAKING

After a nighttime carriage ride from Demeter to the Institute with Chris, Miss Jennings, and Mr. Yardley, Mick collapsed tiredly onto his cot. Leech was gone when he woke the next morning, and Mick realized he was still wearing the "honest poor boy" clothing he'd been wearing for days, though apparently he'd managed to remove his disreputable shoes, which were lying beside the bed.

After a shower so thorough he got side-eye from the other boys for wasting water, Mick hustled to the dining hall to see if there was any breakfast left. There was, but only because the Squad had saved him a plate. All the other food was gone, and there were only a couple dozen students still scattered through the dining hall. At the faculty table, Mr. Edmondson was complaining to some unlucky listener, probably about Americans, Geordies, or women.

"Owl said he saw you in the shower trying to drain the

entire cistern," Leech said, pushing the plate at Mick as Mick settled onto a stool.

Mick dug into the boiled eggs and toast. They'd even saved him enough butter to make the toast delicious. When he got back to his real life, he was going to miss Victorian butter.

And, he realized, he'd miss his friends. He hadn't spent much time with them recently, especially not Leech and Dolly, so he'd been glad to see them. If he managed to get back home, he'd never see them again.

"What's amiss, Gunner?" Dolly asked.

"A girl who is not yet wed," Mick said, forcing a smile. "And what did I miss while I was gone?"

"Watching the professors and the dons wear my feet to nubs," Leech said. "Gunner, I wish to apologize. During the alley waylaying, I envied you at times. The professors were always seeking your help."

"I was just a bomb-sniffing dog," Mick said. "Same as now."

"A what?" Dolly asked.

Mick looked around. There was nobody in earshot, so he risked a connan by describing bomb-sniffing dogs, and how he felt like one, always getting trotted out to find and describe this time lightning or that alley.

Only Dolly seemed surprised by the concept of a bomb-sniffing dog. "That is rather how they've been treating poor Leech," she said. "He's ever so good with stirrings. He's predicted two time lightning incidents."

"And been dragged to hundreds of dead-ends," Leech said.

"Wait," Mick said. "Are you going out alone? Just the Squad?"

"We do our customary patrol, well, as customary," Dolly said. "But if Leech is summoned in particular, then Alison and I don't always join."

"Then it's myself and a legion of greets and dons," Leech said.

"Good," Mick said. "Have lots of people with you. People are getting attacked. Gail and Stephen. Miss Jennings. Me." He wondered whether to add Elmer Maxwell to the list. So much had happened that he'd almost forgotten about Elmer.

"We knew about Gail and Stephen," Alison said. "But not Miss Jennings or you."

Mick gave them a quick run-down of what he was allowed to discuss, which wasn't much. Chris had sworn him to secrecy about glow-glass, August Blake, and Catherine Collins. And, of course, Lord Harrowgrave.

Alison frowned. "Now I worry about you two patrolling without me," she told Leech and Dolly.

Dolly explained to Mick, "Alison is on occasion called upon to help Miss Emmet, and then Owl serves as our thane."

"I walk the streets of London like a faithful hound sniffing the pavement, with her and Owl holding my lead," Leech griped as he stole the last bit of buttered toast from Mick's plate.

"There's Owl now," Dolly said, pointing to the dining hall doors, where Owl was waving to them. She stood and started toward Owl. Still grumbling, so did Leech.

Mick started to stand up, but Alison shook her head. "Miss Emmet instructed me to bring you to her office at quarter past."

When Mick started to dig out his pocket watch, Alison told him it was about 9:50. She yawned and stretched both hands up high over her head. Then she stared up at the high ceiling. Mick followed her gaze. In the bright daylight, the familiar artwork on the ceiling was easy to make out. There was a picture of a golden globe in the middle and four smaller globes at each corner of the ceiling, with golden lines connecting dozens of spots on the small globes to England at the center of the big globe.

"Material, intellectual, temporal, and spiritual," Alison said.

"Huh?"

"The smaller globes. They represent the material, intellectual, temporal, and spiritual spheres. They are 'blended by the divine hand' to form this world. The 'four-into-one.' One finds an illustration of the four-into-one in a great many Project books from the turn of the century. Dreary, dreary books written by people with more ink than information." She sighed. "The entire spiritual sphere, for one, is rubbish about ley lines, which don't exist."

Mick chuckled. "I've never heard you angry about having to read."

Alison lowered her gaze from the ceiling and grinned wryly. "Do you know, I too found myself envying you. Our day in the wagon, with Chris, was such a delight. I wasn't required to read tedious tomes with spidery print. I was, in fact, *forbidden* to read them. Life in the wagon sounds quite appealing of late."

"It's that bad?" Mick asked.

"Oh, occasionally, I find something of use to Miss Emmet or one of the dons. It's only..." She collected her thoughts for a while. "Reading has always been so comforting. When I was a little girl, in the future, I would lie beside my brother in bed and our mother would read to us, and it was marvelous. She made the people and animals sound so alive. And she taught us to read, rather younger than most. And then my alley dropped me into confusion and starvation and terrible dread about J— my brother. Tips, Hoot, and Gristle saved me, and I had to repay them. I could read a little, and they could not, which made me useful. And any kind of reading, even signs in a shop window, reminded me of my mother and brother, usually in a happy way. So when the greet team found me and brought me here, and there was food, a roof, clean clothes, and so many books, well, it all fit together, somehow. But now..."

She paused and stared blankly for a while until her attention returned to the room. "We'd best go or we shall be late."

They went up the backstairs to Miss Emmet's office. Miss Emmet led them at a brisk pace up to the roof near the Turret.

Standing sentry at the Turret's entryway, Chris nodded as they entered.

Inside, the two large round tables had been pushed together. Already seated, nearly shoulder to shoulder, were Mrs. Cutter, Mr. Victor, Mr. Yardley, Miss Jennings, Miss Mitchell, and Gail. The table was eerily silent, and those seated greeted the newcomers with nods.

Miss Emmet, Alison, and Mick sat down, leaving two chairs empty. A moment later, Miss North entered and slid into one of them. Instead of her usual plain gray dress, she was wearing a puffy blue and red gown and a matching hat that made her look like an expensive balloon animal. At least until you saw the scowl on her face that made her look like the sort of person who wouldn't want to hear one *single* word about balloon animals.

Into the silence, Mrs. Cutter said, "We are about to discuss matters of great delicacy and import. Discretion is paramount, as is trust. Does anyone here question the presence of anyone else?"

They all looked at one another awkwardly.

"I do," Alison said.

All eyes turned to her. She blushed and looked down at the table, but then drew in her breath and raised her gaze. "I question my own presence," she said. "And perhaps Mr. Gunn's. We are children, and many would say our judgment is not to be trusted. I am happy to depart if others question it too." She paused. "I am also happy to remain."

She looked down, apparently having used up her bravery. Mick was impressed.

"I consider Miss March wise—and worldly wise—beyond her years," Miss Emmet said. "I also consider her necessary. She has done much analysis, including laying eyes on a great many texts that I have not. We have very little time in which to act, and we dare not increase our ignorance."

A few people nodded, and nobody protested.

"We need Mr. Gunn's alley sight," Chris said from the entryway, "And he has impressed me with his discretion and deduction."

Mick looked around the table. Again, there were a few nods and no protests.

"Very well," Mrs. Cutter said. She looked at Chris. "My dear, are you going to continue hovering at the threshold?"

"Yes," Chris said flatly.

Mrs. Cutter sighed. "Very well. I suppose we must first explain the Undertaking to Miss Atkinson, Miss March, and Mr. Gunn." She looked at Gail, Alison, and Mick. "Do you agree not to repeat anything that we tell you must remain secret? Please say that you do."

They all said they did.

Mrs. Cutter looked at the others. "The rest of us should take that oath as well. We shall not speak of any of these matters to any person not at this table unless the adults at this table agree that it is absolutely necessary. Agreed?"

The others all agreed.

Mrs. Cutter drummed her fingers on the table thoughtfully. "Where to begin? You've all met Lady Penbrook and heard her sermon on the Nye twins, I think?"

When they nodded, she said, "That is because you were identified as people who might be of service to and, one hopes, be well served by an undertaking dedicated to the principles that effort and ability are more important than birth and connection and that effort and ability are not found exclusively in those with beards and skin that turns red in bright sunshine. We call it 'the Athena Undertaking,' or simply 'the Undertaking.' It was begun by the Nye twins. Gemma later named it for her sister and for all the things that inspired her sister to take the name 'Athena.'"

A lot of things fell into place then for Mick, including Miss Mitchell's remarks at the Ladies Society about Athena's spear and many of Miss Emmet's cryptic comments about various factions of the Project.

"The Nye twins," Mrs. Cutter continued, "were ferociously intelligent and ferociously committed to never returning to the torment and terror of their childhoods. To never again being vulnerable to the contempt and cruelty of lesser people with greater means. The twins laid the foundations for the Undertaking. Since their deaths, a great many people have devoted their lives and treasure to continuing and strengthening it, including those gathered here. We are subtle, we are careful, and we are strong."

Gail didn't look too surprised. Alison looked like she had a lot of questions but was forcing herself to stay silent.

"Of course, one needn't be an alley rat to believe the world can be, and ought to be, more just. But," Mrs. Cutter waved a finger for emphasis, "if one comes from the future and has already lived in a place that takes at least some of that justice for granted, it is easier to have faith that such justice may one day be attained."

Mick thought about that. "Isn't that changing the future?"

"Doubtful," Miss North said. "It is vastly easier to change tools than to change thinking. If one gives people a better hammer, they will use it. If one gives people a better idea about how to treat people with respect, they will most likely resent one until the day they die. One could more easily move technology forward a century than decency forward a year. Especially if the Ladies Society committees are involved."

Mrs. Cutter grinned at Miss North. "My dear, if you wish to abandon your duties at the Ladies Society, do let us know so that we may devise an orderly succession. If you delay your resignation too long and murder one of those priggish biddies, you might be sent to the gallows and your duties there might fall to me. I refuse to consider the possibility."

Miss North chuckled. "I shall endeavor to murder no one, not even Beatrix Milner."

"That one you may murder without reproach from me," Mrs. Cutter said. "I shall gladly help you dump her body in the Thames."

Miss Mitchell and Miss Jennings guffawed.

"In your time at Hidden Thorns," Chris asked Miss North, "have you come much in contact with Catherine Collins?"

Miss North frowned. "I have conversed with her from time to time. She seems a clever woman, if overly given to badinage with bachelors."

"Are August Blake or Lord Harrowgrave among those bachelors?" Chris asked.

"Certainly," Miss North said. "Though his lordship is not much given to badinage."

"Miss Collins was a student at the Institute," Miss Jennings offered. "She and I are roughly of an age. We were never close, not even tory chums, but I shouldn't say we were ever at odds. She went alley-blind, or so I believed, and went to Lady Grenville's not long before I became a don."

"I remember her now," Mrs. Cutter said. "Canny girl. Precocious with languages. She clearly had a gift for mathematics but never showed any love of the subject. Shame she went alleyblind." She paused and turned to Miss Jennings. "'Or so I *believed?*' Past tense?"

Miss Jennings nodded. "I now rather doubt she went alleyblind."

"On what basis?" Mr. Victor asked.

Miss Jennings explained about the glow-glass theodolite and how Miss Collins had been using it.

"And this theodolite would be useless to an alley-blind person?" Miss North asked Mr. Yardley.

"It is useless to anyone without exceptional alley sight," he said. "At least to observe alley phenomena. The glow-glass theodolite would still work to observe mundane phenomena, but not so well as a conventional theodolite. The glow-glass dulls conventional light, you see."

"So she counterfeited alley-blindness?" Mr. Victor asked. "To what end?"

"Perhaps she wearied of gray dresses and patrol," Mrs. Cutter said. "When I was a girl of fifteen, I took little interest in patrolling. And I was at great pains to conceal my gift for mathematics. Unladylike, you know."

"Or perhaps she had already decided she wanted to pursue schemes that the Institute would not permit," Miss North said.

"Then she and Lord Harrowgrave are birds of a feather," Mr. Victor said.

"The Project will regret smuggling that one into an earldom, I suspect," Mrs. Cutter said.

Right, Mick realized. Lord Harrowgrave was an alley rat, so he couldn't have been born an Earl. He wondered how the Project had done it.

"As Miss Collins attended the Institute," Mr. Yardley said, "we must be able to learn her drop date, yes?"

"About a year after mine," Chris said, "though she was but an infant."

"It's a simple matter of consulting the records," Miss North said. "Is it significant?"

"If this clever young man is correct," Mrs. Cutter said, looking at Mr. Yardley, "it could be of great significance."

Alison and Gail were looking at one another intently. Then their heads swiveled to Miss Emmet, who gestured that they should speak.

"It's she?" Gail asked. "She's the one anchoring the threads?"

"To her drop point?" Alison asked.

Mr. Yardley looked surprised and then nodded enthusiastically. He looked at Chris. "Did you drop roughly Christmas of 1832?"

"Not quite two months afterward," Chris said.

Mr. Oliver looked at Miss Jennings and Mrs. Cutter, who were both nodding. "It fits together, does it not?" he asked.

"Very much so," Mrs. Cutter said.

"Please explain," Miss North said.

"Whoever is causing the time lightning appears to be

anchoring all the threads at a point in time right around Christmas of 1833," Miss Jenkins said.

"And my two intrepid researchers into the temporal arcana there," Miss Emmet said, nodding to Gail and Alison, "have found several texts that insist that the best way to anchor an alley thread is to use one's own drop point."

"And we are quite certain," Mr. Victor said, "that the purpose of anchoring so many threads is the Realignment? To once again be able to shuttle the alleys?"

"We are quite certain of nothing," Mrs. Cutter said. "But, to date, that is the only hypothesis worth considering."

"How close is Miss Collins to succeeding?" Miss North asked.

Mr. Yardley exhaled thoughtfully. "Our calculations continue to suggest the Realignment will occur when the delay from lighting to alley reaches approximately five days. And it is now just over two."

"But accelerating," Mrs. Cutter pointed out. "Every time that Miss Collins—or whoever may be the responsible party— manages to affix a thread to some anchor point, she brings the moment closer. Much closer, I suspect. I should be astonished if more than another half dozen threads are required to reach Realignment. Were I a gambler, I would bet on fewer."

"And it is one thread per affected alley, correct?" Miss North asked.

"Correct," Miss Jennings said.

"How many threads has she anchored already?" Mr. Victor asked.

"We cannot be certain," Miss Cutter said. "She may have succeeded with threads unknown to us. She may have failed with some that are known to us."

"And we have no idea how she does it?" Miss North asked, leaning forward to rest her elbows on the table.

"We have some notion of the theory and have devised quite a few rather excellent equations," Mrs. Cutter replied. "But we know far too little about the practical steps. On that front, learning that Miss Collins is using the glow-glass theodolite is one of a very few useful scraps of intelligence."

"By all accounts," Miss Emmet offered, "the practitioner must have not only prodigious alley sight but also considerable familiarity with the manipulation of alleys."

"But where on earth does one *acquire* such familiarity?" Miss North asked in exasperation. "How is it that Cassandra Halliwell learned how to do such things when no one else did? She wasn't especially clever. And now Miss Collins? No professor here could have taught her, even were any of us so inclined. Since the Collapse, no rat has been able to do what she is doing. And those who did know are long dead."

"It cannot be so impossible as we have been led to believe," Mr. Victor said. "Someone taught Miss Collins, just as surely as someone taught Cassie Halliwell. Someone of position and influence in the Project because Cassie did not get those future journals on her own."

Mick remembered that Cassandra Halliwell had apparently known when lift alleys would appear because someone had given her future journals that should have been sealed deep in the Vault somewhere beneath the Institute.

"Is not Lord Harrowgrave the obvious suspect?" Miss North asked. "Miss Collins and Mr. Blake are his creatures, and his lordship has ever been ambitious and unscrupulous."

"He has the position and the ruthlessness," Mr. Victor said. "But has he the alley sight?"

There was a long silence until Mick nervously said, "Probably not."

All eyes turned to him.

"And why not, Mr. Gunn?" Miss Emmet asked gently.

"His eyes aren't bright enough," Mick said.

He got nothing but confused expressions in response. "All alley rats have, sort of … glowing eyes," he said. "Unless they're alley-blind, I guess. Some only a little bit, so that it looks like it might just be regular light reflecting a little funny. Some are really bright so that it looks like they have gas lamps behind their eyeballs. I used to think I was imagining it because nobody else sees it. But it's real. And I think brighter eyes means better alley sight. At least usually." He shrugged. "I think."

"Who has the brightest eyes among us?" Miss North asked.

"Other than me?" Mick asked. "Gail."

Gail winked at him, which was nice.

Miss North turned her gaze to Gail and asked whether Gail could see the glow. When Gail shook her head, Miss North returned her gaze to Mick. "And after Miss Atkinson, whose eyes shine brightest?"

Mick shrugged. "It's all pretty close. Yours, Mr. Victor's, and Miss Jennings' are brighter than the rest, but not by a ton. Not by a great deal, I mean."

"And Lord Harrowgrave does not have bright eyes?" Mr. Victor asked.

Mick shook his head. "Everybody's here are probably brighter than his except…" He trailed off, not wanting to sound mean.

"Except mine," Chris said matter-of-factly.

After a thoughtful moment around the table, Chris pointed out, "Lord Harrowgrave needn't be tutoring Miss Collins

THE FLICKERING BRIDGE

himself. He is a powerful person. Powerful people have others to do their bidding. Butlers and barristers, chambermaids and chamberlains, all ready to hand for whatever task needs doing."

Mick could tell that made sense to the others.

"And does Miss Collins have bright eyes?" Mr. Yardley asked.

Mick realized he didn't know. He'd mostly seen her from too far away, or from the back. The only time he'd been close enough and looking at her face, she'd been wearing a veil. Had she done that on purpose, to hide her eyes? He explained why he didn't know.

"Are your eyes the brightest eyes you've seen?" Miss Emmet asked.

Mick shook his head reflexively. "Cassandra Halliwell's," he said.

That made everybody look at one another unhappily.

"Which is a reminder," Mrs. Cutter said, "that although it is important to know how the Realignment is being brought about, it also is important to know *why*. Why would anyone want to shuttle the alleys again, knowing the risks it poses? Is it the same madness of despair that drove Miss Halliwell? Is it power? Greed?"

Maybe, Mick thought, *they've figured out a way to go forward in time. Maybe they just want to go home.*

"I'd submit that the most important question is how we may prevent it," Mr. Victor said.

"Well," Mr. Yardley said quietly, "we may soon have the beginning of answers to many of those questions. Mr. Gunn's descriptions of the time lightning at the Observatory have given us information that lets us rather confidently predict that the time alley associated with that lightning will open not long past noon tomorrow at Greenwich Observatory. If Miss Collins returns then, we may be able to observe her closely and learn what she is doing."

"I bet she'll be there," Mick said, his brain finally putting his memories into a sensible order. "I think she's usually at the lightning and the alleys. Maybe always. I think that was her, and probably Capt— Mr. Blake at the cricket match." He looked at Gail. "The alley rats in the fancy clothing who snuck away."

Gail scrunched her face up in thought and then nodded to indicate it was possible.

Mick continued, "I bet it was also them near Chesterfield House, when Miss Jennings got attacked. Gail and I saw a man from behind, in the carriage. That could have been Mr. Blake. And somebody else got in that carriage, on the side I couldn't see, just before it left. Maybe that was Miss Collins. And then we saw them both again at the Ladies Society right after, and that's really close to Chesterfield House."

"And," he added after a pause, "near Gaoler's Home Outpost, when we got attacked, one of the dons said he saw a tall man and a short man watching from a window. What if it was a tall man and a regular-height woman, maybe in men's clothes?"

"Preposterous," Chris said. "What unnatural woman would wear men's clothing in a public place?"

That got louder laughs than it deserved.

"And before, when Gail got attacked," Mick realized, "there were people on the bridge watching. Didn't you say they bent over like they'd dropped something?"

Gail nodded. "And, if that was the glow-glass theodolite falling to the bridge… And it was damaged…"

"Perhaps that was why the time lightning stopped," Mr. Yardley said. "The other mechanicals and I were losing sleep repairing that dratted theodolite, so Miss Collins couldn't have been using it."

"We didn't see them at the Hungerford Bridge during the time lightning there, did we?" Alison asked. "Not that they weren't there, of course, but—"

"I saw Lord Harrowgrave's carriage there afterward," Mick said, "when we were walking home. The shiny black one with the big brass 'H.' Remember? I tried to point it out."

"If Mr. Gunn is correct," Mrs. Cutter said. "Then I'd say we can expect Miss Collins—and Mr. Blake—to make an appearance tomorrow at the Observatory. If so, I propose that we observe her without making ourselves known, in the hopes that we learn what she is doing. If we manage that, we may be able to stop it."

"We are, most likely, only a few more threads away from the Realignment," Mr. Victor pointed out. "Perhaps we should attempt to stop her, even detain her."

Mrs. Cutter nodded thoughtfully. "Perhaps. But she is likely Lord Harrowgrave's instrument, and instruments can be replaced. Stopping her likely would not stop the Realignment."

"It would delay it," Miss North said.

"Most likely," Chris said. "But it would also encourage Lord Harrowgrave to be more secretive. We know Miss Collins. We can find her and spy upon her. But if she were to be replaced, we might never know by whom, leaving us powerless to stop the Realignment."

Mr. Victor sighed heavily. "All very true. Then again, tomorrow's alley might provide the final thread necessary to finish the Realignment. If so, learning the method will profit us nothing, and it will be too late for us to prevent the Realignment."

"Take heart," Miss Emmet told him with a tight grin, "if the

Realignment happens, it will again be possible to return to the past deliberately, and thus it will never truly be too late for anything ever again."

Mr. Victor shuddered.

Mrs. Cutter and Mr. Yardley looked at one another and passed a piece of paper back and forth several times, each scribbling something on it before returning it.

After the final pass of the paper, Mrs. Cutter said, "We think it most unlikely that a single additional thread will suffice to cause the Realignment."

"Quite a gamble," Miss Emmet said calmly.

"We must all of us be gamblers now," Mrs. Cutter said. "But I believe this is a sensible wager, however terrifying."

After a long silence, Miss North said, "Shall we do as Mrs. Cutter suggests?"

Slowly, the adults nodded.

"Now, what of this must we keep secret?" Miss North asked. "A great deal of this, we *must* tell other people, even people not in the Undertaking. We shall need assistance at every turn. And we cannot hope to keep it all secret in any event."

The adults murmured their agreement.

"I think perhaps it is as simple," Mrs. Cutter said, "as not mentioning that we have any idea of the involvement of Mr. Blake and Miss Collins. Or, especially, of Lord Harrowgrave."

"Nor even that the same man and woman have been present so frequently at the time lightning and related alleys," Mr. Victor said.

Chris turned away from scanning the roof to look at everyone. "I cannot presume to tell you who needs to know about the Realignment. However, I beg of you to tell only those who truly need to know. Those who do not know cannot tell, not even by innocent error."

There were murmurs of agreement.

"One more thing," Chris said. "We need a name for only those of us at this table and the few trusted souls who are with us in spirit."

"Excuse me," Alison said hesitantly. "But is the Vicar one of those trusted souls?"

"Indeed he is," Miss North said. "However, perhaps his greatest contribution to our cause is to maintain at all times a semblance of genteel traditionalism that soothes the members of the Project and, indeed, members of the public in those rare moments when the Institute somehow catches the public's attention. So he must often maintain a discreet distance from conversations such as this."

Alison nodded, looking relieved. Mick felt relieved too.

Chris continued. "As I was saying, we can no longer simply call ourselves—or, more's the point—simply *consider* ourselves the Undertaking. It is far from certain that all members of the Undertaking are with us. And we cannot always trust those who are with us to act with the necessary discretion and wisdom. Lord Harrowgrave's reach is long, and his grasp is both subtle and firm."

The others agreed. There was a brief debate, and Miss North's suggestion of "Palladians" won the vote. Alison whispered to Mick that "Palladian" had something to do with Athena.

"We are resolved, then," Mrs. Cutter said. "We have our name, and we know our gamble. Let us cast our lots and hope that we learn more than how to regret our choices."

CHAPTER 15

THE THREADS TIGHTEN

Some said the lonely, marshy patch of London briskly rolling past Mick's brougham was called the Isle of Dogs because one of the King Henrys had taken his dogs hunting here, though Chris said it probably got the name because people misheard its original name, the Isle of Docks. There were definitely a lot of docks. "Drunken Dock" was an especially good name, Mick thought as their brougham passed it. "They should have called it the Isle of Drunken Dogs," he said.

"That's what the French call England, I believe," Chris replied.

It could also have been the Isle of Smokestacks, Mick thought. There were plenty of those belching black soot into the overcast sky.

Mr. Yardley was above in the driver's seat because he'd refused to squeeze himself inside the small, two-seater carriage. Chris was sitting next to Mick with a heavy, cherrywood box in her lap that apparently held a telescope and the glow-glass cap.

They were on their way to spy on August Blake and Catherine Collins at the Royal Observatory by using the glow-glass telescope, this time from a lot closer than Demeter Farm. Gail was with a bunch of Eyes and dons across the river at the Observatory itself.

Near the southernmost tip of the Isle, Mr. Yardley turned the horses onto a side street, down a narrow drive, and stopped in the grubby backlot of a big brick factory with two big smokestacks, one sending up constant smoke, one issuing not even a puff.

"The Covens factory," Chris said. "Steelworks and ironmongery. They do some work for the mechanicals now and again because the Project controls the factory, though I doubt anyone associated with the factory has any notion of that."

Mr. Yardley opened the brougham door and took the cherrywood box from Chris, who led them along a muddy path beside a tall, crooked fence. Soon, they reached the sleeping smokestack, its bricks grimed with soot and ash. Mick realized it wasn't attached to the factory.

"Joshua here," she said, pointing at the smokestack, "took offense at something the previous Covens factory did. Burned it to cinders, thorough as birth flame. Nobody perished, by some miracle. Mr. Covens decided not to trust Joshua again, so they built a new smokestack when they built the new factory."

Mick was starting to wonder why Chris was bothering to tell him all that when Mr. Yardley came to a stop beside a ladder attached to the smokestack. "Lightest first," he said, looking at Mick and gesturing to the ladder.

Mick tilted his head back and realized it was a really tall smokestack and that the ladder went all the way to the top.

"Time and tide, Mr. Gunn," said Mr. Yardley cheerfully. "Time and tide."

Mick began climbing the cold, dirty rungs, soon rising high enough to gain a view of the tidal Thames and the domes of the Royal Observatory on the far shore.

Chris followed him up, and eventually so did Mr. Yardley, who strapped the telescope box to his back.

After the first ten feet or so, the ladder was encircled by a cage of metal bands that were probably designed to make it harder to fall off, but they just made Mick think about how easy it would be to fall off.

"Steady on, Gunner," Chris said from beneath him.

When Mick got within about fifteen feet of the top, he realized there was a narrow covered platform wrapped around the top of the smokestack, with a hole in its floor where the ladder went through.

"Ahoy, grubby peepers," Chris called up.

A kid's face appeared in the hole, peering down at them. It was, indeed, a grubby face. But cheerful and alert. A second kid's face appeared, also grubby, also cheerful. They had to be Eyes, especially since they didn't have alley rat eyes.

"Ahoy, Chris," one of the kids said.

Mick, Chris, and Mr. Yardley all climbed onto the platform. Mr. Yardley had to squeeze awkwardly through the hole in the floor to avoid banging the telescope's box on the sides, and then had to tilt his neck awkwardly to avoid banging his head on the platform's roof.

The Eyes grinned at Mr. Yardley's contortions, and Mick struggled not to do the same.

Chris removed a small satchel hanging from her shoulder and dug out a pair of meat pies of some sort. The Eyes each snatched a pie and turned it into a light dusting of crumbs. Mick wasn't sure he'd ever seen anyone eat that fast.

"A joey," she said, handing over a small silver coin. "Even split, mind. Now off with you."

The Eyes looked at each other, grinned, and slid onto the ladder, disappearing from sight, though their hooting was loud enough to be heard even when they reached the ground.

"They're good kids," Chris said. "But I fear they spend too much time up here with only the seagulls for conversation. Then again, they go to grammar school every afternoon when it's safe to cross the river, and the seagulls may have a broader view of the world than their instructors."

The platform was surprisingly cozy. It was about six feet wide and wrapped around the top of the smokestack like a doughnut-style batting weight slipped onto a baseball bat. The roof was tin, the floor was steel or iron mostly covered in whitewashed planks, the walls were whitewashed boards without too many gaps, and big, mostly unbroken, windows ran around the whole ring. Some of them even opened.

There were two pairs of binoculars in a box fastened to the inner wall. There was no telescope, but there was a mount, and Mr. Yardley was fussing with it. Satisfied at last, he fastened the telescope firmly in place. Then he swiveled the big end of the telescope to face inward and began attaching the glow-glass cap.

Mick took the opportunity to walk the circumference of the platform, amazed by the views. He could see London in every direction, and the mostly open countryside farther to the east and south. Their location gave them particularly good views of the Thames leading in and out of London as well as a number of important docks, including the West India and East India docks. If you wanted information about what was coming in and out of London by water, you were in the perfect spot. In some cases, you could even see over the walls surrounding the various docks. No wonder there were Eyes up here. And maybe not just kids, either, he realized, noting a tattered man's over-coat hanging on the wall.

"Eureka," said Mr. Yardley cheerfully. Mick circled back to the south side of the platform, which looked across the Thames at Greenwich, including, of course, the Royal Observatory.

"Have a look, Mr. Gunn," Mr. Yardley said.

Standing on a small, battered box so he could use the tele-scope, Mick pressed his eye to the eyepiece. The telescope was focused nicely on the grassy western slope of the Observatory hill where the time lightning had appeared. There was no sign of a time alley, but there wasn't supposed to be for another few hours. There were already a few people strolling along a pathway leading up the hill. The telescope was focused to give him a view of the entire hill, since they didn't know exactly where the aperture would appear. He couldn't see people's faces, but he could tell whether people were wearing men's or women's clothes, especially the hats. The women's hats were often huge. He wondered if it was fun to wear hats that big. It looked like a literal pain in the neck, but things often felt different than they looked.

He asked Chris if she enjoyed it. "Things are usually more amusing when one chooses to do them than when one must do them," she said. "I sometimes enjoy wearing garlanded frip-peries, and I almost always enjoy ceasing to wear them. But above all I enjoy deciding *whether* to wear them."

"I take it from the subject of conversation," Mr. Yardley said with a hint of impatience, "that no aperture is yet visible?"

Mick said there wasn't.

"It's scarcely quarter past ten, Oliver," Chris pointed out. "You and Mrs. Cutter were quite definite that the aperture would begin to form no earlier than quarter to one."

Mr. Yardley sighed. "Well, yes, the numbers are quite clear. But..." He trailed off with an irritated wave.

Mick knew that feeling. Time alleys made sense and followed rules until they didn't. And when they didn't, something bad was probably happening.

"Mr. Thompson of the Observatory Outpost," Chris said, "has sworn that someone atop the roof of the outpost will raise a red flag as soon as the dons receive intelligence of an aperture. That should be within moments of its happening." Chris grabbed a pair of binoculars and handed the other pair to Mr. Yardley.

"It is now," she checked her pocket watch, "10:17 of the a.m. At twenty past ten and every twenty minutes thereafter, I shall inspect the roof of the outpost. If I spy a flag, Gunner will scrabble over to the chronoscope and breathlessly report all that he sees. Oliver, at half ten and every twenty minutes thereafter, you will do the same, and Gunner will respond in the same fashion. Agreed?"

Mr. Yardley nodded. "Although a chronoscope is actually an altogether different device. At least two altogether different devices, now that I think on it."

"If it will sweeten your disposition, you may consider me abjectly humble in my apologies to you and the world's chronoscopes," Chris said.

Mr. Yardley grinned.

"Gunner," Chris added, "you should consult the chronoscope—"

"Ahem," Mr. Yardley said.

"You should consult the *telescope* every quarter hour. Having just done so, your next inspection will be at half ten. All of us may need to make more frequent inspection when the appointed hour draws closer."

Except for needing to climb all the way down the ladder to pee, they spent the next two hours fidgeting and seeing nothing relevant. At 12:30, they began to check more often. The first signs of the time alley came at 1:06, and the aperture was fully formed by 1:25, a fairy path Eight near the base of the hill. Two fashionably dressed people, a man and a woman, appeared nearby. They were almost surely Mr. Blake and Miss Collins. There was no sign of the theodolite.

Chris told Mick that plenty of people were focused on Mr. Blake and Miss Collins, and that he needed to keep his eye on the aperture. He did so, describing everything he saw, which was a series of developments and patterns right out of the pages of *Broome's*. Mick didn't see a dropper, but he was pretty sure that Miss Collins and Mr. Blake suddenly disappeared into thin air for a couple minutes before reappearing. Chris and Mr. Yardley both wrote that down, though Mick wasn't sure they believed him. Or that he believed himself. And if it had happened, what did it mean? Were they already shuttling the alleys? Had they gone to the past and returned? To the future? To the moon to chill with Smaug and Santa? His brain spun at high speed for a while, but his thoughts didn't resolve into anything sensible.

When the aperture closed, Mr. Yardley got intrigued by something about the timing of the aperture and started muttering math out loud with increasing excitement before announcing that he had to return to the Institute to talk to Mrs.

Cutter. Mick liked that idea. The wind had gotten stronger, and the platform had started to sway a little. Plus, he had to pee again.

About two weeks later, Mick was again in a small room with Chris and Mr. Yardley, waiting for something of interest to appear in a glow-glass telescope. This time, Miss Emmet and Alison were with them, and they were all gathered in an office belonging to Bryce & Adams, Accountants.

The furniture was the sort of heavy wood and smug brass that looked like it starched its underwear and glared at kids and dogs for breathing too loudly. When Mick pointed that out, Chris said that Bryce and Adams both worked very hard to give that impression. She said the two men did some extremely creative things with money for the Project that probably would have been illegal to do with small sums in an office with beat-up furniture and an unfashionable address. However, since they did it with enormous sums in well-appointed offices near Scotland Yard and since they had gone to university with lords, it was entirely legal, and essentially a patriotic service to Queen and country.

It was a Sunday, so the offices were empty and there had been no need for awkward explanations about their oddly assorted group or the rather large glow-glass telescope that Mr. Yardley had finally gotten in place on a window looking down at the Hungerford Bridge. According to all the numbers, the time lightning was due to appear there later that afternoon.

Mick was checking the telescope often, mostly to keep an eye on his friends and others from the Institute. It was often a struggle to pick them out of the dense crowd. Since it was

Sunday, all of respectable London was out and about, wearing its finest clothing for its neighbors to envy. The finery provided bright flourishes to a day that was otherwise gray as granite and chilly as an offended priest. Most of disreputable London was also out and about, seeing if it could beg or steal some coins from respectable London.

Gail was at the Hungerford Market stairs, more or less where Mick and his friends had stood to watch time lightning on the bridge the last time. She was flanked by Miss Mitchell and Mr. Victor, with a couple more dons standing discreetly nearby and no doubt a half-dozen Eyes as well.

Leech and Dolly had been walking slowly back and forth between the banks of the Thames since Mick had been watching. They were under the watchful eyes of Mr. Cooper and Mr. Huxley, the dons from the Gaoler's Home Outpost. Leech was one of a half dozen or so streets and greets who were especially good at sensing alleys. Dolly had said she was there to keep Leech from getting pickpocketed, but Mr. Cooper and Mr. Huxley could have done that without her. Mick figured Dolly was there because Mrs. Cutter liked her and wanted her there for some reason.

"Explain it again," Miss Emmet said to Mr. Yardley. "Mr. Gunn, do please step away from the telescope and pay heed for a moment."

Mick went to sit beside Alison on one of the two brown leather couches facing one another across a long, narrow coffee table. Miss Emmet was sitting in a matching leather chair at one end of the coffee table, and Mr. Yardley was pacing behind the couch farther from the window. Chris remained standing by the open window, carefully scanning the bridge through binoculars.

"Where should I begin?" Mr. Yardley asked.

"How shall we know whether the alley following this time lightning will be the one to cause the Realignment?" Miss Emmet asked.

"Well, 'know'..." Mr. Yardley said hesitantly.

Miss Emmet waved her hand. "'Believe,' then. But a belief based on reason, if you please. Miss Atkinson and Miss March have very kindly scoured the library for information on these topics and have managed to collect a great deal of lofty gibberish that is neither intelligible, nor even altogether sane."

"I suspect some of those authors were indeed crack-brains," Mr. Yardley said. "Still, the mathematics describe a reality that sounds more than a little mad, likely meaning that at least some of the books provide sane descriptions of an insane reality."

After a moment of silent pacing, Mr. Yardley said, "We speak of alleys and apertures as if they were the same thing. From our regular world, that has a certain sense. Here, we can only see an alley when its aperture opens. But the alley is far more than its apertures." He paused. "Think of an alley as a huge, hollow thread, one large enough to walk inside like a corridor. Imagine it has a door at either end, and no other doors. Some books describe the, ah, transition between the thread world and our world as a 'vestibule.' If the relevant door to the vestibule—what we call the aperture—is closed and locked, no one can see into the thread, and no one can enter it. But it's still there."

Everyone nodded. They had covered this ground before, using various metaphors.

"When an alley picks up a rat up in the future and drops the rat in the past," Mr. Yardley continued, "the alley's thread carries a chronal charge, somewhat like a copper wire carries electricity." He paused. "Of course, I must stress that chronal charges do not behave much like electricity. For example, and most crucially, some of a thread's chronal charge endures long after its aperture closes. At least some charge can endure for quite a while as we count time here in the ordinary world." He paused again, this time at the far end of the couch from Miss Emmet. "None of that is, scientifically speaking, quite accurate." He sighed ruefully. "Not that any of it is truly scientific."

"But helpful nevertheless," Miss Emmet said. "Pray continue."

"The books say it is easiest and most effective to enter the thread whilst the aperture is open in the usual way. But, so long as adequate chronal charge remains in the thread, a sufficiently skillful rat may open and enter the thread. We don't yet know *how*, but Miss Collins clearly does."

"And once in that thread, what does she do?" Miss Emmet asked.

"It appears that from inside the thread, she does what any skillful rat may do. She unfastens and refastens one end of the thread at a time. It appears that one typically does so with the more distant end of the thread. Let us say a thread connects, say, 1853 to 1953. If a rat enters from 1853, the rat can … travel, one might say, to where the thread touches 1953, unfasten the vestibule touching 1953 and relocate it to some other time. We believe that moving the vestibule in that way is what causes time lightning, or at least contributes to it. My own suspicion is that some of the charge escapes during the process and bursts into our world as time lightning."

"And one can move either end of a thread, yes?" Miss Emmet asked. "It needn't be the more distant one?"

Mr. Yardley nodded. "Correct. However, the fastenings are

what connect the threads to our world. If a rat enters a thread in 1853 and unfastens that end of the thread, the rat then cannot use the thread to return to 1853."

"Unless she refastens one of the ends to 1853, correct?" Miss Emmet asked.

"In theory, yes," Mr. Yardley said. "But there appear to be limitations on that sort of thing. It would seem that threads can only be fastened and refastened so many times before they lose their charge, and such 'dead threads' are useless for the purpose of time travel."

"Also, if you'll recall, Miss Emmet," Alison said, "it is apparently quite difficult to fasten a thread at an exact point in time." She turned to Mick. "Apparently, alley rats can develop a sense of how far they are moving an alley, but only within a few weeks at best."

"And more likely within a few months or even years," Mr. Yardley said, nodding in agreement. "Unless, Miss March?"

Alison blushed. "Unless they are refastening threads to their own drop points."

"Indeed," Mr. Yardley said. "For some reason, a rat's own drop point supposedly calls to a rat much as a homing pigeon's home calls to the pigeon. Some describe it as a literal, physical tugging."

"And that's why it was such a big deal to figure out that it was Miss Collins doing this?" Mick asked. "Because we know her drop date, and that means we know where she's moving the threads?"

"To December 28, 1833," Mr. Yardley said, nodding. "It would appear that, in the days of shuttling the alleys, the very few rats who ever mastered the skill would collect threads and anchor them to a single point in time. Once a rat has anchored alleys that, together, carry enough temporal charge, the rat can begin to weave the threads together. The weaving appears to slow the dissipation of their chronal charge. And having them anchored in one place allows the rats to travel back in time."

"How so?" Miss Emmet asked.

"Once a rat anchors all of the alleys to a particular place and time," Mr. Yardley explained, "let us say a particular intersection in London at roughly fifteen minutes past noon on December 28, 1833, then the rat can travel back through one thread fastened to that anchor and transfer to another alley that might be fastened at its other end to, say, 1848 or 1852. The anchor spot serves as a sort of railway junction."

"And creating an anchor spot that serves as this sort of railway junction is what we are calling the Realignment?" Miss Emmet asked.

Mr. Yardley nodded.

Miss Emmet sighed. "I thought that I had managed to understand that even before the Collapse, rats could not travel backward in time more than perhaps a half dozen years, and that they either could not travel forward at all or could do so only a few days. What you are saying seems to signify that one could travel decades in either direction."

Mr. Yardley blinked. "Ah, no. My apologies. Those restrictions still apply. I fear this is another example of the confusion arising from treating threads and apertures as the same thing. I am speaking of travel *within* the threads. *Inside* a thread, one can indeed travel decades, perhaps even centuries. Or, I suppose I should say, one can travel to parts of the thread that ... *touch* times decades or centuries distant from the time at which one enters the thread. But to travel *within* a thread is not at all the same as actually *leaving* the thread and stepping into the real world. To step from a thread into the real world, the aperture must open, and it appears that apertures simply will not open later than a rat's entry point—at least, as you say, not more than a few days later. Nor will they open more than a few years earlier than the rat's starting point, at least not unless there is a truly colossal release of chronal energy, which could very well kill the rat by destroying the thread. Nor, I should add, can a rat, as it were, compound the procedure to travel back more than perhaps five years. That is, if one begins one's journey in 1853, one can travel back to, say, 1848 and then can—likely *must*—return to 1853. But one could not travel back to 1848 and then again to 1843 and then 1838 and so on."

After looking at Miss Emmet for permission to speak, Alison said, "Before the Collapse, some very accomplished alley shuttlers tried to compound the procedure as Mr. Yardley describes. They all met with failure, and many seem to have gone to their deaths."

"Thus," Miss Emmet asked Mr. Yardley, "for a rat traveling from 1853, the purpose of anchoring all the threads in 1833 cannot be to travel to 1833, or indeed any year before roughly 1848? It rather must be to use the anchored threads as a sort of railway junction to travel, ultimately, to a year such as 1848?"

Mr. Yardley nodded. "Just so. Though the rat must first 'weave' the various threads together so that the anchor will indeed serve as a, ah, railway junction. Naturally, there are all manner of perils attendant upon such weaving. Weaving too many threads appears to make them volatile, likely to come unfastened at one or both ends, with potentially fatal results. And it is inevitably fatal if both ends come loose, of course, because in that case, there is no contact between the thread and this world, and the alley rat is trapped in the thread."

"And if a thread that is woven to other threads is stretched too far?" Miss Emmet asked. "That too can be perilous?"

Mr. Yardley nodded. "Extremely. It could cause catastrophic failure of every thread in the weave. At best the rat stretching the thread would be stranded in the past."

"And at worst?" Miss Emmet asked.

"The rat would be killed," Mr. Yardley said. "However, if done correctly, it would also safely deaden all the threads in the weave without imperiling the rat doing the stretching, or anyone else. The rat would simply re-anchor the threads in an even more distant past, then return to the real world at the same time he accessed the threads."

"And that is how you propose to stop the Realignment?" Miss Emmet asked.

Mr. Yardley nodded enthusiastically. "We still do not fully understand how Miss Collins enters the alleys. But, especially in light of the tireless researches by people such as yourself and Miss March, we are confident that we understand how Miss Collins has been unfastening and re-fastening the threads. All the books suggest that, bizarre as it may sound, the threads themselves ... listen to the alley rat and somehow, ah, encourage or guide the process. So once Miss Collins opens the door, we can, in essence, walk through it and move enough threads far back in time far enough to safely deaden the weave before returning to 1853."

"And we needn't move all the threads?" Miss Emmet asked.

Mr. Yardley shook his head. "Once threads are woven together, causing instability in some threads will spread that instability throughout the entire weave."

"How many are 'some'?" Miss Emmet asked.

"It depends on many things," Mr. Yardley said. "After today's aperture, I hope that we shall know a great deal more, including precisely how far back the threads must be moved. At the moment, our best estimate is 1808."

"Why not 1708?" Mick asked. "Just to be sure?"

"Catastrophic failure, Gunner," Alison said. "It might well kill the rats doing it."

Mick blushed. Right. Mr. Yardley had just said that.

"Best to avoid that, then," Miss Emmet said breezily.

Unsettled by the talk of death, Mick returned to the telescope to make sure his friends were okay. They were. There was no sign of time lighting and no sign of Miss Collins. But he couldn't quite make himself sit down. And the stepstool was too small for him to pace on, so he found himself climbing up its two steps and then backing down them, over and over.

"Look every quarter of an hour, Gunner," Chris said gently from a few feet away. "It will come in its own time."

Mick nodded and returned to sit next to Alison on the sofa.

"But," Miss Emmet said, emerging from silent contemplation, "though it may come in its own time, if we fail, it will leave on Miss Collins' time. Which is Lord Harrowgrave's time."

"We'd best not fail, then," Chris said, watching patiently at the window.

CHAPTER 16

CURED OF ENVY

When yellow-white time lightning began to flash along the Hungerford Bridge later that afternoon, Mick watched closely, describing everything he saw for others to take notes. Meanwhile Chris kept an eye on non-alley events.

Mick used the glow-glass cap, though doing so seemed unnecessary, almost silly. Even without the glow-glass, the time lighting was flashing like every summer thunderstorm all at once, causing bright bursts on the office's window panes. It felt like it had to be raining buckets, even though not a raindrop was falling. Even Chris could see the time lightning, including the vivid flickers and slashes of pink and the ever-accelerating purple blobs racing from one bank of the river to another.

Mick was glad that he'd seen his friends and their dons return to the Hungerford Market nearly an hour before the lightning started. He hoped, yet again, that all the alley rats had gotten clear of the bridge soon enough. Nobody really knew what would happen if time lightning struck an alley rat.

When the purple blobs reached dizzying speeds, Mick pulled his eye away from the telescope, stepped down from the stepstool, turned away from the window, and shut his eyes tightly. "It's going to be really bright," he warned.

Soon, there was a flash so brilliant that Mick briefly saw the veins in his eyelids. When he dared to open his eyes, it was once again an overcast London day, the sun sleepy behind the clouds. The brightest thing left on the bridge was the Sunday finery of London's more flamboyant residents.

Mick swung the telescope toward the market, finding Gail and Miss Mitchell, then Leech and Dolly. They looked safe enough, and he supposed they were. For now. But in five days, Miss Collins would try to trigger the Realignment for Lord Harrowgrave. And whatever reasons Lord Harrowgrave had for wanting the Realignment, Mick was pretty sure keeping Mick's friends safe wasn't high on the list.

For several days, Mick answered questions about time lightning and alley phenomena. He didn't think he was doing a good job. The questions mostly felt like, "Was it more like This Thing You Don't Understand or This Thing You've Never Even Heard Of? Did it seem more like a Leftward Inverted Nonsense or a Right-Spiraling Phase-Shifted Balderdash?"

While trying to answer questions, he learned a bit about what others were doing, including many of the Palladians. Somewhere, Miss Mitchell and Miss Jennings were drilling a dozen dons on how to move the threads back far enough to undo the Realignment, but not so far they'd strand themselves in the past or get themselves killed. Other dons, and a few mechanicals, were helping Mrs. Cutter and Mr. Yardley calculate how far back to take the threads. Chris reportedly had seized control of the telegraph room in the dons' wing and was dividing her time between that room and the Hungerford Bridge. Gail was alternating between answering questions like Mick and helping Alison and Miss Emmet stare at old books and curse quietly. Leech and Dolly and sometimes Owl were out looking for unexpected stirrings, just in case.

On the day before everybody expected Miss Collins to try to trigger the Realignment, the questions stopped.

Although Mick braced himself all through breakfast to be interrupted by a summons, he was allowed to eat his porridge and sausage in peace, as were Leech, Dolly, and Owl, though poor Alison was off battling books somewhere. It was the most time they'd had together for a while. He was grateful to just sit with them for a moment.

"I take it we're all cured of ever envying one another ever again?" Leech asked as he forked his last fragment of sausage.

The others smiled faintly.

"Let us rather envy the arrows," Dolly said, "who pass unaware though it all." She raised her water glass in mock toast.

"Envy the arrows," they said, doing the same.

The rest of the morning, Mick tried playing footie but couldn't focus on the game. He tried to read a novel, but the words wandered around the page. In the end, he went out to the Institute's garden and sat on his favorite bench, enjoying contemplating whether the temperature was just right or a degree too cold. When the sun wasn't behind a cloud, it was definitely just right. After a while, Owl wandered over and sat with him for a bit, not saying anything. Mick got the sense that, like a lot of kids, Owl was also fidgety and out of sorts. You didn't have to be a Palladian to know that something big and scary was happening.

"School hasn't started, has it?" Mick asked. "Like a real term, I mean?"

Owl laughed. "Despite the holiday's date, we've more than a week till Michaelmas term."

"Good," Mick said. "Then I'm not behind yet."

He stared for a minute at the toddlers playing in the grass twenty or thirty yards away under Mr. Phillips' attentive gaze. Seeing the little kids with Mr. Phillips reminded Mick of confronting Cassandra Halliwell. Mick, Mr. Phillips, and Miss Weathers had stopped Cassandra Halliwell from getting into a lift alley that had opened in the garden, but little Julia had toddled right in and dropped a hundred-plus years into the past. Mr. Phillips had been slashed up badly, and Julia had been lost, and it had been pretty awful. But all of that had happened by surprise. This time, Mick knew what was going to start happening and when. The question was whether they could stop it. He wasn't sure which was worse. But at least one of them was already over.

Although, if the Realignment happened, maybe nothing would ever really be over. Maybe some psycho alley rat could just get in an alley, drop back in time, and try again and again.

Mick sighed and said to Owl. "Of course, if we had school, I could be busy not studying, you know? I'd have something not to do."

Owl laughed. "You could get an early start. That way you won't have as much studying to avoid once term begins. Never avoid doing tomorrow what you can avoid doing today."

Mick laughed too. But then he made the mistake of thinking

about tomorrow. Even more than usual, tomorrow couldn't be avoided.

After lunch, Mick was handed a bundle of clothes by a don who told him to get dressed and go to the garden gate. There, Mick found Chris waiting for him. Her clothes made her look like a mildly prosperous young man who worked with his hands but not with his back, maybe a cobbler or a tailor. Mick's made him look like her relative.

Chris led him on a zig-zagging route through much of north London, some on foot, some in cabs. One of the cabs eventually carried them south across the Thames via the London Bridge. Mick was pretty sure Chris was trying to avoid being followed or even seen, including picking routes that bypassed as many outposts and lookouts as possible. Which was ... interesting. It meant she was trying to avoid being seen by Eyes and dons, even though she usually spent her days going to see and be seen by those very people.

In the last cab, Chris made Mick slouch below the windows the entire way. He was starting to get stiff by the time Chris tugged at the driver's string and the cab came to a halt. From there, they walked a crooked path before eventually knocking at the back door of the rectory of a church facing Waterloo Road.

A serious woman in a plain, respectable dress opened the door and, without speaking, ushered them down a back hall to a small room that had been packed with cots and bedrolls on the floor. Mick counted four cots and four bedrolls.

"Thank you, Mrs. Nelson," Chris said.

"You are most welcome, young sir," she said with a faint

smile before backing out of the room and disappearing down the corridor.

Chris had hardly spoken during their trip. She'd spent the cab rides flipping through scraps of paper carrying what looked to Mick like coded messages, a painful mix of numbers, random letters, and weird symbols. As soon as they arrived in the little room at the back of the rectory, Chris sat down on a cot, leaned her back against the wall, and resumed contemplating the scraps, along with a map of the area around the Hungerford Bridge.

After watching Chris frown to herself for a while, Mick asked, "Can you tell me anything?"

Chris looked up at him, smiling slightly. "Precious little, I fear. We have a great deal of information about what is to happen tomorrow, much of it unclear or incorrect. That includes some rather clever lies. At the risk of flattering myself, I believe some of those lies were crafted specially for me."

"Can I help?" Mick asked.

"If your uncanny alley sight permits you to see into the souls of men and women, I should be most grateful," Chris said.

"I regret that it does not," Mick said, trying to sound like Miss North.

Chris chuckled. "Then I fear there is little you can do for the nonce, save amuse yourself, perhaps with the help of one of Mrs. Nelson's friends." She waved the back of her hand in the direction of a shelf of books on the far wall.

Mick sighed and reviewed the shelf, quickly deciding against anything that had "sermon," "essay," or "virtue" on the title page. Volume nine of *The Life and Opinions of Tristram Shandy, Gentleman* started off with a good phrase about the powers of time and chance but quickly got incomprehensibly old-timey.

"I've always suspected he was an alley rat," Chris said.

"Who?" Mick asked.

"Sterne," Chris said. "The author."

Mick looked at the title page again. Laurence Sterne was indeed the author. Chris was twenty feet away and, as far as he could tell, hadn't lifted her eyes from her map and her scraps. Impressive.

It didn't matter what book he picked. He couldn't concentrate. Chris told him he couldn't leave the room or even peer out the window through the sheer curtains. So mostly he lay on one of the bedrolls and dozed. Chris left after about an hour, after making him promise to stay in the room and keep away from the window. After that, there was more failing to concentrate and more dozing. As the sun through the sheers turned orange with sunset, Mrs. Nelson brought him a slice of gamey shepherd's pie, which Mick made himself eat before dozing again.

Mick woke up to find the room filled with light and shadows from oil lamps and quickly filling with dons. Miss Mitchell and Miss Jennings were there, as was Mr. Bateson, the don who looked like Mick's cousin Mateo. Mick recognized the other three dons as people who had been training to re-anchor the threads. He pulled out his pocket watch and was surprised to find it was already a quarter past ten.

"Where's Chris?" he asked Miss Jennings.

"Doubtless drunk in a gin parlor," she said with a wink.

Mick took that as a polite way of saying she didn't know or couldn't tell him. At some point, he fell asleep again and didn't wake up again until the whole group started stirring around seven the next morning. Chris was there but already dressed, so he didn't know if she'd been there all night or had gotten back five minutes earlier. She looked tired and worried, but so did everybody else.

After the dons carried the cots and bedrolls to another room, they brought in a couple tables and swiveled their tops into place before bringing in mismatched chairs. They closed the door, with one don always standing outside to make sure nobody could eavesdrop.

"Father Nelson owes his living to his wife and to the Project," Chris told Mick between bites of brown bread as she readied herself to leave again. "Otherwise, we should find ourselves having to answer a great many more questions about the hubbub." Resting her hand on the doorknob, she announced to the room, "I shall return by noon. Be ready to leave at half twelve, whether I have returned or not. You each know the plan, and you will be informed if your role changes."

The next hour or so involved the dons murmuring the same plans at one another over and over. It didn't sound to Mick like he would have any role beyond tagging along and saying something if the time alley did something weird. The broad strokes of the plan were pretty simple. The time alley, a horse kick Nine or Ten, was going to open on the Hungerford Bridge between 3:15 and 3:45 that afternoon, roughly two-thirds toward the north bank. Protected by dons and Eyes, teams of greets were already patrolling the bridge and the areas nearby for any signs that timing might change. There were two groups of dons assigned to the alley itself: the one with Mick, and the one with Gail, which was somewhere on the north bank of the Thames near the footbridge. Each team could apparently stop the Realignment by itself, but it sounded like Mick was with the "A" team and Gail was with the "B" team.

A few hours before the alley was supposed to open, both teams would step onto the bridge, one from each side, and take up position near where the alley was going to open. If they could get onto the bridge, that was. It sounded like Chris expected problems with that, so she had at least one back-up plan. Mick wasn't sure what it was, though, because that was about when the dons nudged him out of the room, handed him a stool, and told him to knock on the door if anybody came near it.

Mick settled onto the stool, listening to the indistinct murmur of the dons' whispers on the other side. He kept alert for long, boring hours, but nobody came near.

At about 11:30, Chris appeared at the far end of the hallway and disappeared into the room. The murmuring got louder and then quiet again. Chris came back out and patted Mick on the shoulder. "More patience will be required, I fear, Gunner."

Chris left again and didn't return until nearly 1:30. When she went into the dons' room, the murmuring behind the door got louder and then went quiet. Then the furniture scraped around for a little bit, and everybody came out.

"With us, Mr. Gunn, and briskly," Chris said as the dons walked down the hall ahead of them. She nudged his shoulder and winked. "We're off to save time itself, and it's poor form to be late for a thing like that."

CHAPTER 17

THE BRIDGE SHUDDERS

Their party scattered as they exited the rectory's back door. Chris went off alone, and the dons divided into three pairs, with Mick joining Miss Jennings and Miss Mitchell. As they walked, Miss Jennings explained that the dons were all headed to the Old Bargehouse stairs, but they were splitting up and taking weird routes to be harder to follow.

"What's Chris doing?" Mick asked.

"Surveying the footbridge," Miss Mitchell said.

"At eleven o'clock this morning," Miss Jennings told Mick, "some men appeared at the footbridge, some of them dressed like coppers and most of them looking like they ought to be under arrest. They've been blocking the entrances since then. Nobody gets on, and everybody who was on has been shooed off."

"What?" Mick asked. "Why?"

"By order of the officers of the Royal Society, upon the authority of Her Majesty Victoria Regina," Miss Mitchell said, apparently quoting someone. "In furtherance of scientific inquiries of the most profound and delicate nature."

"The Royal Society?" Mick asked. There was a memory in there somewhere. "Isn't that…"

In a plummy voice, Miss Jennings said, "By a most remarkable coincidence, Lord Harrowgrave does happen to be an officer of the Royal Society."

"Well, so that's kinda proof he really is the one behind all this, right?" Mick asked.

"Indeed," Miss Mitchell said grimly.

At the Old Bargehouse stairs, Miss Mitchell led them to a steam-powered narrow-boat. Before stepping down into the small cabin below, Mick glimpsed Eliza Richardson, the mechanical, standing at the stern of the boat, chatting with Elmer Maxwell. Elmer was in his usual working clothes, and Miss Richardson was wearing something like what Mrs. Maxwell usually wore. In the already cramped cabin, four dons scooted over so the newcomers could sit with them.

After about a quarter hour, a little guy with a big, bushy beard scuttled down the short stairway. It took a second for Mick to realize it was Chris in canal boater's clothes and a fake beard. The beard was pretty bad, now that he looked.

"Welcome aboard the *Lagertha*," Chris said. "Miss Richardson reports the engine is eager to carry us onward. We await only the signal."

"Is the engine powerful enough to propel all of us and that monstrous muzzle too?" one of the dons asked.

Chris chuckled along with everybody else and trotted back up the stairway.

Everyone waited nervously, mostly in silence. Occasionally someone would venture to say something, but it was never enough to spark a conversation among the group. But it did give Mick time to ask Miss Jennings what was happening.

"Entry to the bridge is still blocked at both banks," she said. "We're going to pant to the south pillar of the footbridge and clamber up. There are stairs to take us up to the bridge from there. Our counterparts on the north bank will do the same."

"They've got a steamboat too?" Mick asked.

"Rowboats," Miss Jennings said. "But they need only row from the Adelphi Wharfs."

Mick tried to picture the bridge and its pillars. "Won't they see us coming?" he asked. "The people on the bridge?"

Miss Jennings looked at Miss Mitchell, who shrugged and said, "We hope they will be too distracted to notice us. Or at least to stop us. We must rely on others for that."

"The signal we now await," Miss Jennings added, "is that our distraction will be ready when we need it."

A few minutes later, the female dons stood and reached into the folds of their plain but respectable dresses. With a practiced set of complicated gestures, they undid some snaps and unfastened the high-waisted skirts so that they hung from a thick band of fabric halfway up their stomachs. They then spun the skirts halfway around, tugged at the fabric now in the front until they had the hems in their hands. Mick had half-expected to see whatever over-the-top fluffy underwear Victorian women had to lug around, but it turned out they were wearing wool slacks that wouldn't have been out of place on a fashionable young gentleman. The skirts were lined with canvas or something like it. Some complicated movements turned the skirts into rucksacks. They shoved their floppy hats into the rucksacks, closed the rucksacks, and strapped them to their backs.

The resulting look was weird but pretty cool, a sort of farm wife in the chest, hiker in the back, and dandy the rest of the way down, although their shoes were far too practical for any self-respecting dandy. The female dons tied their hair back with leather laces, except Miss Mitchell, whose hair held itself in place.

Miss Jennings said to Mick, "The snaps are technically connans, but they are also a godsend."

A painfully long time later, a steam whistle shrieked from directly above, startling Mick and a couple of the dons. The boat began chugging forward.

Chris reappeared, unfastening her ridiculous beard and hanging it on a peg near the door. "Not long now," she said.

Even chugging slowly, their narrowboat reached the footbridge's southern pillar about a quarter hour later. While Elmer and Miss Richardson held the boat steady against the tide, Chris looped a mooring rope over one of the sturdy iron hooks anchored to the pillar, apparently for just that purpose. Miss Mitchell tossed a rope ladder with grappling hooks through an archway partway up the pillar a few times until the hooks caught properly and Miss Jennings could tie off the ladder at the bottom. Chris swarmed up the fifteen or twenty feet of treacherously twisting rope ladder and then held it steady at the top as all the dons clambered up except a big guy with a real version of Chris' fake beard. Then it was Mick's turn, with the big don boosting him and then steadying the rope ladder from the bottom. The big don came up afterward, and Elmer Maxwell unfastened the rope ladder and the mooring rope. Soon, the narrowboat was chugging away.

Mick looked toward the far pillar, and saw figures clustered inside one of its arches as well. They were too far away for him to see them clearly, but it had to be Gail and the other group of dons.

From the bridge above, angry bellows and tin whistles filled the air.

Chris grinned tightly and whispered, "That'll be our distraction."

As a group, they inched quietly up narrow granite stairs, which were slick with water and moss. Near the top, everybody stopped.

From the rear, Mick leaned to one side until he could see Chris standing at the door. She waved everybody down until they were out of sight. After a moment, there was a loud rapping at the door, the squeal of unhappy hinges, a faint thwacking sound, and a thud. The hinges squealed again, a little more quietly.

"Oy," Chris called softly from above.

Everybody crept back up the stairs to find Chris standing over an unconscious police officer, whose hands were bound behind him.

"Assaulted an officer of the law, have we?" Miss Mitchell said.

"Doubtful," Chris said. "This is the bully rook who kidnapped Miss Atkinson. I suspect he and the so-called coppers out there have visited the police station only as guests of Her Majesty."

"Well done, nonetheless," Miss Mitchell replied. She then led everyone in synchronizing their watches.

Chris then pointed to the big, bearded don and then to the

fake cop. The big don picked up the fake cop in a fireman's carry and cautiously hefted him down the slick stairs.

Chris had Mick kneel and peer out through the door to the bridge that she had cracked slightly open.

"Is there an aperture yet?" she asked.

Mick said he couldn't see enough of the bridge to tell, and Chris eased the door open bit by bit until Mick was pretty sure he was looking at the right spot. There were four fake cops and four real thugs clustered seventy or eighty yards south of the northern pillar, and someone who could have been Miss Collins was walking back and forth, almost testing the air with her hands. A man who might have been Mr. Blake was standing off to the side. Farther away, some other fake cops and real thugs appeared to be facing a cluster of people at the bridge's north entrance.

"Anything?" Chris asked. "Alley-wise, that is?"

"No aperture," Mick said. "And it's a horse kick, so it'll be hard to see, probably just a frame and a shimmer. I don't hear any alley song yet, either."

He got baffled silence. He briefly explained alley song, and they looked at him like he had ferrets crawling from his ears, except for the big don. "Siren song," the big don said. "He's speaking of siren song. Did I not tell you? And never anything but scorn and pity I get from you lot, but there he is, the alley sport himself, and he hears it too."

"Larson, everyone on the bridge will hear *you*," Miss Mitchell said quietly.

The big don blushed. "Sorry," he whispered.

They were all silent then, as Mick stared out the crack in the door, watching Miss Collins wave her hands in front of herself like a beginner mime.

And then ... *Yep.* A faint shimmering haze, like a patch of sequined fog, and the quiet singing in his skeleton of the alley calling to him, calling him to do something delightful and deadly. "Alley," Mick said.

"Three-eighteen and forty-one seconds," Miss Mitchell said.

A little later, Miss Collins stopped waving her hands in front of her. Then, looking for all the world like a gallant gentleman opening the door for a lady, she pulled her hand toward herself and used her other hand to gesture that Mr. Blake should step forward. Which he did.

And vanished.

Everybody drew in their breath in shock.

Following Mr. Blake, Miss Collins stepped forward and also vanished.

"Good lord," one of the dons said. "Knowing it will happen and *seeing* it happen ... Not at all the same thing."

"Three-twenty and six seconds," Miss Mitchell said in an almost calm voice. "Once Miss Collins and Mr. Blake are finished anchoring the threads, they will return. That should be within roughly ten to twelve minutes, though we have been advised that time moves differently in the alley realm than in our world. Once Miss Collins and Mr. Blake have emerged, we shall have no more than a dozen minutes to enter the thread and so that we may re-anchor the threads. The signal will come shortly. After the signal, we shall give our comrades two minutes to create confusion, and then we shall charge. On my mark and not before."

They all fell silent for a few moments. Mick was about to ask what the signal was when the sky exploded.

Chris grinned at Mick. "Some rather stern Eyes have been up in the bridge towers these past two days and nights, using the bridge chains as pillows. And Mr. Vines has been in the north tower. Bleeding uncomfortable for them. But the Eyes have been rewarded with fisticuffs, and Mr. Vines has just placed a three-minute fuse in a cask of gunpowder and lit it. Even if he lives to see a hundred, it may be the greatest joy of his life."

From both directions on the bridge came more shouting and police whistles, but Mick had been jostled away from the door, so he couldn't see what was happening.

All the dons patted their pockets or took deep breaths. Soon, Miss Mitchell started counting down from ten, and Chris pulled Mick out of the way by his collar.

Miss Mitchell called, "Go!" and the dons burst through the door onto the bridge. Without thinking, Mick tried to follow, but Chris was still holding his collar.

"Haste is their only option," Chris said. "You and I, however, must gather our wits, such as they are." She looked at her watch. "Let me see. August and Miss Collins disappeared into the ether at three-twenty and six seconds, so they should finish anchoring the threads and reappear roughly thirty minutes past the hour. When they reappear, Miss Mitchell and her team will disappear into the ether themselves and begin re-anchoring the threads. The trick will be to ensure that no one interferes with them, and it appears that our prospects are excellent. Observe either end of the bridge, and you will note that the forces of virtue are ascendant. But observe them from here, with the door nearly closed, just as now. If you are forced to flee here, for whatever reason, try to climb the ladder leading up to the tower directly above. That should remove you from the fray. One of the Eyes should still be there. If he challenges you, the password is 'bridler.'"

She made him repeat the password twice and told him twice how to reach the ladder that led up the tower. "But," she said firmly. "It is better for you to remain here, out of sight, and out of the fray. Do remember to look over your shoulder occasionally, however. One assumes the villain whom Mr. Larson left downstairs will eventually free himself."

She rested her hands on his shoulders and looked unblinkingly into his eyes. "I am hoping your part in this is done, Gunner. But if it is not, things will have gone badly amiss, and you will be needed urgently, and we shall seek you here, or the tower above." She squeezed his shoulders. "Courage. And calm."

With that, she slipped out, pushing the door nearly closed behind her. Listening nervously for footsteps on the stairs behind him and trying to ignore the coaxing of the alley song, Mick knelt by the door to see what was happening on the bridge.

From what he could see, there was a lot of pushing, yelling, and people getting their faces pressed into the bridge. Which, Mick decided, looked like good news because he didn't recognize the faces being pressed and did recognize some of the people doing the pressing. Mr. Victor was one of them, and there was a young professor from the Institute near him. Mick watched Chris move through the bellowing and the brawling with the same fluid speed she showed on the obstacle course. She slowed down only twice, and both times somebody slumped to the ground in her wake.

He checked his watch. 3:29:34. Miss Collins and Mr. Blake were supposed to be leaving the alley soon. His gaze switched rapidly back and forth from his watch and the subtly shimmering haze of the alley, and the whole time, the sweet, dangerous alley song filled his bones with summoning.

Several minutes ticked slowly by, and he saw no sign of Miss Collins or Mr. Blake.

Then, without warning, his head filled with the screams of a wounded animal, and he felt overwhelmingly dizzy. Most of the dizziness soon passed, but the screams continued, and when he looked up, the alley shimmer was tinted a purplish black.

Something had gone wrong with the alley. Really wrong.

Still a little woozy, Mick forced himself to stand up and pushed his way through the heavy door. Half-running, half-staggering, he hurried toward the time alley and his friends clustered around it.

Mr. Victor looked up from subduing somebody in a policeman's uniform. "Mr. Gunn? What on earth—?"

Mick pointed over Mr. Victor's shoulder toward the time alley. Mr. Victor turned and swore. They both started jogging toward the alley, Mr. Victor slowing his pace to match Mick's unsteady steps as they covered the remaining seventy or eighty yards. Partway there, Mr. Victor suddenly sprang a few feet to the side. A hatless man in a dirty shirt skidded past before turning with an angry look in his eye and an angry knife in his hand. The man didn't have time to raise the knife before Mr. Victor kicked him in the knee and punched him in the jaw. The blow to the man's jaw dropped him heavily, and he didn't move when Mr. Victor bent over to pull the knife from his hand. Mick noted the dull glint of metal on Mr. Victor's hands. Miss Jennings hadn't been kidding about the brass knuckles.

Mr. Victor jogged to the nearby railing, glanced over, and tossed the knife into the Thames thirty feet below. He and Mick resumed jogging toward the aperture. There was still a great deal of shouting, but only in the distance. "We have enlisted the aid of actual police officers," Mr. Victor said, "to hold back the angry pedestrians who wish to cross the footbridge. A surprising number of people would rather cross a bridge packed with nitroglycerin than walk a half mile to the next bridge." He saw the look on Mick's face. "There is no nitroglycerin. We simply needed a story." He paused. "Are you quite well, Mr. Gunn?"

Mick shook his head. "There's something really wrong with the alley. It's … screaming. And making me dizzy."

When he and Mr. Victor arrived at the aperture, they found both teams of dons clustered nearby, speaking excitedly to Mr. Yardley. Gail was standing with them, listening intently. A little ways beyond the aperture to the north, Miss North and a few other professors, including the music professor Mr. Phillips, were talking among themselves. Dr. Quinn and Miss Weathers were with them.

Slightly beyond and to the side of them were a bunch of fake cops and thugs, handcuffed or tied to the railings of the footbridge. Mick was pretty sure he recognized both Blue and Green, and he definitely recognized one of the big thugs who had attacked him near Gaoler's Home. Blue and Green didn't seem to notice him, but the big thug was glaring at him. Mick looked away quickly. His eyes landed on the opposite side of the narrow bridge, and for the first time he noticed Leech, Dolly, Owl, and Alison, along with Tips, Hoot, and Gristle. Were they supposed to be there?

Miss Mitchell noticed Mick and waved him over. Miss North detached herself from the other professors and reached the conversation among the dons and Mr. Yardley about the same time as Mick and Mr. Victor.

"You hear it too, right?" the big don, Mr. Larson, asked Mick. "The song is sickly, yes?"

Mick nodded.

Miss Mitchell looked at Mick and then at Mr. Victor. "Neither Miss Collins nor Mr. Blake have emerged from the alley. Something went awry shortly after they were supposed to exit."

"How long are we past the moment we anticipated for their exit?" Mr. Victor asked.

"Roughly seven minutes," Mr. Yardley said.

"And your team," Miss North asked Miss Mitchell, "had a dozen minutes to enter before the alley is closed to them? Does that signify that but five minutes remain?"

"They have all dozen yet," Mr. Yardley said in his deep voice. "The sands don't begin to run until Miss Collins and Mr. Blake step out of the alley."

"Mrs. Cutter agrees with that?" Mr. Victor asked.

"We have both been quite convinced of it these last seven or ten days," Mr. Yardley said. "But she is watching from the offices of Bryce and Adams, so we cannot consult her."

"I suspect she is making her way here," Mr. Victor said.

"Doubtless," Mr. Yardley. "If we are fortunate, she may arrive in ti—"

Mr. Yardley fell silent as Miss Collins suddenly appeared in the center of the aperture's dark shimmer, wobbling on one knee and muttering to herself.

"Three-forty-one and forty-eight seconds," Miss Mitchell called out sharply.

Miss North crossed to Miss Collins, stopping about two yards from the edge of the aperture haze. "Miss Collins, what on earth has happened?"

Miss Collins looked up at Miss North, her eyes unfocused but aflame with alley glow. "He tried to prune a dead thread," she said in a raspy, quiet voice. "Needless. Dangerous. I couldn't save him." An anguished look overwhelmed her face. "I tried to fasten the dead thread to a live one. Unwisely. Unwisely. And too long. Time is so different in there." Her face went slack. "It is so cold without the charge." She slumped forward, falling heavily to the hard planks of the bridge.

"Stop!" Miss North yelled. "Hands in pockets."

Mick froze as did nearly everybody else who had involuntarily started toward Miss Collins.

"I remind you," Miss North said loudly, "if you step into the haze, you may be pulled into the alley. No one is to step into the haze who has not trained to enter the alley and return safely. And even they will not—*not*—do so without discussion. The situation has changed, and perhaps so too must our plans. Dr. Quinn, please keep watch on Miss Collins, but do not approach her until you may do so safely."

Dr. Quinn nodded, as did Miss Weathers beside her.

"She appeared at three-forty-one and forty-eight seconds," Miss Mitchell called out. "Twelve minutes after that will be three-fifty-three and forty-eight seconds. Burn that time into your eyelids."

Miss North, Mr. Victor, Mr. Yardley, and the dozen dons circled up a safe distance from the slightly brighter purple-black haze. Gail and Mick shrugged at one another and joined the circle.

"Silence," Mr. Victor said firmly into the agitated chatter of the dons. Everyone shut up. "Mr. Yardley, is the relevant amount of time still twelve minutes? Is three-fifty-three and forty-eight seconds still our deadline?"

Mr. Yardley breathed deeply. "I believe so, yes."

Miss North said, "Miss Mitchell, the time?"

"Three forty-four and thirty seconds … mark," she said.

"And, Mr. Yardley, there are still four threads that need re-anchoring?" Mr. Victor asked. "Miss Collins mentioned a dead thread."

"Still four," Mr. Yardley said.

"Then the plan is unchanged?" Miss North asked. "Four dons enter the alley, re-anchor the threads, and return?"

Mr. Yardley shook his head. "I'm afraid not. Miss Collins said she anchored a live thread to a dead one. That will confuse things badly."

"In what way?" Miss North asked.

"In the way that things are now enormously confusing," Mr. Yardley snapped. "I cannot tell you with any certainty. Not without more information, not without more time. And we have neither."

"Perhaps Mrs. Cutter—" Mr. Victor began.

"She would be the best person to ask, yes," Mr. Yardley said. "But even if she were to arrive in the next few minutes, she would say the same thing that I must say now. Reliable calculation would take days. If, as we all believe, this our best chance, our *only* chance, to stop the Realignment, we must act now. We must re-anchor the threads so far back that they snap catastrophically. That is the only way to be certain."

"Before 1808?" Miss Jennings asked. "How long before?"

Mr. Yardley smiled a strange smile. "As a precaution, days ago, Mrs. Cutter and I did the calculations separately. We both arrived at dates in late 1767. I thought late October. She thought early November."

Nearly everyone sucked in their breath at once. At first, Mick wasn't sure why. But then he realized—

"The Collapse," Miss Jennings said. She laughed darkly. "We're going to cause the Collapse."

The Collapse. The moment when it had become impossible to shuttle the alleys. The Realignment was meant to undo the Collapse, but now the dons were going to cause the Collapse so they could stop the Realignment. Mick's head spun a little, and not just from the tortured alley song.

"Seven minutes before the alley closes ... mark," Miss Mitchell said. "Mr. Yardley, once we are in the alley, shall we still have the same amount of time to re-anchor the threads in 1767 and return here?"

Mr. Yardley sighed, his face grim. "You will have the same amount of time to re-anchor the threads, yes, whatever time may mean in the alley realm. But there will be no return. Catastrophic snapping, you see."

"Death?" Miss Mitchell asked.

"Not necessarily," Mr. Yardley said. "The energies involved will be tremendous, perhaps enough to exit the alley safely into the real world in 1767. But any who survive will—"

"Be stranded in 1767," Miss Mitchell said flatly.

"Indeed," Mr. Yardley said, just as flatly.

The dons looked at one another for a long, tense moment.

"Very well, then," Miss Mitchell said. "Eight dons, two per thread to ensure that at least one don succeeds with each thread. I shall take the primary thread and shall need seven volunteers."

"Six," Mr. Yardley said. "You may need my help."

Slowly, all the dons except Miss Jennings raised their hands to volunteer. Miss Jennings leaned against Mr. Victor for a moment and stepped across the circle before delivering a brutal punch to Miss Mitchell's ribcage. Miss Mitchell cried out in pain and doubled over.

Everybody stared at Miss Jennings in shocked silence, as she bent down and kissed Miss Mitchell's hair before easing Miss Mitchell's pocket watch from her hand. Miss Jennings straightened and handed the pocket watch to Mr. Victor, along with the brass knuckles she'd apparently just taken from his pocket to use on Miss Mitchell.

"Everyone venerates the Nye twins but nobody *thinks* about them," she said. "Miss Mitchell is not going to spend the rest of her days in an Empire that would gladly reduce her to chattel." She rested a hand on Miss Mitchell's shoulder. "I cannot permit it, Clarissa."

Miss Mitchell protested, but her words were distorted by pain.

Miss Jennings turned to Mr. Yardley. "Miss Mitchell has at least one broken rib and is unfit to step into the alley. I shall go with you in her stead. Mr. Victor, how many minutes remain before we must enter the alley?"

Mr. Victor consulted Miss Mitchell's watch. "Four minutes, thirty seconds."

"That's it then," Miss Jennings said. "Six volunteers. No time for nonsense." With a little arguing and quite a few tears, six more dons, including Mr. Bateson and Mr. Larson, joined Miss Jennings and Mr. Yardley. Miss Mitchell tried to join them more than once, but Miss North held her firmly by the arm, pressing at her broken ribs when she tried to break free. The last time it happened, Miss Mitchell cried out and bent over, cursing.

"Two minutes until the alley closes," Mr. Victor said.

"Good," Miss Jennings said. "Those two minutes will be better spent in the alley than out here."

"One moment," Mr. Victor said. "Miss Jennings, when she

first exited the alley, Miss Collins said something silently. Could you see what?"

Miss Jennings thought. "'He was misinformed.' She repeated it several times."

"That was all?" Mr. Victor asked. "'He was misinformed?'"

"Indeed," Miss Jennings said. She looked at the dons going with her. "I feel quite confident that we shall succeed," she told them. "Indeed, we know that already we have done. So let us also endeavor to survive." With that, she took Mr. Yardley's hand firmly and led him into the alley's shimmer, stepping around Miss Collins' motionless form and disappearing from sight. The remaining six dons clasped hands in pairs and stepped inside, one pair after another, also disappearing as they entered.

Miss North, Mr. Victor, Gail, Mick, and the remaining dons stared at one another blankly.

From the corner of his eye, Mick realized that the aperture was starting to develop a steely silver frame. Definitely a Nine or Ten, probably a Ten.

Then he saw Gail notice the same thing. "Horse kick-alley," she said softly. More loudly, she repeated, "It's a horse kick alley."

Mick realized what she meant. Even a normal horse kick alley that big would pack a wallop. One that was woven to other threads and was being dragged almost nine decades into the past, well, who knew what that meant, except that they should get the hell away from the blast zone. They all started to hustle toward the Hungerford Market stairs at the north bank.

Crap, Mick thought. He looked back at Miss Collins still lying on the bridge. If she was alive, he couldn't leave her there. He turned and started back. The good news, he supposed, was that the alley haze had shrunk to fit the frame, a square prism ten feet to a side but only maybe a foot thick. Miss Collins was now clear of the haze, so he could probably touch her without getting sucked into the alley. He hoped.

Trying to concentrate despite the desperate song of pain from the injured alley, he grabbed Miss Collins' arm to shake her awake, and he was glad when her brilliant eyes half-opened. But they weren't really seeing him, or anything. He realized that there was no way he was strong enough to carry her.

A hand grabbed his shoulder. "Go, Gunner."

It was Miss Weathers and Dr. Quinn. "We have her," Miss Weathers said.

Mick managed to run despite the dizziness, though not in a totally straight line. He was nearly at the north tower when the desperate alley song turned into a roar, which turned into a giant hand hurling him forward, which all turned into dark silence.

CHAPTER 18

MEMORIES OF THE FUTURE

Mick woke to the soothing feeling of being tucked in by his mother.

But that was impossible. Unless he was dead.

He didn't feel dead. He was pretty sure that your forearm didn't hurt when you were dead.

He blinked a few times and found himself looking into the face of Miss Collins, who was arranging something soft under his head. Everything was blurry, and her brilliant brown eyes glowed fuzzily, like street lamps in fog.

She paused, turning her gaze toward the shouting and cursing coming from behind Mick's head. She gasped. "Oh, gods, no," she said, looking stunned. The shouting intensified. "Devil take his soul," she said bitterly. She stood and disappeared from sight, her footsteps thudding on the bridge before being drowned out by the tumult behind Mick's head.

Mick sat up. His left forearm hurt but not terribly. The pain in his head from the injured alley song was gone, and the ringing in his ears and the blurred vision were starting to fade. He risked standing up and felt okay enough. He scanned the narrow bridge for Miss Collins and spotted her about twenty or thirty yards away, moving south at a brisk walk. He tracked her by her long, dark hair until she tucked it into the back of her shirt. He processed for the first time that she now appeared to be wearing men's clothing. He looked down at the pillow she had made him: her dress.

Mick tried to get someone's attention, but everybody was staring over the railing on the Waterloo side, except Chris, who was sprinting to the north tower and disappearing through the door leading down into the pillar. He looked back at Miss Collins. He was going to lose her if he waited any longer. He hurried after her.

By the time she reached the south bank of the Thames, he was only thirty yards behind. As she approached a group of men at the end of the bridge, he slowed down and pulled his cap low. A couple of the men asked her some questions. Her answers apparently satisfied them, and they let her continue toward Belvedere Road.

Mick followed. None of the men challenged him as he left, but one of them did detach himself from the group and fall in beside Mick. "A word, young sir."

The voice was familiar. The teenager from the barrow and the wagon. "Mr. Davies," Mick said.

Mr. Davies tipped his cap. "Indeed, young sir, indeed. I take it you are interested in the footsteps of yon gal."

Miss Collins was winding a crooked path ahead of them, having gone west briefly before turning south and then east again. Mick shrugged.

"I am too," Mr. Davies continued. "Only moments ago, you

and most of the fancy folk fell into a faint, like ladies strangled by their corsets."

Miss Collins turned north. So far, she wasn't checking behind herself very much.

"And whilst you were all a-swooning on the bridge, Chris told me that the young lady there, when she awoke, might abscond herself somewhere, and if so, I was to give her her head but not lose her tail."

Mick translated that to mean Chris had told Mr. Davies to let Miss Collins leave the bridge and follow her. "Just you?" he asked.

"You are a clever nob, intcha?" Mr. Davies asked cheerfully as Miss Collins took another turn. "I'd say a good dozen Eyes have her scent one way or another."

"And so...?" Mick asked.

"So, young sir, if you must be unwise and follow someone, I'm asking you to follow me, not her. Begging your pardon, I'm much better at this than you, and Chris said this one's a sharp blade. If you follow me, you'll be back farther, and she'll be less likely to spy you."

Mick had to admit that it made sense. But he also had to ask, "What if I don't want to?"

Mr. Davies nodded cheerfully. "I'd imagine Chris would want me to leave you sleeping somewhere safe, which probably would be the Blackfriars lookout."

Mick wasn't sure he could trust Mr. Davies, but he was very sure he couldn't take Mr. Davies in a fight. So playing along was his best bet of not getting knocked cold and dumped at the Blackfriars lookout. He fell back twenty or thirty yards to follow Mr. Davies instead of Miss Collins.

It was a good plan, he realized. Miss Collins gradually

started looking back more often, as well as doubling back and changing directions. She spent almost fifteen minutes doing this on Ground Street, right off the river. If Mick had been following her, she would have spotted him right away. But Mr. Davies simply strolled past her, apparently without a care in the world, continuing on to chat with a baked potato seller near the Blackfriars Bridge. Mr. Davies was apparently betting that she was headed to the bridge, as indeed she was.

Mick got in line behind them to cross the bridge. As he looked around at all the people walking or rolling across the bridge, he was struck that there were nearly as many moods as people—happy, sad, bored, angry, all the rest. But, whatever their moods or their errands, they were *there.*

Unlike Mr. Yardley or Miss Jennings or the other dons who had sacrificed their futures to prevent the Realignment.

And Miss Mitchell was still there because of Miss Jennings' swift, ruthless protection. That had been love of some kind. Friendship? Romance? Mick didn't know.

Once they reached the north bank, Miss Collins began to wander, tending gradually westward. By the time night crept over the city and the gaslighters were illuminating the elegant neighborhoods, Miss Collins was walking around Grosvenor Square for the third time. Mr. Davies stood across the street from the square, chatting amiably with a constable who had probably stopped to ask Mr. Davies his business in the exclusive neighborhood. Apparently, the constable bought Mr. Davies' story.

Mick didn't have the right accent to charm the constable, so he hung back on Grosvenor Street, trying to be invisible. At some point, Miss Collins made a decision about where she was going next. She turned onto Charles and then quickly onto the Adam's Mews.

Mr. Davies doffed his cap to the constable and walked south past the mews before pausing at the corner. Mick followed, taking up a new position in the shadows nearby. He'd assumed that Mr. Davies would follow Miss Collins into the mews, but Mr. Davies just tipped his hat in Mick's direction and sauntered out of sight.

"Greetings, Gunner," said a voice from directly behind him.

Mick jumped forward about a yard, landing in the street. But he managed not to scream. And before he'd even finished turning his head, he knew it had to be Chris.

"Hello, Chris," Mick said. "Um, Mr. Davies left."

"Indeed," Chris said.

"She's not, uh, getting away, is she?" Mick asked. "Miss Collins?"

"Eyes are watching every way out of the mews," Chris said. "And in any event, she has gone into the townhouse."

"Oh," Mick said. So that meant... what? Probably that Chris had already known where Miss Collins was going.

"Why did you follow Miss Collins?" Chris asked him in a neutral tone.

"At first, because I didn't think anybody else was going to," Mick said. "And then because I didn't trust Mr. Davies. Not totally, anyway."

"And why not?"

"Partly he's just ... Is 'shady' a connan?"

"It's appropriate."

"Well, on the way to the rectory, you had cabbies drive us weird routes to avoid the Eyes and the dons. And then at the rectory, you said people were lying to you. So I didn't know if he was helping you or helping Miss Collins."

Chris nodded. "Sensible. Miss North and Mr. Victor are quite cross with you for leaving the bridge and wanted me to send you back to the Institute. But I'd say you've done well on a day when so many things were done so ill." After a pause, she added, "You and the Collapsers may be the only ones among us to have done anything correctly today." Even in the deep shadows, it was easy to see her grim expression.

Mick almost asked who the "Collapsers" were but then realized she meant the dons and Mr. Yardley, who had just caused the Collapse trying to stop the Realignment. "So it worked?" he asked. "What the dons and Mr. Yardley did?"

"Time will tell," Chris said with a humorless smile. "But so far it appears that the Collapse happened just as it always must have, meaning that the Realignment has failed." She thought for a moment. "I shan't send you back to the Institute just yet. I have need of your alley sight. So much about Miss Collins involves the bloody alleys that I'll need you with me when we search her rooms."

"You know where they are?" Mick asked, surprised.

"Perhaps not all of them," Chris said. "She rents rather a lot of lodgings, under rather a lot of names. We are bound for her chief residence, in Belgravia."

A hansom cab stopped nearby. Chris moved swiftly toward it, and Mick followed. She let him climb up first and then slid in. The cab was rolling before she finished closing the door.

A brief ride brought them to an elegant building a couple blocks southwest of Belgrave Square. "Her rooms are on the first floor," Chris said. "Her housekeeper and maid are mother and daughter, and both are visiting relations in Camberwell. And her landlady has just been called away on urgent business."

"What urgent business?" Mick asked.

"Whatever the inventive Mr. Ferness conceived."

Before Mick could ask who that was, they climbed the narrow stairway to the first floor. A middle-aged gentleman in a respectable suit let them in as they reached the landing. He was holding a lit burglar's lantern with one flap raised. He used its candle to light another burglar's lantern, handing one lantern to Chris and the other to Mick.

"My associate, Mr. Ferness," Chris told Mick. "You have touched nothing?" she asked the man.

"Naught but the doorknob, the floor, and these lamps," he said. "If it's papers you're after, I suspect you'll find them behind a false front at the base of the vanity in her dressing room. Villiers et Fils created quite a vogue for that trick last decade. Down that hallway, on the left."

"Thank you, Mr. Ferness," Chris said. "Please be so kind as to wait without."

Mr. Ferness stepped onto the landing and shut the door behind himself.

"Good man, that," Chris said. "Sense of humor so dry one must add water for laughter."

"What if Miss Collins comes back?" Mick asked.

"We shall have adequate warning," Chris said, turning down the hallway Mr. Ferness had indicated. "Though I suspect we shall be done and gone long before her return. Lady Penbrook will doubtless delay her with a great many questions."

"Lady Penbrook?" Mick asked, turning down the same hallway. "What's she got to do with it?"

Chris turned to face him, her face surprised. "I assumed you realized," she said. "It was her townhouse Miss Collins entered."

Mick froze. Chris was right, of course. He'd only been there once, and they'd approached it from the other direction. But, yes, that had been Lady Penbrook's townhouse. "Does that mean...?" He couldn't wrap his head around it. "What *does* that mean?"

"That is something I should very much like to know," Chris said grimly, opening the drawing room door.

The heavy drapes were drawn, so Chris opened all the flaps on her lamp and told Mick to do the same. She knelt in front of the vanity, tapping and prodding its base. Mick wondered if they should be wearing gloves. But they didn't do finger-printing or DNA testing in 1853.

Chris made a pleased grunt, and there was a loud click. She placed a curved piece of wood on a fussy little chair beside the vanity. "Top marks to Mr. Ferness, as usual." She stood, holding an elegant walnut box. Mick didn't even have time to ask where she thought the key was before she was picking the lock. When the box clicked open, Chris' lockpick disappeared as magically as it had appeared.

"I shall need to take some time with these, Gunner," Chris said. "Please have a look through the apartment and see if you see anything that hints of alley phenomena."

Mick did so dutifully, though he didn't have any idea what that might be, except maybe the glow-glass theodolite, and there was no sign of that. There weren't any glow-orbs in the linen closet, or any fairy paths under the bed. It was just a bed with lumpy pillows and a lumpy teddy bear.

A lumpy, barf-orange, squinty, lopsided teddy bear.

The same teddy bear Mick had seen every time he looked at his baby sister in her crib.

The teddy bear was missing a lot more fur than Mick remembered. But it was Swaggy Bear. He was sure of it even before he picked it and checked the stitching inside its ears. "J" for "Julieta" in one ear, "E" for "Emilia" in the other.

Carefully, he set the lantern on a bedside table. He tried to sit on the bed but didn't quite get there. His butt and then his back slid down the side of the bed until he was sitting on the floor, staring at his baby sister's teddy bear.

He remembered Dolly's theory about natural fibers surviving the trip through time alleys. He remembered Tía Julieta bragging how she'd made Swaggy Bear out of all-natural materials.

That was why Catherine Collins had always seemed so familiar. Because she looked so much like his mom. Like *their* mom. She was his sister. Emilia.

He sat in a strange bubble of calm as he tried to put the pieces together. Catherine Collins had dropped about twenty years earlier, as a baby. Had she been pulled into the same alley as him, just a little bit afterward? Was that possible? The alley obviously hadn't dropped her the same place it had dropped him, at least not at the same time. But he knew *that* was possible. Alison had dropped two years before her twin brother. In a different city, even.

He wasn't sure how long he sat there, memories and fantasies flashing through his head. He kept seeing the picture of his parents on his dresser at Uncle Dan's, the one from just after they'd met. Their mom hadn't been that much older than Emilia was now. Than Catherine Collins was now. And, yes, Catherine Collins and their mom did look a lot alike.

Mick sat there clutching Swaggy Bear to his chest until Chris found him.

She must have asked him something a few times because by the time he heard her, she sounded annoyed. "Sorry. What?" he asked.

"Any evidence of alley phenomena?"

Mick shook his head. "It's all just normal stuff, I think."

"Very well," Chris said. "I have what I came for. We should go." She paused. "Where did you find that poppet?"

"On the bed," Mick said, trying to keep his voice neutral.

"Please replace it just as you found it so that we may depart." She paused. "Is there anything the matter?" she asked, a note of concern in her voice.

He thought about telling her everything. But this was his discovery. His family.

He shook his head, stood up, and forced himself to put Swaggy Bear back where he'd found it. At the front door, they blew out the candles in the burglar lamps, opened the door, and handed the lamps to Mr. Ferness, who was waiting on the darkened landing. Mick followed Chris carefully down the steps in the darkness as Mr. Ferness turned a key in the lock above.

After catching a cab near Belgrave Square, Chris and Mick rode in darkness without speaking, letting the clatter of wheels and clopping of hooves fill the carriage. After having the driver stop not far from the Institute, Chris led Mick on foot to Cavendish Square.

They settled into the same bench where, on a sunny summer's day, they had chatted about the Eyes after Chris had first escorted him around London. That seemed like a very long time ago. In gaslight, the square felt chill and foreboding. Mick tried to keep alert to the world around him, even though all he could think about was his baby sister's being a decade older than him. And maybe a villain. Though she *had* helped him, on the bridge. Villains didn't give you a pillow after a time alley kicked your ass, did they?

"There are some things," Chris said, "that I must tell you now, not least so that you will not be shocked by them later. Some, I hesitated to tell you because I thought they weren't mine to tell. Also, and I do apologize for being cold-blooded, because I needed you to have a clear head in Miss Collins' rooms."

Mick snorted with laughter, which Chris thought she understood. "As clear a head as you could have after a day like today," she said. "The first thing, though a serious matter, is unlikely to pain you overmuch. Lord Harrowgrave is dead. He was found in a tradesman's offices at the top of the Hungerford Market, stabbed through the neck. The police are mystified that an earl came to such an end in such a place. I am less mystified. A good deal of mystery remains, of course, but today has been a great teacher, ruthless and efficient. August Blake is also dead, we believe. Also murdered, I believe."

Mick remembered Catherine Collins (*Emilia!*) saying something about trying to save August Blake. But that had sounded like an accident. "Murder?"

"I am told there are few things more dangerous, and nothing more useless, than pruning a dead thread. Handled properly, the dead thread was irrelevant to the Realignment. And pruning it required unfastening it at both ends, which apparently can be—"

"Fatal," Mick said, remembering Mr. Yardley's explanation.

Poor Mr. Yardley. He was dead now too, like Miss Jennings, like Mr. Larson, like the other dons. Hopefully, dead of old age after dropping in 1767, not killed while re-anchoring the threads. But dead and gone, either way.

"And yet August tried to prune it," Chris said. "Remember what Miss Jennings saw on Miss Collins' lips: 'He was misinformed.' Misinformed by Lord Harrowgrave, I'd wager. Mr. Blake was not a foolish man, and I cannot imagine who else could convince him to do such a foolish thing. But, then, Lord Harrowgrave had no use for alleys or alley lore unless they increased his power, and I doubt he wanted Mr. Blake dead. So if it was Lord Harrowgrave who misinformed Mr. Blake, he too must have been misinformed. By someone who *does* value alley lore and who might indeed have wished Mr. Blake dead."

Chris paused, one of her eyes bright in the gaslight, the other a patch of darkness. "I'd lay odds on Lady Penbrook," she said.

"Lady Penbrook?" Mick asked with surprised confusion.

"What I found in Miss Collins' hidden box included a pair of ciphered letters. I copied them out, and most likely we shall eventually decipher them. But the most important information was not in the letters, but in the handwriting. There can be no doubt that Lady Penbrook wrote them. I rather suspect that Miss Collins will turn out to be Lady Penbrook's creature more than Lord Harrowgrave's." Chris' expression turned angry. "Perhaps even as much as I was Lady Penbrook's creature, and perhaps even as deluded as I."

She snapped her fingers loudly. "And it is difficult indeed to be so deluded as I. In uzeetatees lenseeum," she said.

Or something like that, anyway. It sounded like bad Spanish, so it was probably Latin. "What?" Mick asked.

"It's the name of a small book that sat forgotten for decades in the mechanicals' little library at Demeter," Chris said. "It explains how to make glow-glass. Not long after it was rediscovered and used to make the glow-glass theodolite, Lord Harrowgrave asked to borrow it for copying, and it was on its way to him when it was stolen."

"Stolen?"

"From the *Baret*, the day Elmer was so terribly beaten. I thought it was odd that I wasn't asked to carry it myself, but Mr. Yardley said the instruction to use the *Baret* came directly from Lady Penbrook."

Mick wasn't sure what that meant, and Chris obviously read it on his face. "I suspect that Lady Penbrook didn't want Lord Harrowgrave to know how to make glow-glass. So long as only the mechanicals knew how, she could control glow-glass. I think she stole the book from herself."

Mick was about to ask why Lady Penbrook would do that when he realized that it made her look like she'd been trying to help Lord Harrowgrave. If her own boat was attacked, and her own employees were assaulted, then he had no reason to think she was behind it. Never mind poor Elmer, who might have been killed.

"So Lady Penbrook is the bad guy?" Mick asked.

"Lady Penbrook is not who we—I—thought. Whether she is bad or good or something altogether different, I cannot yet say. But I do suspect that she is dangerous."

"Do the Palladians know?" Mick asked.

"Much of what I have just told you, yes. They will know the rest soon." She paused. "I suppose I hardly need say that you should not repeat most of what I just said to anyone who is not a Palladian? Lord Harrowgrave's death is public knowledge, of course, or soon will be. But the rest should remain secret, at least for now."

"I can keep a secret," Mick said.

Chris nodded. "That leaves one last thing. It is not a secret. It is simply a heartache. Owl is dead."

"Owl?"

"When the time alley closed, it knocked all the alley rats flat, many unconscious. Even the arrows felt it, but they recovered faster. In the confusion, some of Harrowgrave's henchmen freed themselves. Miss March raised the alarm, and two of the thugs tried to silence her. They were the ones who attacked you near Gaoler's Home, I believe. Miss March's friends from Orphans—a sturdy crew—came to her defense, and that likely would have been enough, especially as handy as Miss March is with that razor. But Owl didn't weigh the odds. He simply leapt upon one of the thug's backs. Bit the man's ear, I shouldn't be surprised. There was certainly a lot of blood and bellowing. The ruffian plucked Owl off his back and heaved him all his strength. And since they were near the railing, well... Your friend struck his head and fell into the river. I ran down the stairs and dove into the water, and brought him out by the nearest stairs. But only his body. His spirit had departed."

Mick remembered waking up after the alley knocked him out. Catherine Collins' face. His sister's face. When the shouting had gotten loud, she had said, "Oh, gods, no." And then, "Devil take his soul." She had seen Owl killed. And been horrified by it and cursed his murderer.

The entire day had been impossible to absorb. Unreal. And now his friend was dead, and Mick was only now realizing that Owl was his friend, not just a kid he knew. Mick stared blankly at Chris' face beside him.

"I wish I had words for this, Gunner," Chris said, her voice breaking.

Mick realized then that some of the dons who had gone into the alley had been Chris' friends. Chris had admired Lady Penbrook and been betrayed. Chris had pulled Owl's dead body from the cold and dirty river. "I'm sorry, too," he said, taking her hand.

Chris squeezed his hand.

They sat in silence for a few moments. Mick spent a lot of that time being numb, but he also spent some of it being ashamed. He'd put so much energy into hoping that somehow the Realignment would let him go home that he hadn't really let himself think about how dangerous the people were who had tried to make the Realignment happen. When people are willing to kill for power, you can't sit back, cross your fingers, and hope it will work out for you. If you do, you or somebody you care about will get hurt. And if that's the price, then even if you somehow get what you want, it won't be what you want.

Eventually, Chris released Mick's hand and stood. "Let us return to the Institute," she said. "We shall use the garden gate. The front door will mean questions for you that you oughtn't face until tomorrow. I can tell the Palladians and the rest of them enough to keep them occupied, and terrified, tonight. And many nights to come."

A little later, as they waited for a scullion to answer the gate bell, Chris looked through the gate at the Institute. "I shan't ask what you were thinking as you held that poppet, Gunner. But your face was not the face of a child at play, or even of a young man remembering being a child at play. I fear that moments of childhood are too often denied you, and all children who learn their lessons in this place."

. . .

The next day, Mick met Alison, Leech, and Dolly in the tory common room. He and Leech had been crying, and it was easy to see that Alison and Dolly had too. Downstairs, they ate a silent breakfast that tasted of nothing.

"There will be a funeral tomorrow," Dolly said. "Alison, if you could have your friends tell Owl's friend at Orphans about it, I suppose that would be good. What was his name, Owl's friend?"

"Jeremiah," Alison said.

"Today," Dolly said, "I should like to go to the Hungerford Market stairs to say farewell to Owl, just we four."

"We should get ice cream if Mr. Cats' stand is still open," Mick said. "Owl said eating ice cream gave him 'memories of the future.' That's a good way to remember an alley rat, right?"

"It's a fine idea, Gunner," Leech said.

The warden probably shouldn't have let them go out unsupervised, but he was an inexperienced, grief-stricken don who didn't even blink before logging them out. It was a fair fall day, warmer than London had any right to expect, and Mr. Cats was indeed still selling shells of ice cream. They ate theirs standing on the market steps, looking out at the bridge, none of them wanting to actually set foot on it.

Eating the ice cream didn't remind Mick of the future. It reminded him of that day in the market with Owl. He remembered Owl's raised eyebrows and faint smile.

"Whatever happened there," Dolly said, pointing to the bridge, "it isn't over. The professors are running from room to room and book to book like grinds on the eve of the sorting exam. They don't believe the problem is resolved." After an unsettled pause, she said, "To Owl. He was brave in aid of his friends."

Mick tried to think of something to add, but Dolly had hit the key point. Apparently, the others agreed. They stared silently at the people walking over the bridge the way people so often walked over tragedy—unwittingly and unable to do otherwise.

All you could do was remember, Mick thought. Remember the future. Remember the past. Carry your friends' and loved ones' best deeds with you as carefully as Mr. Yardley had carried his glow-glass telescope. Carry them and hope that they too might help you see a little better than you could have without them.

www.ingramcontent.com/pod-product-compliance
Lightning Source LLC
Chambersburg PA
CBHW052029240626
47153CB00006B/2021